INTRATERRESTRIAL
Nicholas Conley

Intraterrestrial
Red Adept Publishing, LLC
104 Bugenfield Court
Garner, NC 27529
http://RedAdeptPublishing.com/

First Print Edition: January 2018
ISBN-13: *978-0-615-81433-9* (Red Adept Publishing, LLC)
Cover Art by Streetlight Graphics

This is a work of fiction. Names, characters, places, and incidents either are the product of the author's imagination or are used fictitiously, and any resemblance to locales, events, business establishments, or actual persons—living or dead—is entirely coincidental.

Dedicated to my mother

ACT I of III:
OUR WORLD

"The existence of the rainbow depends on the conical photoreceptors in your eyes; to animals without cones, the rainbow does not exist. So you don't just look at a rainbow, you create it. This is pretty amazing, especially considering that all the beautiful colors you see represent less than one percent of the electromagnetic spectrum."
Sergio Toporek

Chapter 1: In Media Res

The boy in the bathroom mirror had a purple shiner for a left eye, and oddly enough, the boy was him.

Adam Helios couldn't believe it. He'd made it to thirteen years, never having been in a fight before. Sure, he'd talked back when other kids teased him badly enough, but that was all for show. The second that hands balled into fists, he always made excuses and ran to the bus, the next class, or somewhere safe. He was too scrawny to get into fights even though he might as well have had a target painted on his forehead: he was a glasses-wearing bookworm, a science nerd with a soft voice, a foreign kid in a milk-white small town. Fate seemed to have decided that he should be the world's most obvious bully magnet, so he dodged trouble at every opportunity.

Not anymore. Adam was standing on shaky legs in the Ottanga Junior High bathroom. Just two weeks before, in that same spot, he'd been spat at, pushed around, and teased to the point of tears. He straightened his back, trying to look tough for himself, but he still shivered at the messy puddle of emotions inside him.

The new Adam who was looking back at him from the mirror was a stranger. Part of him *liked* that. The old Adam, the Adam he recognized, was a loser. At the same time, though, his stomach churned at the thought of his parents sitting there in Principal Hamer's office at that very moment, fighting over him.

He ran cold water over his face, burning his bruised eye and feeling the dampness soak into his sweaty pores. He wasn't ready to go back to the principal's office. He'd fled from there because of a pit of guilt in his stomach, pretending he needed a bathroom break, scurrying down hallways that had emptied hours before, and finding solitude. However, fear rather than guilt made him *stay*—fear of the mysterious twitching inside his brain, a damp light behind his eyes that he didn't understand.

The Star Voice had spoken to him again. His ears were still ringing. Adam looked into the reflection of his eyes, and the trembling cadence of the Star Voice sent chills down his spine.

"Don't be afraid," the Star Voice said. *"The transition will be pain, and then the next stage shall begin."*

The voice had been speaking to him for days, but no matter how hard he tried, not getting scared was awfully hard when the school therapist wanted to write him a prescription or when Dad shot him those nervous looks or when Mom leapt into a panic when he mentioned a strange voice. The last few weeks had been hell. Then today, when that snobby rich kid, Joe Sanderson, broke Adam's bicycle—

"Who are you?" Adam whispered, prodding his temples to dig the voice out of his skull. "Please. Just show me you're real."

"Soon. Don't be afraid."

The bathroom door swung open, and Adam's gangly, zit-covered classmate, Greg, stepped inside, reeking of bad cologne. On his way to the urinal, Greg kept his eyes pointed toward the floor, refusing to acknowledge Adam's presence. That wasn't very unusual, for although Greg's high-pitched voice and awkward demeanor made him every bit as socially unacceptable as Adam, he often blasted out Adam's more embarrassing qualities as a scapegoat to fit in better with the popular crowd.

Adam reached out, trying to feel human again. "Hey." As much as he disliked Greg, he still wanted Greg to like *him*. "Mrs. Parker make you stay after school again?"

Greg shook his head and spat into the urinal. To Adam's disbelief, Greg was shivering in his presence. Normally, Greg would have mocked Adam or told Adam that he would never have a girlfriend. Adam wondered if Greg was looking at him differently after having seen the fight.

Maybe he's afraid of me now. Do I like that? Adam couldn't decide whether to be friendly, to act like a badass, or to retreat. He reached to adjust his glasses, an old nervous habit, but his glasses weren't there. *Oh yeah.* He'd forgotten. Joe had shattered them under his heel.

Greg moved to wash his hands, his chin lowered to his collar, avoiding eye contact.

Adam hurried out of the bathroom. The weird new dynamic with Greg was getting too uncomfortable. Besides, he'd been hiding for nearly ten minutes. He had to go back, face the icy condemnation of the adults, deal with whatever punishments they wanted to strike him down with, and most importantly, get far away from the Star Voice.

He scurried down the brown-carpeted hall, unnerved by the long shadows stretching in from the windows. He'd never been at school so late that he saw the sun going down. At Principal Hamer's office, he stopped. Joe Sanderson sat by the door, an ear angled toward it. Inside the office, shouts fired back and forth, most of the loudest outcries coming from Mom's booming lungs. Through the blinds, Adam peeked in at his parents, making quick eye contact with the sorrowful blue eyes of his father, and jumped backward.

The seat next to Joe was open, but Adam definitely wasn't going to sit anywhere close to his most hated enemy. Joe licked the scab on his lip and wiped away blood. "Hey, pussy. Back from your lil' potty break?"

"Wow, Joe." Adam shook his head. "Your insults are always so original. You're a clever kid."

Joe had clearly been on the losing end of their fight. Normally gelled, his black hair was spread out like a lion's mane, both of his eyes were puffed out, and his handsome, square-jawed face was swollen, bent out of shape, and painted with dried blood. Joe's nose was swollen blue and bent enough that Adam thought it looked broken, though he'd never played sports or been too interested in studying medical textbooks, so he didn't know for sure. Adam still couldn't believe that he'd not just won but actually escaped the fight without getting brutalized. Even though Joe Sanderson was a seventh grader, his muscles could have belonged to a high-school football jock or even a gorilla.

Joe extended a middle finger. "Whatever, douche." He wiped blood from his upper lip. "My parents are gonna sue yours. By the time they're done bankrupting your ass, this country's gonna have to send you back home to that dirty alley you people come from. If I could break that stupid bike again, I would."

Adam didn't have the heart to toss any more witty comebacks. The blatant racism struck a nerve. Joe's parents were both wealthy lawyers with a lot of status, and the threat seemed all too real.

"Leave me alone, Joe."

"Too late for that. Say"—Joe peeked through the office window—"I forgot that your parents were regular white people. Huh, *that's* weird. Guess you'd be the only one going home to your lil' gutter in India then, huh?"

Adrenaline burned through Adam like acid. He looked away from Joe's puffy face, swallowed a lump in his throat, and stepped up to the door.

Right at that moment, the entire frame rattled from Mom's nuclear outcry. "I'm telling you Adam's not *like* that!"

"Mrs. Helios—" Principal Hamer started.

"Listen, my son is a damn good kid!" Mom shouted. "And I don't believe for one goddamn second that—"

"Camille," Dad said in his always calm Southern tone, "relax, darlin'. We don't know what—"

"Like *hell* I'm going to relax! Listen, you two. I don't care who you are or how much money you make. Your asshole of a son has been bullying Adam for years, and—"

"Hey!" Joe's father shouted back. "Who are you calling an asshole?"

"Your son, obviously," spat Mom.

"Mrs. Helios," Joe's father said, "there *will* be legal consequences for this. What your foreign street urchin of a son has done to our Joe is reprehensible. I suggest that you cease speaking more about the matter, lest you further incriminate yourself and—"

Principal Hamer raised his voice. "Listen, all of you. I understand that this is a difficult situation, but we need to remain levelheaded. Both Joe and Adam are *children.* Neither of them means wrong. If we don't cooperate peaceably, how can we expect them to? Now, from what I understand, this situation escalated when Adam's bicycle was—"

"You know, Adam *made* that bicycle," Mom snapped. "He's been putting together that bicycle for over a year, picking out each individual part. It's one of his favorite hobbies, other than his outer-space telescope stuff. After all of the work that Adam put into that bicycle, the thought of your asshole son breaking it makes me want to bash the kid's teeth in. How's *that* for incriminating?"

"Camille, please," Dad said.

"The situation began before that, Mrs. Helios." Principal Hamer tapped on his desk. "Adam pushed Joe in the hallway earlier this morning. He was walking next to Chandra Goswami, one of our new students, and after Joe talked to her, two of our teachers say that Adam pushed Joe into the wall."

"I'm sure he had a reason," Dad said.

Adam tried not to notice that Joe was smirking. Adam looked down at his own blood-speckled shoes. *Because Joe called her ugly—that's why I pushed him. He was making fun of her, putting tears in her eyes, the same way he always makes fun of me.*

"Our dear son was badly hurt when your boy abused him," Joe's mother said.

"Serves him right," Mom said, sneering.

Adam remembered pushing Joe in the hallway. He remembered how proud he'd felt about standing up to Joe. *Serves him right.* He hadn't expected Joe to tear apart his bicycle in retribution.

"Have you considered," Joe's father said in a voice so oily it made Adam sick, "that your adorable son might have some... mental illness, perhaps?"

"He's a good kid," Mom said. "Heart's in the right place. That's the only thing that matters. I know that Adam is a strange kid, and maybe he's not *cool* or whatever, but for your son to break his fucking bicycle—"

"Camille, honey," Dad said. "You've gotta relax."

"Are you kidding me? John, this is our son we're talking about! Can't you defend *something* for once in your life?"

"Honey—"

"Don't *honey* me. I'm so sick of your passiveness. You'd let these people walk all over you if I wasn't here."

Adam cringed and moved away from the door.

Joe snickered and swiveled to face Adam, malice in his eyes. "Uh-oh, loser. Looks like your parents got some pro-o-oblems."

"No, they don't," Adam whispered.

"Yeah, they do. You hear them fighting? You know, my mom is a divorce lawyer. Maybe she could help."

"C'mon, dude. Just leave me alone." Adam crossed his arms.

Joe stood up and planted his hands on Adam's shoulders. Then he shoved, and Adam fell to the floor, barely catching himself. Though Adam's blood boiled at the sight of the bully sneering down at him, he didn't act. Despite the pride he'd felt at seeing his black eye in the mirror, he was still the same weak little Adam as before.

"I hope it was worth it." Joe scoffed. "Defending that ugly new girl that you got a crush on, I mean. Cause tomorrow, I'm gonna get the whole class to make fun of her nasty-ass face again."

"Shut up." Adam brushed himself off and listened at the door again.

The back-and-forth shouting between his parents—Joe's parents were silent and watching—had overwhelmed every other noise. Mom and Dad had been fighting every day for a long time. He couldn't remember the last time he'd seen them happy together. Dad was sleeping in the guest room more and more often.

At least a few times a week, every week, Adam heard his name shouted through the walls. The explosive repetitions of "Adam this... Adam that... You need to think more about Adam... Adam shouldn't hear us fighting" often kept him up at night as he struggled not to cause *the big fight*—the one that would end it all, the one that would lead to either Dad or Mom moving out. He would never forgive himself if that happened. As much as he hated Joe, as angry as he'd been when Joe mangled his bicycle, beating up Joe wasn't worth causing the big fight.

"Don't be scared," said the Star Voice.

"At least your husband is being, ah... reasonable," Joe's father said. "Mr. and Mrs. Helios, we're going to leave now. You'll be hearing from us in court at some predetermined time once we work out the basics."

An explosion of bad words went off like a grenade, and Adam forced himself not to listen. The whole situation was his fault. He realized that now. His parents were going to go broke, then they'd get divorced, and it was all his fault.

Joe snickered.

The door swung open. Joe's parents came out first—slick, well-dressed, and elegant, with broad swooping gestures and confident smirks. Joe's father grabbed his son by the collar, lifted him out of his seat, and dragged him down the hall by his arm. An aggressiveness to his manner made Adam wonder if Joe's abusiveness to him was a symptom of something worse at home.

Quivering with anger, Mom emerged from the door and nearly tripped over her high heels on the way out. Her red hair had ripped free from its tight bun and spilled over her shoulders. Her makeup was smeared, revealing dark circles of exhaustion beneath her eyes, and the pale, freckled skin on her face looked as if it'd been stretched so thin that it might tear open.

"Let's go." She slung her dress jacket over her shoulder and dropped her work badge into her purse.

Adam's father emerged behind her, his hands in his back pockets, his broad shoulders slouched as if he were carrying the weight of a tortoise shell. His familiar Atlanta Braves baseball cap was pulled low over his eyes, hiding their blue glow. Dad attempted to wrap a loving arm around Mom's waist, but she stormed ahead. Her heels *click-click-click*ed down the hallway.

"Come on, Adam!" Mom called back as if only remembering at that moment that he was in the hallway. "Let's get going."

Adam moved close to Dad, who offered him a familiar pat on his back. Though Adam felt he had more in common with Mom, he'd always wished he had Dad's simple, good-hearted nature. Dad was an uncomplicated good old boy who just did what he thought was right and didn't analyze things all the time.

"Hey, kid," Dad said, offering his son a wan smile mostly hidden beneath his dark, overgrown mustache. "It's all right. I reckon we should get movin' before—"

"Come on, people, let's *go!*" Mom was already halfway down the hall, rushing in the direction of the parking lot. "I've got to start calling my old lawyer friends from college if we're ever going to make it out of this thing with a roof above our heads. Hurry up!"

Dad sighed. He and Adam stepped forward together, following Mom past the lockers. As they walked, Dad's comforting hand dropped from Adam's back, and the man deliberately walked behind him, which told him his father needed space. Adam wanted to walk next to him. However, the older Adam got, the more distant he felt from his father—and the more Adam thought he himself was a disappointment. Adam knew, deep down, that his old man had probably wanted a son to toss a baseball back and forth with, not one who spent all his free time reading about satellites, staring into a telescope, or correcting adults about how to pronounce the names of distant galaxies or stars. Dad would never say that, but Adam knew.

Adam raced ahead to catch up to Mom. They walked out the double doors at the back of the hall and entered the parking lot right as the sun was dripping inky shadows over the landscape.

The lot was mostly empty. The shattered remains of Adam's bike were parked at the side of the building, barely recognizable as a bicycle anymore. His hands clenched into fists. He looked away from it, swallowing the lump in his throat. Mom stampeded across the parking lot, and he followed her to her SUV. He approached her with a hot blush on his cheeks.

"I'm sorry," he mumbled.

"What?" She jingled her car keys. "Speak up."

"I'm sorry, Mom." Adam lowered his eyes to the ground.

Mom stopped so abruptly that she kicked up dust behind her heels. She swung around to face Adam, and her eyes narrowed then softened. She pulled Adam right up to her and squeezed him tightly, her hair tumbling over his shoulders.

"Not your fault," she said. "God, Adam, sorry I'm in such a mood. It's just that this whole thing really got to me. Listen, I know you're a good kid. You don't have to prove that to me. You didn't deserve to have some bully ruin all your hard work."

Tears were in Adam's eyes. "I don't want something bad to happen to you."

"It won't."

"But I'm scared." Adam's voice was humiliatingly weak, and he ducked his head into his chest to hide his tears. "I have this... feeling."

Mom lifted Adam's chin and stared right into his eyes with fierce confidence. "Don't be. We're fighters, Adam. Always remember: if you believe that everything's going to be okay, if you fight for it, then it *will* be okay. The world doesn't control our lives. We do. We make the decisions. We lead the charge. Remember that."

Adam breathed in heavily. "I know."

"You've always been my Little Optimist. Don't forget that. You've always known how to see the best in things, and I know things get harder when you get older, but you shouldn't lose that. Just remember—everything is going to be okay. Everything is A-okay."

Adam looked down. *Little Optimist.* That was her old childhood nickname for him, from back in the days when he used to run around singing songs and imitating spaceships. He suspected Mom still wished he was still that same bouncy little boy instead of whatever he'd turned into. He bit his lip. He and Mom had been arguing almost as much as Mom and Dad lately, and he didn't want to provoke another fight.

"Sure, yeah," he said, trying to sound relieved.

"Hold it, mister." Her eyes narrowed and snapped onto him like a rubber band. Mom was like a human lie detector, so intuitive that he'd sometimes worried she might be psychic. "What's wrong?"

I don't want to talk about this right now. "Nothing. I said sure."

"No, don't lie to me. Tell me what's wrong."

"It's just... nothing's okay," Adam muttered under his breath and kept walking. "Never mind. I don't want to talk about it."

She stopped him, taking his shoulder. "What do you mean? Talk to me. I hate when you do this silent thing and—"

"I said"—his voice elevated—"*nothing* is A-okay, Mom."

"Adam, honey—"

"I mean, seriously?" He raised his hands. "We're in a world where people get killed every day, and like... we're *still* dropping bombs in other countries, NASA is no longer sending humans into space, our awesome government is controlled by all the big businesses and billionaires—"

"Okay, smartass." She sighed. "Didn't know you'd become a political activist. But listen, kid, as far as you and I are concerned—"

"And Dad's having problems with his back again. I saw him wincing when he lifted the table yesterday." Tears ran down Adam's cheeks, and he wiped them away. "You're always worried about money. Both of you fight every day. Nobody likes me. The only friend I ever had at school... You know what happened to him. And now I'm hearing this weird voice in my head that no one wants to pay attention to... and you're really telling me that everything is okay?" He shook his head. "No, Mom. Stop talking down to me. I'm not your baby anymore. I'm not your Little Optimist anymore, and I'm sick of living with all this crap going on."

Mom stared at him, dead silent, sucking in on her cheeks. Adam shook with frustration, disturbed by how thin his mother had gotten in the past year, since all the fighting had started. Her bone structure, with its jutting shoulder blades and sharp cheeks, was undergoing the transformation from a hidden framework into a visible exoskeleton.

"Adam," she said, "I'm sorry that you..." She shook her head. "Listen, I do understand. Maybe I don't show it, but I'm your mother, so of course I understand."

"Except you're not," Adam whispered. "Not really. That's why you don't get me."

She winced, finally unable to look at him anymore. "Adam, don't say that."

"It's true." Adam gritted his teeth. "My real mother died in India. Right in the Dharavi slum, right in some trash-filled ditch, holding a stupid screaming baby that the agency gave to a couple of white people. Me. Kavi Kapoor. I'm supposed to be dead."

"But you're not dead." She jingled the keys.

"But I *should* be." Adam closed his eyes and reopened them. "If that dumb baby had died in India like I was supposed to, then maybe you and Dad would be happy."

Mom closed her eyes and looked away, breathing heavily. Adam felt a black hole rip open inside him and suck all his emotions into its event horizon. Staring at her, he suddenly remembered being young, playing games with her in the backyard, tossing a Frisbee back and forth and pretending it was a flying saucer. Back in those days, everything made sense. Everything seemed right. Back then, there were no bullies, no confusion, and no Star Voice.

"We'll talk about this later, young man." Her pain was no longer visible, masked by blank, eye-colored shells. "Let's go."

Mom jumped into the driver's seat of the SUV and fired it up. Dad came along behind her, carting the remains of the bicycle. He gingerly stashed it in the trunk, taking care not to scrape the paint. Mom blew the horn. Adam took one more look at its broken gears and decided to never ride a bicycle again. Dad got in the front of the car, and Adam crawled into the back seat, wanting to lie down and hide.

Mom zoomed out of the parking lot and whipped around the turn, clearly not wanting to be stuck in that place any longer than needed. She took off down Whiskey Street, buzzing past a long line of leafy green trees. Dad repetitively tapped the dashboard.

"Honey, you've gotta drive a little slower," he said. "I know you're all emotional and stuff, but I wanna make it home in one piece."

"Emotional and stuff." She snorted. "Our son gets in a fight today, some bully breaks his bicycle, that bully's parents are threatening to sue us, and you're calling me *emotional*. Seriously, John, why the hell are you so calm? Do you really care that little about your own son? About *us*?"

"Of course I care, Camille." He threw his baseball cap onto the dashboard, running his hands along the circumference of his shiny, balding head. "You don't have to give me crap like that. It ain't fair. But we need to look over our options, y'know. Be rational about—"

"Can't you just get *mad* for once, John? Can't you just show a little goddamn emotion, defend someone you care about, show that you actually care about something besides your little handyman business?"

"I *do* care!"

Adam shrank into his seat. *Please stop fighting. I don't want to hear this. Please.*

Mom turned onto Laurel Street, and Dad was fidgeting anxiously. The two of them continued shouting back and forth. Mom turned up the music to drown out Dad's voice, and the cacophony exploded in Adam's ears—then faded into a gentle ringing.

Adam watched his parents argue, but he could no longer hear them. The increasingly high-pitched ringing in his mind overtook every other sound. As the sun continued its descent, he saw—no, not saw, *felt*—stars appearing in the sky. With them, the Star Voice returned.

"Adam. Don't be afraid."

"Who are you?" he whispered, knowing his small voice was hidden beneath the deafening roar of his parents' argument.

"We are your friends. Please find us."

"How?"

"We'll show you the way."

"But—"

"Brace yourself. Fight through the pain. Then follow the light. Meet us between the folds of darkness, and find us in the stars. You're almost here."

Adam's sense of reality whirled like a top, as if his head were spinning off his shoulders. The colors of everything around him glowed, as if a neon bulb were shining behind every object. Though he couldn't hear the noises of his parents' argument, he saw soundwaves shoot from their lips and bounce off every object, leaving little dings and pockmarks in the leather seats of the SUV. He focused on the individual hairs on his father's face, then the shimmering clear polish of his mother's fingernails, and finally the light of the half-dead sun bouncing off the dashboard of the car.

Terror seized him by the throat, and he didn't know why. He couldn't hear the Star Voice, but he felt its presence inside him, grabbing his guts and squeezing them. As Mom drove the SUV to a red traffic light at the busiest intersection in town, his parents' voices intensified. Dad had changed the radio station, and Soundgarden's "The Day I Tried to Live" blasted from the speakers.

"That's such a lame excuse, John!"

"Camille, we gotta stop fighting this way. We've been fighting way too long."

"Well, there's a solution for that, now isn't there?" she snipped. "Maybe we can hire one of these lawyer parents and take care of our dispute *that* way."

"Camille," Dad said in a sharper tone than Adam had ever heard him use. "For Christ's sake, Adam is right back there."

Mom stopped and whipped her head around to look at Adam, her dark eyes stretched taut. Still parked at the traffic light, she reached back to touch Adam's hand. "I'm sorry," she said.

Adam nodded in a feeble manner but said nothing.

She bit her lip. "Adam, I'm sorry. I shouldn't have said that—"

"The light's green," Dad said.

Mom shot Dad a violent look, squeezed Adam's hand, and returned to her driving position. The car behind her honked. She sped forward. Adam looked out the passenger window, sighing to himself. "The Day I Tried to Live" continued playing from the car speakers. He tried to follow the lyrics. *One more time again...*

Then the front license plate of a white truck on the right side of the intersection went from a harmless speck to a looming giant. Adam saw it for only a split second, but he *felt* the collision's impact in a way that registered throughout his entire body. The entire side of the SUV buckled inward and pierced him in the arm, leg, and collarbone. The window shattered to pieces. Chips of glass tore bloody slices out of his flesh. The car tumbled sideways, gravity reversed, and the floor flipped over to become the ceiling.

Please, God... please save me. I don't want to die.

"Adam!" Mom shrieked.

Gravity skewed so bizarrely that Adam could no longer feel the seat beneath him. Dad reached out for him, extending five splayed fingers—and a sudden protrusion of sharp metal sliced off three of them, leaving only bloody red nubs where he'd once possessed useful appendages.

Then the entire car disappeared. Instead, Adam stared into the dimming sky, and his body cut through the wind, soaring over the other cars. Mom's SUV tumbled down the hill behind him while he flew through the air.

He hadn't put his seatbelt on. All those commercials on TV, all those warnings from his teachers, all those times Mom had told him to always put it on, all those times he *had* put it on—and there he was, in the moment it most mattered, flying out a broken window. As his body hurtled through space, he heard a scream so distant that he barely registered it as coming from his own lungs. He smelled blood and gasoline. He saw the last light of the sunset.

Adam's skull smashed into the hard asphalt, and he heard the bone crack open. He crunched into the gravel. His body crumpled into itself like a compacted aluminum can. Warm blood emptied from his wounds, forming a puddle around him.

Back on the street was a tangled mess of automobiles, piled all over each other beneath the traffic light. Streaks of rainbow-colored oil spilled across the dark street. Flames stretched to the clouds like long orange fingers reaching for God. An ambulance hollered somewhere in a vague distance that didn't seem real, and someone was calling his name.

He tried to call back, but his lungs felt like shredded tissue paper covered in hot mucus.

Then his name wasn't his name anymore. Language became an unintelligible mess of noise, garbled together with synthesizers. He understood nothing but pain. He didn't know who he was. He lost any sense of *what* he was. As consciousness faded, as colors dissipated into a murky, bloody haze, he perceived only one thing vividly.

A light burned in the sky—not the sun, but something else, something brighter—and it was beckoning him.

Chapter 2: Recall

He's six years old again, sleeping peacefully in his bedroom, lying sideways in the red wooden racecar bed that his dad made for him. He wanted a spaceship bed, and Dad made a racecar instead, but that's okay because he loves his room—the way it's high above everything, the way it touches the sky so that he can sit in the window and dangle his legs out over the driveway and—

Darkness. Pitch black. A heavy weight pressed down on his forehead. Blood. Fire. The smell of burnt flesh. Pain rippled through him. Skin crawled over muscle, more liquid than solid. Bubbles. Pus. Hot flames licked raw wounds while cold tremors crept through his blood.

He's a happy little boy, that six-year-old, so happy. He's homeschooled, never facing rejection, never made fun of. He still likes himself and hasn't yet learned the talent for self-loathing that will one day be his biggest hobby. In bed, he's cuddling with his favorite plush Jupiter Man doll, wearing his Jupiter Man footie pajamas. Jupiter Man, AKA Christopher Cosmo, has always been his favorite superhero and always will be, forever. It's the middle of the night, and he's awakened by the springs of his bed bouncing up and down. He wakes up and stares at the glowing space stickers on the ceiling.

Mom and Dad are there. Mom is bouncing up and down on his bed, her face spread open in a grin, her red curls like little cherry-colored Slinkies. She's in her pajamas, and Dad is in his boxers. Outside the giant window, millions of stars prick through the black sky like glistening pins.

"Happy birthday!" Mom cries. "Wake up, my Little Optimist! It's your birthday today, the exact hour of it!"

He throws his blanket off so quickly that it flies off the bed. Being seven is so cool, so new to him. He puts his Jupiter Man doll aside and jumps into his mom's arms, and she hugs him. He reaches out for Dad, and they all share in the group hug. Seven. He's seven! Wow, he feels so old now. As he climbs out of bed, his legs wobble beneath him. He stares out the window, thrilled to be up so late. He's never been woken up at midnight before.

"Happy birthday, son." Dad grins then kisses Mom on the cheek.

Adam stares up at his dad, and they smile at each other. Adam wants to be just like Dad when he grows up. Dad is always so strong, so capable. A man of few words, he still always gets the job done and makes racecar beds for his son. Maybe Adam will even grow a mustache and beard like Dad too, though he doesn't know if he wants to get a bald spot like Dad has, but maybe he would because smart guys often seem to have bald spots. He walks up to the window. He loves looking up at the night sky. It's his favorite thing in the world. Whenever he wakes up at night, he just stares and stares at the stars for hours. He loses himself in them. He can—

Darkness became light. Light became pain. The dull, heavy sensation on his forehead became duller, heavier. The worst pain hit whenever he tried to focus on anything, whether a sensation or a thought. Just staying in a dull state was easier. Not thinking. Not wondering. He knew meanings but didn't remember any words. His head felt cracked, split in half.

His brain was broken.

Broken. Broke brain. *Break it in half, gone, gone, gone...*

"Seven years old, Little Optimist o' mine!" Mom laughs. "We're going to let you go back to sleep in a moment—"

"I wasn't asleep," Adam says. "I was awake when you came in."

"Sure thing, sport." Dad chuckles. "And I'm the king of Siam."

Mom nudges him, planting a grinning kiss on his lips. Adam looks at her feet, with her thin white toes and purple toenails, compared to Dad's hairy hobbit feet. He then stares up at the ceiling, with the glow-in-the-

dark stick-on planetary constellations that his parents put up a few months ago.

"Anyway," Mom says, "before you go back to bed, we wanted to wake you up so you could open your first present."

Adam smiles because in the dark corner of the room, right next to the window, sits a big box wrapped in black paper. He loves birthdays—not just his birthday, but everyone's. If anything, he actually prefers other people's birthdays since he loves to pick out presents for them—like last year, when he bought Dad that green polo shirt, or this year, when he picked out the marble statue for Mom.

"Can I open it now?" Adam asks.

Mom nuzzles into the crook of Dad's arm and gives Adam a thumbs-up. Adam creeps toward it, excited but trying to keep from getting too amped up. He wonders if it's the present he's asked for, but he knows Mom and Dad have been having money problems. He knows not to get his hopes up.

"Right now?" he confirms.

Mom nods. "Remember that present you begged me for, Adam?"

Adam's heart leaps into his chest. He looks at the night sky, trying to keep from getting too excited. He wants it so badly.

"C'mon, son." Dad laughs. "You've been beggin' us for a long time."

Adam can't resist. He claws at the wrapping paper, ripping it to shreds. A telescope waits beneath it, the exact thing he wants the most in the world. He opens the box.

"Yes, yes, yes!" Adam squeals.

It's brand new—shiny, metallic black, and almost as big as he is. Dad comes over to help him lift it out of the box, and together they crane its mechanical neck toward the night sky. Adam lunges at his parents and hugs them. They hug him back. They're always there for him. They always take care of him.

"For the record, I have no idea what you like so much about all those stars, galaxies, and whatever." Mom laughs again. "But if that's what you like, then it's what you like."

"Yes, it is! Can I use it? Please?"

"Why do you think we woke you up at midnight?"

Dad helps him finish setting up the telescope. Mom sits on the bed and watches them with one of those really big smiles that she only shines upon others some of the time. Once the telescope is set up, Adam can't wait any longer. He points it up to the sky. He aims it right at Mars, the tiny red dot, and he puts his eye to the lens. His heart bounces up and down in his chest.

Then he sees outer space. Stars, planets, satellites, everything he's ever dreamed about seeing up close. He sees...

He sees...

Darkness. No lights. No sensations. Nothing but dull emptiness. Slowly, he became aware of a deep thudding within his chest, slow and steady. He tried to open his eyes, but the light was too painful to take in. He slammed them shut again.

He tried to imagine where he was or what he looked like, but he found that he couldn't. Instead, he imagined only a little wooden man, like a sort of puppet without strings, falling into a hole in the ground, his limbs flailing about. He wasn't trying to look so ridiculous, but he just didn't have a brain. His limbs floundered and thrashed without any good reason. Then he disappeared in the hole.

Death was a gaping mouth, sucking him down into its snakelike throat. He heard voices, a flurry of unintelligible sounds that his brain could not put together. Everything was unfocused, hazy, and meaning-less—everything but the Star Voice.

"Stay strong, Adam. Don't look away from the light."

A giant star appeared before him, bursting through layers of space and tugging on every nerve of his body, exercising a magnetic pull on every individual atom that comprised his being. Fighting against the pain, struggling against the heaviness on his head, Adam tore open his eyelids. All he could see was a white glow. He screamed.

Chapter 3: Recoil

Camille Campton-Helios woke up screaming, shooting upright in bed. A sandpapery blanket spilled over the side of the mattress, settling on the floor like a coiled snake. Her bare, goose bump–covered legs were coated in cold sweat.

She was also alive, but until her panic had a moment to settle, that fact—no matter how astonishing or unlikely—was the least of her concerns.

Her scream subsided into a strained howl. After several moments, her ears picked up on the calm purring of the medical machinery beside her. Outside the window, a cloudless night sky watched her, and the man in the moon gazed down with a sadistic smirk. As she hugged her legs to her chest, she realized she was wearing a johnny gown and an IV was plugged into her arm. *How did I get into the hospital? What happened? Last I remember, Adam beat up that Joe kid...* That was right. Her son had gotten into a fight with his regular bully, so she and John had gone to counsel the principal and—

Oh my God. The intersection. The car. Adam flying through the window. She had blacked out.

Camille pressed the call button looped around her side rail. Her hands shook so hard that the button slipped through her fingers. She swiped her damp, frizzy hair out of her face and pushed it behind her ears. A glass door slid open, and a short, heavyset nurse walked in with downcast eyes.

"You're okay," the nurse said, feeling in the pocket of her blue scrub top and pulling out rubber gloves. "No bad injuries. Nothing that won't heal. Don't worry."

Camille ran her tongue along the inside of her teeth. She wanted to demand answers, but the day's events had siphoned the gas right out of her motormouth.

"My son," Camille whispered. "Please tell me he's not dead."

"He's alive," the nurse said. "Husband's alive too. Just like you. Now, take a deep breath for a second, and thank heaven for that oxygen in your lungs. Can I get your arm, honey?"

The nurse smiled, revealing gaps in her teeth, then stretched on her gloves. Her badge revealed her name to be Geraldine Hopewell and showed a picture of her in the sort of overdone makeup applied by someone who normally didn't use makeup.

"Mrs. Helios?" the nurse asked.

"Campton-Helios." When the nurse raised an eyebrow, Camille pinched her lips. "I mean... yes."

"Camille?"

"Yeah... yeah."

"Are you here with me, sweetie?"

Camille gulped and shook her head. "No. Yes. You say I'm... okay?"

Geraldine hooked Camille's index finger up to a monitor then wrapped a blood-pressure cuff around her arm. If Camille remembered correctly from her younger days as a per-diem CNA, the device would quickly take her pulse, BP, and oxygen levels simultaneously. The nurse was a remarkably calm woman, which was a rare and beautiful trait for a nurse to have. Camille shuddered at the memory of how frenetic working in a healthcare facility was and how so many workers got burnt out.

Geraldine had the worn, sagging cheeks of a nurse who'd probably been doing the job for most of her life—she'd seen everything and taken care of everyone, and she wouldn't get surprised easily. "Sweetie, you're gonna be just fine." She unplugged Camille from the IV with a quick, nonchalant flick of her wrist. "You've been unconscious, but you're a lucky duck. A couple cuts, some bruises. Though you do got yourself some minor traces of blood in your urine, so we gotta keep an eye on that."

"Urine? How did you—"

"We had a catheter in you. Don't worry, it's out now. And then we did some x-rays, found nothing to worry about—"

"I slept through x-rays?"

"Honey." Geraldine smiled a crinkle-eyed smile, her professional voice melting into a more affectionate tone. "You was out like a god-damn light."

Camille smiled back at her, unable to resist the nurse's working-class charm. Geraldine unwrapped the blood-pressure cuff. Then she noted the numbers, unsnapped her gloves, and rested her wide, callused palm on Camille's leg. "You're alive, hon. Be happy about that."

Camille nodded. "Yeah. But... but..."

"What's wrong?"

Tears formed in Camille's eyes as she took hold of Geraldine's hand. Her pulse raced. "What happened to my family?"

A FEW HOURS LATER, Camille was dressed, discharged, and ready to move. She signed the release forms and agreed to come back for a checkup in two weeks. She moved her base of operations to the waiting room outside the ICU, transforming from patient to worried family member.

She was okay, but Adam and John were another story.

Geraldine hadn't known the details about either of them, other than the fact that both were alive but in critical condition. Adam and John weren't on her unit. No one on that floor had any idea, so Camille had moved to the ICU and was waiting for Dr. Blake to fill her in. On the elevator to the third floor, Camille had felt a sense of purpose, but as she stepped into the empty waiting room, with its dim lights and a flickering TV showing some stupid reality show, knowing she had no idea how long she might have to wait...

I can't do this. Hopelessness grabbed her by the throat and threatened to drag her to the floor.

Her feet bristled with the urge to march into the ICU and make demands, as she always did. Her door-busting attitude was what had gotten her through college and grad school with straight As even though she'd been a high-school dropout before that. She was always prompt, always ten or twenty minutes early for every appointment of her life, with a perfectly organized closet and a rigid morning routine. She kept a tight schedule and expected others to do the same. Her attitude and discipline were what got her through her sixty-hour work week and why the company depended on her even though she was paid half of what she deserved. She wanted to whip the doctors into shape and make sure they did everything right. However, as those urges burned up like oil trails inside her, a greater realization held her back: this time, she could not do anything. At times like the present, her strengths became her greatest weaknesses. Stubbornness became impatience, and defiance became blubbering fear. Somewhere, just beyond that door she wasn't allowed to cross, her son and her husband were being operated on, and all she could do was wait.

She was powerless. Though she'd always been agnostic, she found herself wishing she was religious. Her vision blurred at the thought of living in a brutal, purposeless world with no rules, where one accident could sweep in and tear her life apart. One day, she was a mother and a wife—the next day, she could be a childless widow. Camille stared at the television, wishing it would crash down on her head.

No, I can't think that way. Stay positive, like Adam always is. Or always used to be, anyway. The Little Optimist who'd once always cheered her up with his positive, bizarre-but-oddly-logical insights about the world had become a bitter adolescent, a shut-mouthed loner who didn't open the gates for anyone.

Well, he certainly won't be very talkative ever again if he's dead.

Twitching like someone recovering from a seizure, Camille stood up, sat back down, then stood up again. She walked back and forth across the waiting room several times then noticed a dusty Keurig in the corner. She prepared herself a cup of black coffee with a teaspoon of sugar and brought it back to her original seat. She held the coffee to her face and breathed in the soothing aroma of the caffeinated release.

They're dead. Both of them are dead. I know it. She tried to focus on the coffee. She swished it around in its Styrofoam cup, watching the coffee gently bob from side to side as if it were trying to escape the cup. She took a sip, but it was too hot and burnt her tongue. She put the cup down on the magazine shelf next to her.

Glancing at her phone, she winced at the sight of forty-three missed calls and countless more unread text messages. She scrolled through her social-media feed, and her stomach lurched at the multiple headlines and photos about her accident, sprinkled casually amidst the usual coverage of political posts, goofy memes, and high-school football games. Their town was a small one, where everyone knew everything. As much as Camille loved attention, her cheeks reddened at the thought of her family being front and center in the town gossip.

That was particularly true when it came to Adam—shy, delicate little Adam. Camille's guts twisted up at the memory of how she'd reacted when Adam had told her about the "Star Voice" in his head, how she'd flipped out and panicked. She reacted in exactly the wrong way, causing him to retreat from her. Since then, he'd avoided all mention of that Star Voice, but she'd known something was still going on. News of the fight with Joe had shocked her, but it hadn't surprised her. *Not that any of this matters now because he's probably dead by now. You're the mother of a dead child. He's gone, and it's your fault because maybe if you'd gotten him help, maybe if you'd actually* listened *to him—*

After a click, the door opened. When a tall Caucasian man with a glistening shaved head walked in, wielding a clipboard like a shield,

Camille knew instantly he was Dr. Benjamin Blake. After having worked that CNA job as a college student, Camille's blood always ran cold at the sight of white coats.

The doctor approached her in the way that professional health-care workers always approached people with whom they were about to share bad news. His shoulders were slumped, eyes lowered, hands stroking his dark goatee. Camille jumped to her feet and shook his chapped hand far too aggressively for his liking, for his grip soon became as limp as an eel wanting to slip back into its hole.

"I'm Mrs. Campton-Helios," she said. "Dr. Blake?"

"Yes. Yes, Mrs. Helios, a pleasure to meet you. I'm afraid I have some, ah—"

"Bad news." Camille cleared her throat. "Spill it."

Camille hoped she was wrong. She hoped that she was an idiot, assuming the worst, fearful for no reason, and that Dr. Blake was going to tell her everything was fine. She even prayed for that, albeit silently—she actually *prayed* to a god she didn't believe in, begging Him, Her, or It for the lives of her family. Before Dr. Blake spoke, he sucked in a massive breath of air.

"I'm sorry," he said.

"What?"

"You're right. Yes. I have bad news."

"About whom?" Camille asked, her tone sharpening as if in accusation. "Which one might die tonight, Adam or John?"

Dr. Blake shook his head. "Both."

Chapter 4: I am I

H*e's walking next to her. Chandra Goswami is her name, this new girl from Nebraska with the amazing brown eyes that stare at him and don't blink and don't look away. She has a scar from her lip to her nose, the final signature of a cleft lip. That's why Joe Sanderson makes fun of her, but Adam doesn't care. She's still beautiful, the most beautiful girl he's ever seen, and when she says, "Hi, Adam," he wants to jump with happiness. When she smiles at him, he can't believe it because a girl has never looked at him this way before.*

"I, uh, I like your name," he says.

"Really?" She giggles. "Why?"

"Um, I guess 'cause it reminds me of NASA's Chandra X-Ray Observatory," he mumbles. "It's really cool. Do you know about it?"

"Nope." She shrugs. "You can tell me about it?"

They're walking together down the hallway. Side by side, they pass through the doors of Ottanga Junior High, walking home together. Just the two of them are there, guy and girl, and everyone can see them. They see *Adam Helios, the walking spaghetti noodle in glasses, walking home with the cute new girl. Adam unlocks his custom bicycle from the bike rack and holds it by one handlebar, wheeling it along beside him as he walks. They walk down the sidewalk, and the breeze from a passing car—*

Cars.

Avoid the cars!

Cars kill. Death, death, death.

—rustles her hair. She points at his rusty, awkward-looking, homemade contraption of gears and pedals, and Adam stiffens as he prepares for her to make fun of it.

"Did you make that?" she asks.

"Heh. Um... yeah." He adjusts his glasses. "I, uh... found the parts at a junkyard, mostly. I just went there, like, every week. I collected what I needed, looked up online tutorials and... yeah. I know it looks sketchy."

"Dude," she says, "that is the most seriously awesome thing I've ever seen. You did that? You must be really smart."

He looks down. "Me?"

"Yeah. I like smart guys." She nudges his head up.

"I'm not smart. I just like reading about stupid stuff." He notices he's biting his fingernails and puts his hand in his pocket. "I'm sorry, I should get going. I don't want you to get annoyed with—"

"You don't have to go." She reaches out and touches his back. "Y'know, I'm new, I don't have any friends here. Can you, like... Do you wanna hang out, maybe? You can say no if you don't wanna."

Adam smiles. "Okay." He walks beside her. Right at that moment another fast car races by and—

Car, Car, Car. Death, Death, Death.

Death!

Ringing. High-pitched ringing. Everything was ringing.

He seemed to be lying down, but he couldn't sit up, couldn't move an arm, leg, finger, or toe. He breathed, his chest heaving in and out, and a cold numbness surrounded his mind in the shape of a human body. In the pocket of his cheek, he felt cold, hard rocks that had probably been teeth a few hours before. Cold metal chunks were embedded inside him, streaked with blood. His eyes were open, but he couldn't see. Everything looked white.

He couldn't move. He could *think*, but he couldn't speak, breathe, or react. His entire body was paralyzed.

Unintelligible muttering surrounded him. He blinked, and the blood on his eyes gave way to vision. The white starlight flooding his mind dimmed, replaced by the comparatively dull glow of a fluorescent light bulb.

Dark shadow people with masks and blue uniforms surrounded him. He heard metal clicks. Something rubbery poked at his side—the prodding finger of a latex glove. One of the shadow people popped open the cap of a permanent marker, and its inky odor gagged him. The marker's cold wet tip pressed down against the lumpy, inactive clay that was supposed to be his body.

The accident. The car crash. They were operating on him.

And he was awake.

His heart raced, and his brain fired with signals to move, to scream, to thrash around wildly, to call for help. *I'm awake! Don't do this to me. Put me out. Put me to sleep!*

One of the shadow people held a scalpel. Glowing goggle lenses peered down upon him. Adam silently pleaded for an escape, but no escape came. He was only thirteen years old. He'd always been a good kid, at least until that day. He'd done nothing to deserve such a horrific fate. If he could go back, if he could stop that car—

Cars. Lots of cars.

He walks through the junkyard with Chandra, the same junkyard where he found all his bike pieces. Hundreds of crushed, decimated cars, like a post-apocalyptic wasteland. Others would find it depressing, but Adam loves to see the mechanical guts of these cars, to analyze their inner workings. Maybe that's why everyone thinks he's so weird.

"Were you born in India?" Adam asks.

"No, I wish. That'd be cool." She shakes her head. "But I've visited there a few times. The food is awesome, but the traffic is crazy. People drive without headlights. My parents are from India, of course. Kolkata. Where in India are your parents from?"

"I..." He bites his lip, not sure how to respond. "No. I dunno."

A million needles stab his heart at the thought that she might reject him for being adopted by American parents instead of coming from a true Indian background. He's quiet, not answering her question, but Chandra doesn't force him to talk. Instead, she just slips her hand into his, and be-

fore he realizes it, their fingers are interlaced. No girl has ever held his hand before. The two of them climb to the top of a big hill and take a seat on the hood of a rusted red Dodge with no wheels on it, just as the sun slips below the clouds and stars glimmer in the dark sky. The Dodge hasn't been there before, but the place is familiar. From the crest of this hill, he can see the entirety of the junkyard spread out before him, all the broken-down cars, and beyond them a landscape of trees that goes on for miles.

"You like this spot?" she asks.

"I come here all the time, yeah. It's where I like to think."

"About what?"

He shrugs. "Stupid things. The same sorta stupid things that all dorks like me think about."

"Dude. Stop pretending that everything you like is stupid. Tell me?"

Adam taps the car's hood, head lowered. "Life." He points up at the burgeoning night sky. "The universe. I like looking at the stars. I always have. At first, when I look up at 'em, I feel lonely. But then..."

"Then... what?"

The Adam who sits on the hood of that Dodge, the Adam who exists just a few days before the car crash, before the fight, the Adam who may never exist again—now that he got in that stupid, stupid fight—that old Adam smiles at the first girl who has ever talked to him and squeezes her hand, and she doesn't let go. "Then, I think about how huge the universe is," he says. "And how small I am. It makes me think how, y'know, bullies don't matter, drama doesn't matter, none of that is important. And I think, maybe, in a universe so frickin' huge, maybe a person can only create their own path. No matter where we are on this whole big planet, we all see the same sky. And when I think about it that way, instead of feeling lonely, I feel—"

"Free?"

"Yeah. Totally."

And they sit there, on the hood of that old red Dodge, their blue-jeaned legs touching just barely enough that he can feel that Chandra is

*shivering as much as he is. The stars looking down on them are luminous,
bigger than usual, brighter than usual. Adam doesn't tell her about the
Star Voice because he doesn't want her to think he's crazy.*

"So are you gonna be an astronaut someday?" she asks.

"Maybe." He laughs. "I'd like to. Or at least something to do with satellites, maybe, or something to do with space. Everyone always tells me I
should be a scientist, that I act like one or something."

"What was it that made you like space so much?"

He shrugs. "I dunno. Jupiter Man, I guess."

"The—wha?"

"Jupiter Man." He chuckles then looks away when he realizes she
doesn't get the reference. "He's a comic-book character, y'know, like... a superhero. The guy with the big purple helmet. He shoots lights out of his
hands that carry him through space on, like, this big streak of light."

"Oh yeah!" She giggles. "But why him? Why not Batman, Spider-
Man...?"

"I dunno. I think he's, like... not just that he's so different, like I am,
but y'know, he was inspirational to me as a kid. Christopher Cosmo—see,
that's his real name, and he was born on Earth, but then he got adopted
by the peaceful aliens of Jupiter, who all have giant green heads. Then one
day, Jupiter gets attacked by this big angry alien race of giant bug monsters
called the Byzaxamites—"

"Byzax-a-what?"

"Byzaxamites, yeah. And the bugs, see, they were gonna destroy the
whole planet, and they shoot out this disease that causes the Jupiter aliens
to all get sick. But Christopher, since he's actually an Earthling, his genetics are different, and so he's immune from the disease that the bugs shoot.
So he flies into the Byzaxamite ship, and he breaks it all up, so it drives
them away forever. But because Christopher goes into their ship—which
gives him his powers, by the way—he's now carrying the bug disease, so he's
now poisonous to his family on Jupiter, and he can't ever go home. He never sees his family again... to save them, see, he had to leave them behind."

"That's really sad."

"Yeah. And he's really sad about it too. But he tries to do something good with it all, and so with his new powers, he becomes Jupiter Man and goes around the galaxy saving other planets and stuff. He's such a cool character I really look up to him, which I know is silly, but... yeah, I dunno. He—"

In the distance, a car races by, playing Soundgarden's song "The Day I Tried to Live." Adam's always liked that song. He has connected to it. His head follows the music, listening to it. He takes off his glasses, closes his eyes, focuses on the beat, and—

"Adam?"

Adam looks over, and before he knows what's happening, Chandra's lips are pressed against his cheek. He's startled, totally caught off guard, and he squeezes her hand, wondering if he should try to kiss her on the lips or not. The junkyard of dead cars surrounds them, their hearts beat together, and the stars look down over them both. Right after this happens, right when he's getting ready to try to kiss her, there's a ringing in his head, and the Star Voice—

The scalpel.

The scalpel sliced into his skin. A whole parade of masked faces was standing around him. Adam tried to close his eyelids, desperately tried to close them, but even those tiny little muscles were no longer under his control. He had no choice but to watch them operate on him.

The Star Voice spoke. *"Adam. We need you to save us from the sickness."*

A brilliant light spread outward from the corner of his vision and hovered just out of sight. Something stood in the center of that light, some kind of jagged figure that vaguely resembled a man but was carved from obsidian rock. White flames danced around every crevice of the rock-man's body, disappearing in the light behind it. The rocky humanoid walked away, leading him somewhere. When he tried to focus on the rock person, it disappeared, but when he relaxed, it was there again.

"*Follow us. Follow the light.*"

Adam's body wouldn't let him move. He could do nothing, trapped beneath the scalpel and beneath the weight on his forehead.

"*Adam, leave your body behind.*"

At first, the statement seemed insane, but as Adam focused on that single thought—*leave your body behind*—he felt the dull heaviness of his body start to flutter away. His ears rang with a piercing echo. His vision became brighter. The obsidian figure in the flames loomed before him then disappeared in a flash of white. Then Adam left his body behind and hovered over himself like a floating shadow.

Chapter 5: Bad News

Camille clenched her fingers around the seat of her chair and waited. *Just tell me how bad it is or how long they have. Spit it out.*

Dr. Blake sucked in his cheeks, tapped a pen against his clipboard, and stared at his notes. The waiting room was an empty vacuum, other than the flickers from the TV in the corner, now playing one of those weird and inappropriate Millennial-era cartoons that Adam watched at night. Camille felt the urge to bite her fingernails, an old childhood habit that had died many years before.

"Ms. Helios, I'm not sure what to say. They're not so—"

"They're going to die, right?" Camille said. "If they are, Doctor, then you'd better tell me so I can start grieving because if my family is dead, I might as well stick a gun in my mouth right now."

"No," he said. "It's not so black-and-white. Both of them have a chance. But it's shaky."

Camille exhaled a sigh of relief so heavy that it knocked the wind out of her. Tingles ran down her spine. Her son and her husband had a chance. No matter how bad Dr. Blake's news was, no matter what he told her now, she had room for hope.

"Okay," she said. "Wow, okay."

"Which one should I talk about first?" Dr. Blake asked.

"You serious?" *For Christ's sake, this is like* Sophie's Choice *or something.* "Okay, Adam. Tell me about Adam."

Dr. Blake looked away from her in a way that made Camille want to spit in anger. "Your son, he... he's currently being operated on. Mrs. Helios—"

"Camille." She got enough formality at work and didn't need it here—not while all this was going on.

"Camille, then." The doctor gulped. "I don't know how to put this gently, so I'll give you the facts. Adam's skull was cracked open. His body is pretty torn up, but the most extensive damage is to his spine and his head. We think that he has suffered a traumatic brain injury."

Camille lunged forward, and Dr. Blake jumped back. Her fingers wanted to wrap around the doctor's throat, to blame him for what had happened, to blame *something.* However, she couldn't blame him. He wasn't the one who had been driving. The fault wasn't Dr. Blake's.

It was *hers.*

She started to speak, but a sob bubbled up in her throat, and she couldn't form words without choking. Dr. Blake held out a tissue box, but she refused it. She hated crying in front of people. Her father had always told her that showing weakness was pathetic. As much as she now realized what a foolish statement that was—and hoped she'd never passed that painful legacy of repression down to her son—his lectures had made their mark on her.

"Fuck," she said.

"I'm sorry," Dr. Blake said. "We won't know the extent of the damage until more work is done. During automobile accidents, the sheer force of the collision can often cause the brain to collide against the hard, internal bone of the skull. And on top of that, when his skull cracked open... As I said, Camille, we don't know if he's going to make it. It's shaky. And if he does make it, we can't guarantee that there won't be extensive brain damage. I know this is hard, but we're going to need you to think really long and hard about your options."

Camille wiped her eyes. "Options?"

"In case your son has to go on permanent life support."

"Oh my God."

Camille walked away, positioning herself in front of a window, looking out at the night sky—Adam's sky, the sky he always loved so much. *Life support.* She couldn't handle that—not after having worked as a CNA, not after having taken care of people like that—not after having seen what had happened to Adam's old friend Theo Schlesinger, the only real friend her son had ever had. The idea of Adam being trapped in his body, unable to escape, unable to do anything...

"Is there an advance directive?" the doctor asked. "Did you have any plan in place for this? I know, probably a long shot."

"No. I never thought..." She rubbed her eyes with a sleeve. "Is he in a coma?"

"He's currently in a coma, yes. Depending on the state of his brain damage, he might be experiencing cerebromedullospinal disconnection—"

"Cereba-what? Please, no medical jargon right now. I can't take it."

"It's called locked-in syndrome. Paralysis of all voluntary muscles except for the eyes. He might—"

"Stop." Camille shook her head, her body trembling with terror. "What about my husband?"

"Ah, yes." Dr. Blake breathed a sigh of relief, noticeably thankful at not having to talk about the poor little boy with locked-in syndrome. His bedside manner wasn't terrible, but it wasn't great, either.

Camille stifled her mouthy comments. *That's my little boy you don't want to talk about, you prick.*

"Your husband, yes," Dr. Blake said. "He's in slightly better shape."

She clenched her fists. "What the hell does *slightly* mean?"

Dr. Blake moved backward. "Sorry. I mean his brain has sustained no damage. However, his stomach was punctured, and he's lost a lot of blood. Three of his fingers were severed in the accident—"

Adam's diagnosis had stabbed her in the heart, and John's twisted the knife. She thought about the first time she'd met John, how he'd smiled so confidently at her and held her face with those broad, manly hands right before he'd kissed her for the first time. She thought about how much he loved throwing his baseball, playing guitar, fixing things.

She loved his hands—or *had* loved them. Now three of those fingers were stumps. She paced back and forth.

"And your husband's eye, well..." The doctor hesitated. "I'm sorry, Camille, but we were unable to save his right eye."

Camille choked. His right eye. The eye that always looked at her, winked at her, and called her beautiful even when they fought. That wonderful blue eye. Gone.

"Is he going to... Is he..."

"If we can stop the bleeding, he has a chance." Dr. Blake shook his head.

If. Not yes, but *if.* Also, if he did survive, he'd be a man with one eyeball and one working hand. Camille faced the window again so that the doctor couldn't see her crumbling. In the past six months, she'd actively considered divorcing John. She went so far as to look up divorce lawyers. Now, all that seemed so stupid. Every argument they'd had seemed so minor in comparison to the love they'd shared for over a decade.

Dr. Blake stood up and started to reach out to console her. Then, as if sensing her anger, he pulled back. "I'm sorry. I have to go back in there."

"Can I see them?"

He shook his head. "Not until they get out of their respective operations."

"Is there anything I can do?" When he shook his head again, she pushed closer to him. "Please, please, please, there must be something. *Something.*"

He started to speak and then stopped. After a long pause, he said, "Not really."

Camille wanted to believe he was lying but felt he was telling the truth. Her family might die or might be disabled, but all she could do was stand around like a statue and wait for more bad news that she had no control over. She waved Dr. Blake off, and he left the waiting room.

Their conditions were her fault. She was the one driving. She'd always been so impulsive, so daring, and such a go-getter, and her family would pay the ultimate price for her defective personality. If she could just go back and switch places—have *her* be the one who died while both of them survived—she'd do it in heartbeat, but life didn't offer such choices. Instead, it offered grim punishment. Camille sat down on the floor, pulled her legs up to her chest, and bawled her eyes out.

Chapter 6: Abduction

Adam floated into the air.

The situation was so weird that he thought it was a fantasy, a dream—maybe a nightmare. He hovered over the slender, wounded shape of a boy on an operating table. Something about the boy's face was familiar. He gasped when he realized it was him. Except it wasn't... not really. The Star Voice had cut his mind out of his body, and the weird little wax-looking thing lying on the operating table beneath him was just a slab of meat. *Dude, I look like something from a horror movie. Holy crap. Oh yeah, and there's my eye...*

Compared to the other injuries, the black eye was at least a wound he remembered. The boy on the table still had that purple shiner where his left eye should have been, but after the car crash, that was among the smallest of the boy's problems. The kid was covered in ghastly cuts where shards of glass and metal had been plucked out of him like chicken feathers. His dark skin was painted bright red. His mouth was open, and molars were missing. Bones were broken—fractures that, even in his disembodied state, he could still feel on some level. Worst of all, the side of the boy's head was cracked open like a coconut, and a surgeon was operating on it. Three other medical workers stood around, handing the surgeon instruments and checking the boy's vitals. *I remember when Mom tried to teach me that stuff. Blood pressure, pulse... I don't remember.* Their blue gloves were slathered in foul-smelling blood. Since he was separated from his body, he could once again understand their language. English.

"I don't know what we can do for this kid," the surgeon said.

"Is he...?" another replied.

"No. But he's hanging by a thread. I don't know, I... God. What a tragedy."

"I'd rather die," the other said. "Seriously, I'd rather have the plug pulled on me than have to live the sorta life this kid will have. Quality of life over quantity, y'know?"

"Stop. We don't know that yet."

"True. Okay, but most likely..."

The heartbeat monitor beeped faster and faster. Adam didn't want to hear them anymore, and as he thought that, their voices dissipated into a vague hum. The boy on the table blinked. He was still alive. Even though Adam was in the air, the body he'd left behind was still alive. That raised more questions than it answered.

Adam tried to move. His old body didn't respond to this command, but whatever "he" had become did pull back, floating farther into the air and feeling... thinner. More gaseous. Less real. He felt the pulsing energies of the surgeon's mind, like little electric tingles, as well as the minds of the other men and women in the room. He saw every pore of their skin, and every thrust of their hearts spurted invisible fireworks. *Boom, splash, boom, splash.* Then he saw inside their skulls. He saw their brains and all the neurons firing. A spark of light was inside each of them, each flashing some unrecognizable color that didn't exist in the Crayola box. Adam wanted to scream but had no lungs. He felt as if he were going to disappear into nothingness.

The Star Voice spoke. *"Find us, Adam. Follow the light."*

The Star Voice calmed him. Adam turned his ethereal, nonexistent vision toward the voice and looked at it with what felt like eyes even though they weren't. The door of the operating room slid open for him, and standing in the corridor was the burning figure, the obsidian man covered in shimmering white flames.

Adam didn't know if that figure was the Star Voice, but he knew the two things were somehow connected, which meant he had to follow it if he wanted answers. That didn't make the whole thing any less scary.

He didn't know anything about the figure or the voice. If the figure was some kind of devil, the whole situation could be a trap. He'd never paid much attention to that sort of talk, but he was wondering.

"Adam Helios, you know everything—and nothing—about me. Follow us. We need you, and you need us."

Adam followed the brilliant flames. His consciousness dropped to the floor and regained a sort of corporeal form. He was still transparent and intangible, but he could see the hazy outline of something that resembled his old body in that it had hands, legs, and feet again. He could stand instead of float. *Oh crap, I'm totally a ghost now. That's what's happening.* His gaseous heels pushed down against the linoleum, almost as if they were solid, but the floor felt oddly squishy. Ghost or not, he was relieved to be walking like a human again.

"Who are you?" Adam asked the Star Voice.

"I am one of many, with many ones inside me."

Adam walked down the hallway, following the starlight that floated ahead of him. No one saw him as he passed the nursing station, nurses busy with charts, phone calls, and carts full of medications. A nurse in blue scrubs hurried toward him with a terrifyingly huge syringe. Adam gasped, bracing himself for the impact, but she passed right through him as if he were a shadow. He turned to see if she had noticed, but she kept walking, totally oblivious.

"Where are we going?" Adam asked.

"Somewhere beyond the confines of this world."

"I'm scared."

"It is good to be scared," the Star Voice said. *"Fear is a quality shared by all of the bravest beings in the universe."*

Adam looked down at his ghostly figure, the transparent imitation of the feeble boy he had been. "I'm not brave. I'm only thirteen."

"Bravery is defined only by accepting responsibility and protecting those in need. Come, Adam. We are almost there."

Beneath Adam's ghostly feet, the linoleum felt softer than pillows. He moved through the walls, following the starlight. As he passed through the waiting room, he saw his mother crying, her eyes as red as her hair. She was curled up on the floor, sobbing, broken down in a way he'd never seen before. He didn't see Dad though he knew Dad was alive—he could hear his heartbeat somewhere in the distance—but perhaps Mom didn't know that.

Adam reached out to her, and his arm started to fade away.

He pulled back in horror, and his arm rematerialized. With more caution, he tried stepping toward her, and he noticed his gaseous body dissipated the closer he came to her. When he tried again, stepping even closer than before, his head exploded with pain. The terrible heaviness from the operating table crushed his skull. When he ran back, the pain went away.

Mom got up, wiping her eyes, and made herself a cup of coffee. *That's Mom, always with the coffee.* She took out her phone and began furiously texting someone, as active and stubborn as ever.

Adam stepped back, guilt tugging at his heart. "I'm sorry, Mom."

Adam couldn't cry, but he felt the sensation of what should have been tears. He moved away from his mother and followed the starlight again. He sensed, very strongly, that in order to help Mom—even to protect her, maybe—he had to sacrifice any physical connection to her and instead follow the Star Voice. He *had* to. The Star Voice was telling him that, somehow. The only way to change his fate—the only way to do what was right—was to leave behind the ones he loved. Just as Jupiter-Man had done, he had to do the same.

"I'm sorry," he repeated.

Adam moved away from the waiting room, following the fiery obsidian man through the hallways until the figure became nothing more than a pure white light, shapeless, formless, but real. The figure brought him down a flight of stairs. They crossed through the lobby, with its fountains, armchairs, and desks. They moved right out the front doors of the hospital.

A slight drizzle was falling outside though all the raindrops passed right through Adam's form, seeming as fake as a virtual-reality game. He followed the Star Voice all the way to the scenic rolling hills in front of the building, where he could sense the wet grass beneath his feet but not actually feel its dampness. The Star Voice brought him to the crest of the biggest hill. Adam peered back over his shoulder, gazing up at the looming stone towers of the hospital that contained his physical body, his parents, and countless others. *I always thought it looked like a castle.* He turned forward again. The lights of Ottanga glistened in the dark hills, hundreds of little yellow orbs shining through the rain, arranged in mathematically precise grids. Everyone he knew was some-where within those lights, either going to bed, watching TV, or already sleeping. The castle watched over them all.

Above him was the night sky that he loved, an infinite black mas-terpiece of beautiful constellations that embodied all Adam's dreams for the future. Adam raised his head, smiling at the sight of a flickering red satellite, looked back at the Star Voice, and—

It had disappeared.

He leapt back in terror. The Star Voice had abandoned him. It had separated him from his body, trapping him in limbo, and he was doomed to an eternity of holographic life. The world closed in around him, his throat clenched, and he felt like a tiny head silently screaming in the darkness.

"Help! Don't leave me like this forever!"

He was lost. Trapped. Then, up in the sky, he saw the Star Voice again, the shadow of the obsidian man hovering in its center. It had overtaken the moon, becoming like an enormous white sun in the night sky.

"Adam, come to us."

The sky faded to a color darker than black. Silvery spiderwebs interweaved through all the constellations, leaping between the stars and connecting them. A liquefied transparent film stretched across the sky and gained color, firing red bolts of electricity across light years of space. Comets flew in semicircles. An enormous shadow dropped over the grassy hills, and although Adam couldn't quite see any source for the shadow, he knew what it was.

The entire night sky had become a spaceship, a real, live UFO, which meant the Star Voice was—

A glowing orb popped open on the underside of the sky, and it shone down upon Adam like a spotlight. That energy burned a dark circle into the dirt in a five-foot radius around Adam. Nasty-smelling smoke spiraled upward from the charcoaled grass and was sucked into the spotlight. A giant tube of glowing energy encircled Adam then shot upward into outer space. Suddenly, without any control over what was happening, he was lifted into the air, his heels dangling over the grass.

A tractor beam. He floated up into the light, leaving the ground behind him. Terrified thoughts of green-skinned, big-headed aliens filled his mind. A slew of sci-fi movies came back to him in vivid, horrible detail: *Independence Day, War of the Worlds, Prometheus.* Instinct took over, and he tried to escape, but he could not break free from the glowing tube holding him.

Adam spun in circles hopelessly as the light carried him so high that the flagpole outside the hospital became a twig. Soon, the treetops were beneath him. The mighty stone hospital became nothing but a pebble-colored dollhouse. Ottanga, the town he'd spent his entire life in, was a spinning kaleidoscope of tiny lights that became smaller and smaller. A flock of birds hurried past him, squawking.

"Help!" Adam cried. "Tell me who you are!"

No one heard. He was alone in the sky, ripping through the clouds. He heard the roar of an airplane then watched it fly over his head, as oblivious to the UFO as the nurse in the hospital had been oblivious to him. Miles beneath him was a highway filled with the speeding head-lights of cars traveling either back from a late shift at work or across the country on an overnight road trip. As he hurtled higher into the atmosphere, the ground that had been beneath him became nothing more than a green-and-brown island surrounded by rolling waves.

The air heated up and compressed as if he were trapped in a microwave. Suddenly, the familiar tug of gravity disappeared, and he felt weightlessness beneath his heels. Darkness disappeared into whiteness, but beyond that whiteness he still saw the ocean of stars across which he was fated to sail.

"Are you ready?"

Adam didn't know if he was ready. All he wanted to do was go back to that morning and be the same stupid, nerdy little kid he had been before. He shouldn't have gotten out of bed. He shouldn't have had a crush on Chandra or defended her when Joe bullied her. He shouldn't have punched Joe. He should have stayed in his room, working on bicycles, being alone, being lonely, being a normal human being. That choice was no longer available to him, though, and he knew it.

So Adam looked up at the sky, up into outer space, transfixed by the light of the enormous star, spaceship, or whatever-it-was that was sucking him inside it. The beautiful white orb pulsed with veins of electricity, roared with fire, and stretched out a series of long, transparent arms that hooked onto him in a tangled embrace.

"Are you ready?"

"I guess so," Adam whispered.

"Good."

Then Adam left the familiarity of Earth behind him. His planet became a small blue ball, and he disappeared into the light.

ACT II of III:
UNEARTHLY

"Nothing is inconsequential. Each grain of sand holds amazing secrets. Each event contains mysterious messages. Every encounter with another being is a point of contact upon which the universe pivots. When we enter into this frame of mind, reality as we see it becomes a vast opportunity to experience the interconnectedness of all creation. From this perspective, we come to the realization that every piece is integral in the unfolding of creation, including us."

Rabbi David A. Cooper

Chapter 7: Dawn

Adam opened his eyes to find himself inside an enormous black sheet dotted by little glowing pinpricks. His regular life, with its solid shapes and human faces, seemed as untouchable as a fairy tale. He was somewhere else, in a place of total silence—no sounds of cars, no birds chirping, not even the rustle of a breeze. There were no clear smells nor tastes, and the only feeling was a cold, invisible stillness that needled every pore in his skin.

He was in outer space.

His body—yes, somehow he had a body again, or at least something that felt and looked like one—hovered as if he were submerged in water. He was wearing the same jeans and T-shirt he'd put on that morning, though the shirt kept floating up annoyingly to his armpits until he tucked it into his belt. He tried to swim, and his head tumbled forward in a somersault. The tractor beam had released him, turning him into a satellite carried only by gravitational waves.

A silent comet shot between stars then disappeared into the blackness. He sucked in a deep breath of air then expelled it. *Huh, I'm breathing? That's weird.* He'd been reading science magazines since first grade, and he knew full well that molecular oxygen was a rarity in space. That didn't seem important compared to the more alarming realization that if he really were in space, his eardrums and lungs should have already ruptured.

Adam gazed up at the moon's rocky white curve, closer than he'd ever seen it before. He'd never appreciated its fine, gritty texture. From that close, the Man in the Moon didn't look much like a face anymore.

"Wow," he whispered.

Adam's heart stopped at the sound of his voice. *First I'm breathing, now I'm talking? No way, dude. Space doesn't work like that.* None of the vibrating air molecules on Earth existed in the vacuum, which meant that sound couldn't exist in space, but somehow, he was breathing, could hear things, and hadn't died yet.

"Unless this isn't space," he whispered, testing the air molecules again. "It could be my imagination. Or it could be... could be..."

He swallowed, still weirded out by his own voice. He *could* be inside the spaceship. He'd always envisioned aliens using flying saucers, but perhaps that UFO was more like a transparent bubble of sorts. He gripped his chest, his heart chopping against his ribs like a pickaxe. Either way, it sure looked like space.

He turned around, and behind him was the astonishing blue glow of the planet Earth, an aquatic orb covered with milky white clouds and mountainous juts of land, suspended like a mounted globe in an impossibly huge planetarium. *Yeah, except this time, it's the real freakin' thing.* A balloon of hot emotion swelled inside his lungs, choking him with a feeling somewhere between amazement and soul-crushing dread at how his oh-so-important life now seemed so useless in the face of an entity so huge. Seeing the entire globe outside himself was even weirder than looking down at his own body had been. He stared at the brown outline of North America and nervously attempted another whisper.

"I'm alive."

His voice held still in the air. He wanted to hear it again, to know it was real. He smiled then reached up and traced the line of his mouth, suddenly realizing how amazing it was to have control of his body again.

"My name is Adam Helios, and I am *alive*," he said. "I made it. The crash didn't kill me."

Adam spread his arms out, and the Earth could not be contained within them. Billions of little white Christmas lights dotted both coasts of the United States, right where the big cities were. His smile widened. Tears welled up in his eyes. A joyous laugh emerged from deep in his chest.

"Oh my God, I'm alive!"

He fell backward, floating as if he had a life jacket, and watched the stars. In the distance he saw Mars, and farther away he spotted Venus, Mercury, and Uranus. Every moment of his life seemed so distant, as if it belonged to another person entirely. He rolled around in the cosmic breeze, laughing as it carried him.

"Is this for real?" he asked, hoping the universe might answer him. "How is this happening? Hello, Star Voice?"

Despite the uncertainty pinching his nerves, he laughed again. Even if he was at the end of his life, even if he was only moments away from dying in the vacuum, getting to experience outer space was worth it. After having his head cracked open in a car crash that same day, he couldn't contain the joy he felt at living out his greatest fantasy.

"Take that, you nasty old car crash." He grinned. "One point for Adam. Zero points for Mr. Car."

Due to the lack of gravity, his arms floated in front of him instead of at his sides. Even when he brought them down, they floated right back up. That reminded him of a zombie, so he crossed them behind his head, fell backward, and floated upside down along the circumference of Earth. *How am I alive? How am I moving?* Though he wanted to focus on positive things, an increasing number of disturbing questions occurred to him. His new body certainly felt real, and it looked *exactly* like his old one, right down to his chewed-up cuticles, his ashy elbows, and the annoying length of his bangs, which were falling into his eyes since Mom had rescheduled his haircut for next week. However, feeling and seeing his body out there, in space, made him wonder what was happening to his real body back on Earth.

Is this what happens after people die? Shuddering at the thought, he pulled upright as best as he could and stared at the lines on his palm like a baby who hadn't yet recognized his own hand. He poked at its center and closed his hand around the finger. When he looked down again, the blue planet was rapidly regressing from a beach ball to a marble. The tractor beam had picked him up again. He tried to swim back to Earth, feeling certain that going too far from his home planet was probably a bad idea, when suddenly the galaxy flashed white.

Adam fell backward, spinning as if caught in a whirlpool. The colors of space had inverted as the vacuum glowed white and stars became black dots.

The Star Voice spoke in a quiet, ringing tone. *"You are here, Adam."*

Adam jittered with terrified laughter. "I guess so."

"You are not as scared as you were before."

"Nah." His voice was shaking. "My mom always used to tell me that I was a glass-half-full kinda person."

Adam didn't think the Star Voice would buy his bravado, but he couldn't help old habits. In the face of something so terribly unfamiliar, all he could fall back on was familiar behaviors—jokes, comebacks, anything to make light of the situation. At least the Star Voice, whatever it was, understood English. Somehow.

"Answers await you, Adam."

The cosmos bent, buckled inward, and became dark again, regaining its original appearance. The Star Voice was no longer present, but in its wake, it left the entirety of space shimmering with incandescent fractals that reminded Adam of a snowstorm. Soft voices emerged from the fractals—radio transmissions from Earth, news programs, popular songs. Then the fractals lost their luster and became limp. Their droopy, sagging corpses dropped, disappearing into a starless stretch of blackness below—a sort of "nothing spot." Adam stared at that Nothing Spot, its void of empty colorlessness sucking the blood from his cheeks.

Adam hesitated to stare too long at the Nothing Spot beneath him. It possessed a gravitational pull that seemed directly connected to his eyesight. If he stared at the darkness too long, it pulled him toward itself, dragging his skin downward, grinding his bones together, cooling his blood temperature, darkening his vision. When he looked away, he felt normal again, and the darkness disappeared.

He floated upward. *Jeez, I better not look at that creepy thing again, huh?* For the time being, he decided to just pretend the Nothing Spot wasn't there, at least until he figured out what it was.

By that point, he was floating over the red deserts of Mars—way too soon, considering that it should have taken him one hundred fifty to three hundred days to get there from Earth, and that would be assuming he'd taken off from Earth at a dizzying speed of fifty-nine thousand miles per hour. That strangeness bothered Adam, but then Mars's rosy desert landscape distracted him. It resembled pictures he'd seen of Arizona. As he stared at the planet's twin moons, Deimos and Phobos, both every bit as wonky and deformed as they appeared in pictures, his breathing slowed to a nice, steady pace.

Out of nowhere, a legion of metallic orbs descended upon him from above. The orbs had no rivets or screws to speak of, resembling enormous pinballs, each the size of a fist. They lit him up with aimed red laser lights, their perfectly circular forms spinning in circles around each other. Adam kicked and thrashed, desperate to swim out of their laser focus, but they zoomed in closer and quickly surrounded him like a pack of wolves.

"Hey, um, hello? Can you understand me?" Adam's shaky voice betrayed more than he wanted.

He glanced over at the Nothing Spot, and his blood ran cold. Creepy though the orbs were, the Nothing Spot was worse. He faced the orbs again. *C'mon Star Voice, say something. Tell these weirdos to leave me alone.* The orbs touched his shoulder blades and the backs of his knees, vibrating like massage devices. Then, with an electrical jolt, the orbs latched onto his bones like magnets, his flesh only a thin, inconsequential barrier—like a strip of paper—between bone and metal. Once they were all attached to him, they carried him through space.

"Can you hear me?" Adam cried. "C'mon guys, put me down."

They didn't respond. Adam didn't know if the orbs were alien creatures or alien technology, but he suspected the latter. He didn't struggle as even the slightest movement against them shot pain through his joints. The orbs carried him past the dark side of Phobos, an uneven monstrosity of rock that possessed none of the spherical elegance of Earth's moon. Adam missed *his* moon. Earth's moon was safe, normal, and predictable. Phobos's weird appearance was just as uncomfortable as his present situation.

The orbs lowered him into Stickney Crater, what all the Earth scientists had named the gaping hole in Phobos's side. As they went deeper into the crater, the moon's dusty surface cracked open in a jagged line, both sides of the fracture grinding up against each other like teeth. A splattering of spaghetti-shaped gray tendrils crawled out of the crevice. They reached out like desperate little hands. The orbs that had locked onto Adam's bones continued to push him toward the crevice, right into the embrace of the tendrils.

"Stop! Don't do this!" Adam cried, his voice reaching an embarrassingly high pitch. "Please, please don't put me in there."

They didn't stop, didn't listen, didn't care. One of the tendrils hooked onto Adam's ankle, and he squirmed to free it.

"Please!" he cried. "Don't put me in there!"

With the same electrical jolt as before, the orbs unlatched him, dropping him into the tangled snake pit. Adam desperately kicked, pulled, and punched at the tendrils, but they were made of something that resembled stone—albeit a sort of fluid, liquefied stone—and they only coiled more tightly around him. Flittering through space, they carried him into the crevice. The stone mouth of Phobos shut behind him, killing the light. Lost in the darkness, Adam screamed in terror. For a moment—a brief one, but a very real one—he actually wished he was back on the operating table, back in the world he knew, getting his brain chopped.

Chapter 8: Back Home

After two furious hours of pacing, text messages, and teary phone calls to her girlfriends—as well as three impulsive fits of banging on the doors of the ICU, demanding answers that no one was willing to give her—Camille resolved to stay in the hospital that night. She asked the nurses for some blankets, a pillow, and a fresh pair of socks. What she received were three thin white blankets, a top sheet, a mushy pillow, and a pair of blue slipper socks with little smiley faces on the heels. She also got one of their flimsy little toothbrushes, which was admittedly a nice bonus.

If not for everything that had happened that day, she could've laughed at her own ridiculousness: brushing her teeth in the hospital bathroom, pulling on the silly blue socks with their big white smiles. In the bathroom mirror, she examined the bruises on her hips, legs, and arms, as well as the minor bruises on her neck and shoulders. Inside one of her grinning blue socks, she had two cracked toenails from where her driving foot had collided with a pedal. Her son had a traumatic brain injury, her husband was missing fingers and pouring out blood like a broken milk carton, and she had cracked toenails. The unfairness of it all was sickening.

She stared into her own dark, evil eyes with intense hatred for the woman reflected in the mirror, who oddly enough was her. She didn't think it right that she was the only one lucky enough to walk away from that car crash when she was the one responsible. They were probably going to die—both of them.

Stop it, Camille, don't go there. They're not *dead yet.* The bathroom reeked of antiseptic. She returned to the waiting room, which was still empty, and the TV was playing a commercial for a cleaning product. Always the improviser, she spread out the sheet and blankets into a makeshift bed on the floor. She turned the lights out then curled up inside her impromptu sleeping bag.

The bed wasn't particularly comfy, but it was better than just carpet. It would work as long as her storming emotions allowed her to get some rest. That was still up for debate.

She pulled herself into a tight ball, listening to the muffled sounds of the TV and the distant hum of traffic outside the hospital. She closed her eyes. She rolled over. She lay on her stomach, her back, then her side. Nothing seemed to work. Her guilt wouldn't let her fall sleep.

If John were there, he would've said, "Get some shut-eye, darlin'."

She rolled over, her heart aching at the memory of his voice. Opening her eyes, she imagined John sleeping next to her, lying with her on the floor of the hospital, just as worried as she was. She could see him, everything from the shine of his skin to the stubble on his cheeks, and if she tried hard enough, he almost felt real. She ran her real foot along the imaginary hairs on his imaginary leg.

"I'm sorry, John," she said out loud.

"Nothin' to be sorry about," he replied. Beneath his bushy mustache, Imaginary John smiled. "Mistakes happen."

John propped his head up on one elbow, staring into her eyes with unconditional love and acceptance. He was a big-boned man with a thick neck and a noticeable beer gut but powerful arms, legs, and shoulders. Pictures showed he'd been balding since his college days, and whatever hair was left was wispy, but he had a sharp jawline that any movie star would have been jealous of. The warmth in his eyes, the way he looked at her as if she were the only person in the world...

She wrapped her arms around Imaginary John, and they embraced beneath the covers, huddling together on the waiting-room floor. She sobbed into his furry chest. *He's not real, you stupid woman. The real John is going to die.*

She looked into his face again. "I'm the worst wife ever," she whispered. "The worst mother."

"Far as I'm concerned, honey," John said, "you're the best damn woman that ever walked this Earth. Not a chance in hell that you can prove nothin' different."

Her breathing was ragged with tears. "But I've been so mean to you. I've been resentful of you for so long, for such stupid things, when I could have been savoring that time, loving you, giving you the kind of love you deserve."

"Just as much my fault as yours."

"But John"—she pulled him closer—"you're going to die because of me."

"Ain't dead yet. And neither is Adam. Just keep the hope alive."

She kissed him, aching at the thought that she couldn't even remember the last time she had kissed the real John, much less made love to him. She hugged him, pawing at him, wanting him to be real. Then the door to the waiting room opened, John disappeared, and she was alone. In one moment, she'd been cut down from her role as a hardworking businesswoman, wife, and mother. All that remained of her was a shattered middle-aged crone lying on the floor of a hospital waiting room, wearing stupid blue slipper socks with smiley faces on the heels.

With the lights out, she couldn't distinguish the person who'd entered through the open door. Highlighted only by the dim flickering light of the TV screen, the cloaked figure approached her. In the shadows, it looked like a young boy with a disproportionally large head and an awkward demeanor.

Camille's heart rushed into her throat, and she sat bolt upright. "Adam?"

"Um, no." The shadow person switched on the lights, and it was Dr. Blake. "Sorry."

Camille lowered herself back to the pillow. *I'm such an idiot.* Of course Adam wouldn't be walking into the waiting room after a traumatic brain injury, even if he was alive. In fact, he'd probably never walk again. That fact struck such a horribly painful nerve in her that she immediately chased it away as soon as it arose.

"What's up?" she asked. "I need some kind of info, doctor, or I'm going to go nuts."

Dr. Blake nodded, consulted his chart, then awkwardly crouched down to her eye level. "Mrs. Helios, I have news about your husband."

Chapter 9: The Face

Within the shadowed crevice of Phobos, gravity regained its power, and Adam's feet descended onto a perfectly flat floor. Adjusting back to a weighted state buckled his knees. *Wow, I feel like I just gained five hundred pounds.* The surface had no dust, no residue. When Adam bent down to touch it, it was as clean as glass. Because no light was there to pierce the impenetrable darkness, he saw nothing except whatever monstrous spikes, teeth, and spines his fears conjured up.

Adam struggled to breathe. He heard a low hum, like a machine being turned on, and a lightning bolt of panic stopped his heart. He reached out, seeking something to touch, though he was terrified of what that something might be. He smelled freshly cut steel. Clicking noises emanated from the shadows.

Just when Adam was starting to wonder if everything had been a dream, lights sparkled before him. An iridescent string of yellow and blue flickers snaked toward him as if an especially long branch of a Christmas tree had come to life and was curious about who had decorated it. At the end of that glittering appendage was a glowing sphere that moved to face Adam and seemed to stare at him for several moments in tense, heated silence. Then it twisted sideways and stroked the side of his face with its long, cold neck. Adam jumped back. The tendril copied his motion. Its movements were those of a living creature, not a machine.

Adam stepped away. "Don't hurt me. I don't—"

A louder hum cut him off. Illuminated by the blue and yellow sparkles, the spaghetti-stone tendrils spread out around him like spider legs. Flashing green lights popped up at the end of each tendril, just barely bright enough to reveal that all of them were connected to a vibrating metal ball hovering in the middle of the cavern, that central fixture about the size of a small car. Everything about the room was so weird that Adam's eyesight struggled to take it all in.

Adam stepped toward that centerpiece, hesitating when he noticed hundreds of spiky pieces of metal dangling in the air like hanging mobiles. The shimmering chunks of steel merged together with the blunted ends of each tendril, satisfyingly snapping into place like Tetris blocks. These configurations then became simplistic metal reproductions of a human head—exaggerated but unmistakable, with circular eyes and half-circle mouths, much like a child's bad crayon drawing.

"C-c-can you understand me?" Adam said.

Adam gasped at the spread of cartoonish metal heads that surrounded him, each one joined to the end of its own stone tendril. They almost seemed to be making fun of him, like a group of metal bullies. *Or maybe they're just trying to communicate with me, no reason to get so suspicious.* Some of the faces had small eyes while others had enormous ones. Some had big lips, and others had nothing but a slit. One of the tentacles, whose mouth was fixed in a constant grin, rubbed up against Adam's shoulder like a cat craving attention.

What all those appendages had in common was their physical connection to the metal ball in the center. They were not separate entities nor machines. They were the living arms of a single creature.

So far, it seemed friendly. That made his heartbeat slow down a bit.

A face with uneven eyes and a downward half circle for a mouth zoomed up to Adam and stared at him. It looked so goofy that Adam had to stifle a laugh. Adam ran his fingers down the length of its stone neck, which was coated in tiny siltlike particles of metal, which were too small and thin to cut skin. Its mouth turned upward into a ridiculous smile. That time, Adam laughed aloud. The appendage wrapped around his lower arm and squeezed him gently.

"Okay," Adam said, totally bewildered, as he scratched behind the tentacle's metal ears. "I give up. We're gonna be friends, right?"

Adam cringed at how stupid he sounded. The other appendages circled around him and then scuttled back, almost as if it was afraid of him instead of the other way around. *Well hey, maybe it is. I probably seem like a weirdo to it too.* Then, acting in unison, each of the many metal mouths opened and spoke in a heavy, reverberating tone.

"Hello, Adam Helios," hundreds of voices hummed.

One of the tentacles laughed. Another cried, sobbing cold metallic tears onto the floor. Adam stepped back and covered his eyes. The bizarreness was just too much, too fast, and it all kept getting stranger. His palms smelled like rust.

"You are the... Okay, oh my God. Wow." Adam inhaled then looked up again. "You understand English. I mean, the Star Voice was one thing, but... okay, so I'm really speaking to an alien that speaks English. I don't freakin' believe it."

One of the tentacles nudged him with an exaggerated wink, then they all spoke at the same time again. "It's good to see you, Adam. You may call me the Face."

Adam gulped and addressed his next statement to the humming metal ball at the center of the sphere. "So let me get this straight. You're... the Face. Not Phobos, but the Face." Adam pointed all around him. "And I'm, uh, inside you. Inside an alien named the Face."

One of the heads nodded.

Adam scoffed then blushed. "Okay. *And* you speak English?"

"No. I do not." The Face's many voices echoed about the cold, round room. "But you speak English, and so your—" The tentacles froze to look at each other, confused. "Ears, yes, that's what they're called? Your ears hear me speaking your language because that allows us to communicate. I do not have a... name, either. None of us have names. But your subconscious has named me the Face, and so to you, I am the Face."

Adam walked forward, and the tendrils spread outward to allow him entry, as if he'd parted the Red Sea. Adam smiled. *If I were a little more confident, I might do a twirl here, maybe a bow, some kind of dance move.* As weird as the whole situation all was, he was pretty sure the strange face-tentacle-moon-creature wasn't going to kill him.

"So what are you?" he asked.

"I am a part of this vessel." The Face's voices bounced off the walls. "I come to you, Adam Helios, from a world that is far beyond the reach of the minds on Earth. And we, this vessel, all of us—"

"Aliens," Adam whispered. "That's what you are, right?"

"Yes. To you, we are aliens, much as you are alien to us. We need your help."

The ball at the center throbbed, like a massive metal heart, and glowed orange. It sent pulses of light like projector beams onto the sphere's walls. Adam turned around, and behind him, a black circle was being reflected onto the wall, reminiscent of a giant porthole in a submarine. Inside that blackness were six tiny white stars, forming a perfectly triangular constellation. Adam reached out to touch them, and though the stars swerved away to avoid his grasp—*like a shy puppy,* Adam thought—the triangle did not break.

"You are aboard a vessel," the Face said, "that is comprised of the combination of six separate conscious beings, unified into a whole... a greater being. Merged together, our minds become a vessel that travels the cosmos, powered not by technology, fuel, or electricity—"

"What are you powered by, then?" Adam asked, mesmerized by the six white lights. "Water? Coffee?"

"*Imagination* is our battery, and it is also the only substance that our vessel is constructed from," the Face answered. "Science and technology are limited by the physical world, but imagination has no limits, no distance it cannot traverse. Through our imagination-powered vessel, we have spent many years seeking communion with other worlds, and on these worlds, we find other beings like yourself, Adam Helios, the child of Earth... and we connect to them, beings like you, not through physical contact... but by merging with your subconscious thoughts, using *your* imagination as a tool to allow you to perceive us."

Adam crossed his arms, trying to make sure he didn't lose any details. "Wow, okay, dude. Give me a second to take all of this in." *Six lights. Six alien beings powered by imagination.*

In the projection, the triangle of lights flew back into the darkness, and thin strands of silken, beautiful white webbing connected each light. The triangle soared across the darkness, swerving around planets, between moons, and through geomagnetic storms.

"So when you encounter, uh, aliens like me"—Adam pointed at the triangle—"you make contact with us through our imagination instead of physical contact. I think, right? So Phobos, outer space, these wacky tendrils... None of this is real. It's just like a picture that you've made from... my mind?"

Three of the many steel heads nodded yes. "This vessel, our collective union, our instrument of travel, our greatest selves combined into one superior being... *this*, Adam Helios, is what you have until this point been referring to as the Star Voice. But I see into your subconscious, and I sense that there is another name that you are now coming to prefer?"

"The Consciousness," Adam whispered then jolted backward in alarm. He wasn't sure how much he liked the fact that some alien could pick out random thoughts from his brain, especially without telling him. "That's what I—for some reason, I feel like I should call your vessel the Consciousness instead of the Star Voice, now that I know more about it. But I dunno why any of this... I don't understand."

"You are here because you chose to follow the light," the Face said. "We are also here because of our choices. Now, we ask for your help."

The Face's illustration of the triangle of lights, the vessel, the Consciousness, soared through space. Adam couldn't breathe. He felt smaller than he ever had before. A weirdo like him didn't deserve to be the first Earthling that those aliens contacted. *Man, you guys should have picked someone else.* He turned to the Face and—

"No, Adam Helios," the Face murmured as the tentacles petted his arms. "Do not put yourself down that way. We picked you for a reason. From the moment our vessel arrived on your planet for the first time, we became... sick."

The Face's little movielike animation showed the star-triangle vessel appearing above a tiny version of Earth. Then the six little lights dimmed, sinking and dropping away. From the blackness of space, an unseen cloud, smelling of a public toilet—and so unmistakably angry that Adam could feel its tension prickling on his skin—drowned the lights within its inky embrace. Adam instantly recognized that this dark cloud was the Nothing Spot, the same one he had looked away from. The Nothing Spot drowned out the lights, poisoned them, and turned them into dull, gray asteroids.

Watching the Nothing Spot infect the six lights of the Consciousness made Adam nauseous. The rotten smell didn't help, either.

"I totally saw that thing," he said, turning toward the heated ball at the center of the Face. "It tried to get me too."

"That Nothing Spot, as you think of it, is the sickness that has contaminated us." The Face's heads turned toward the floor. "Much as the Consciousness is the living entity formed from all of our unified hopes and dreams, this sickness is the living culmination of... fears. Something else. Something foreign to us."

Adam touched the crumbling remains of the six lights, which didn't dodge him that time. They broke apart into crumbs, gritty and chalklike. He shook off his hands. "Does this sickness have a name, like you?"

"Remember, Adam Helios, we do not have names except within your mind. But your subconscious has named it the Destroyer."

The word *Destroyer* echoed softly, sending chills down Adam's spine. He glanced at the Face's depiction of the Nothing Spot and looked away. The many tentacle faces all scrunched up their brows in a pleading expression.

Adam shook his head. "Why did you choose me?"

"Time is not the same for us as it is for you. We see the threads of reality that compose everything around us. We see where each thread may travel, how each action may result in a series of consequences. We knew that the automobile accident was going to occur. We saw that, due to the circumstances that you underwent and were about to undergo, you were highly capable of saving us."

"Oh God." Adam rolled his eyes. "Don't start that crazy prophecy talk. There's no way I'm some kinda chosen one. I don't buy that crap for a second."

"No, you are not a chosen one." One smiling tentacle shook its head while another punched him lightly in the shoulder.

Adam's shoulders slumped, and he realized he was surprisingly disappointed by this lack of supernatural purpose. *It actually would have been kinda cool to be the chosen one, now that I think about it.* He tried to mask it by rolling his eyes. "Good. Whatever."

"But you *were* in the right place at the right time. Your accident, which freed you from the earthly distractions that would have normally kept you from making full contact with us, occurred at just the perfect moment in space and time for us to pull you out of your brain and into our vessel. Furthermore, your imagination is strong enough that we were able to use its power to bring you to us. Not many beings in the universe have an imagination as colorful as yours. These two factors were the reason we brought you here."

"So, wait." Adam's brow furrowed. "You're telling me that I'm here because I daydream too much and I was in a car accident at just the right time." *Not because I'm special, not because I'm smart, nothing like that. You picked me because I was unlucky enough to get my stupid skull cracked open.*

"Yes." The ball hummed loudly, and the string of yellow and blue lights circled around Adam's head. "You are our best chance. But even you might not be capable, and if you fail, then the Consciousness will die."

"Jeez, thanks." Adam looked at each of the faces and threw his hands in the air, feeling like the butt of an elaborate joke. "Listen, I'm not good enough for this crap. I can't even talk to girls without making an idiot of myself. You don't want me."

"We do, actually. Whether you do this or not is your choice," the alien said. "You can always go back to Earth. That is up to you. We are simply moving around in your imagination, after all."

"Good." Adam squeezed his fists. "Just send me back. I'll just take my chances at the hospital. Who knows? Maybe I'll even get better. Watch me." He bit his lip, suddenly thinking about what going back to the hospital entailed—but at least knowing he couldn't fail at that task since the only life at stake was his own. If he tried to save an alien space-ship, he definitely *could* fail, and their deaths would all be his stupid fault. "I'm sorry you picked a loser, but that's what I am. I'm no hero."

The stone tendrils wavered. "Who do you think you are, Adam Helios?"

"I'm a weirdo." Adam said, stepping on his right foot with his left one. "I'm the kinda stupid kid that stares in a mirror and wishes I could be someone else. I look at myself, and I talk to myself 'cause I have no one else to talk to. Nothing I say ever comes out right. I'm the kinda person that's always gonna be alone, and I've just gotten used to it be-cause I'm not like what... I'm not what people are supposed to be like. I'm not tough, I'm not strong, I'm not witty—I'm just a loser. I'm sor-ry, Mr. Face, but you picked a loser to help save your spaceship, vessel, whatever you call it. I can't even stand up for myself, much less save some kind of alien consciousness."

"I appreciate your candor, Adam Helios." The tentacle heads smiled, all of them, and their round eyes spun in circles. "But I disagree.

You are a wonderful example of your species." The Face's center radiated heat. "You have both the stubborn courage of your mother human and the simple goodness of your father human. And even more importantly, you are a *compassionate* human being. Just. Moral. Decent. Do not underestimate yourself, for you do not even *know* yourself, not yet. That is the fatal flaw of many members of your species, but you do not have to submit to it."

One of the Face's tendrils rested on Adam's shoulder and winked at him. Adam couldn't remember the last time he'd felt so appreciated. So far, that weird moonrock creature was a lot nicer than most people he'd met.

He lowered his head, smiling to himself. "Yeah, whatever. Okay, I'll save your stupid spaceship."

"Thank you. Like every other conscious being in the known multiverse, you always have a choice, and that choice is what defines you."

Adam couldn't believe it, but he felt increasingly more comfortable around the alien than he did around human beings. Thanks to reading so many comic books and science magazines, the term "multiverse" was familiar to him, but he'd never heard anyone say it aloud before. Usually, he was the one saying words like that while adults laughed at him. In the Face, he'd finally found a peer, even if that peer was probably a thousand times smarter than him.

He stepped closer to the center of the Face and touched the throbbing steel ball that he suspected was indeed its heart. It was warm and purred at his touch.

"So if I'm gonna do this, what can I call the other five aliens, besides you?" he asked. "Spock? Chewbacca?"

"I am the Face. My siblings are the Courage, the Optimist, the Mad Glee, the Motherboard, and the Rage."

Adam laughed. The Face's faces didn't reciprocate, and he blushed. *Of course they don't think their own names are funny, doofus.* "Okay, wow. So what do you want me to do with all of you?"

"You will take a piece of each of us, which will be called a *spark*, a spark of our hope. And once you have collected one of these from each of us, you will give them all to the Consciousness itself. There, with our hopes unified, the vessel may once again fly... and the sickness will be vanquished."

"Cool." Adam shrugged, imagining himself as a cocky action hero, cool in every situation. "Sounds easy. I hope?"

"Be wary." The Face's heated center cooled down. "In the absence of hope, some of us have become destructive and violent. All of us are dying from the sickness that plagues us, and in our despair, some of us have even sided with the Destroyer. You must force the others to re-member who they really are."

"Me... convince? You kidding?" Adam didn't feel so cool anymore. "I really don't know if I can do this."

"Do you still want to proceed?"

"I guess. I... um." He straightened his back, wanting to impress his new alien friend. "I mean, yeah. Of course."

"You are our only chance. We don't have time to find anyone else. But remember, you must beware the Destroyer."

"Jeez." Adam shuddered. "He can get me too?"

"The Destroyer knows you are here. It is hungry for you. If you give it the chance, it will devour every part of what was once the human named Adam Helios until nothing remains but a shallow husk of who you were."

The Destroyer. Adam swallowed acid, and tingles once again crept through his veins. "What if I mess up?"

"Adam Helios, if you are going to help us, it is time to begin. And that means it is time for you to take what you need from me then leave me behind." The Face's voice deepened. "Reach inside me. You must take my spark."

Sensing that wasn't a request but a demand, Adam's hands circled the warm ball, and a hidden latch opened on its underside. From inside it, Adam pulled out a tiny shard of what looked like indigo-colored crystal. As he touched it, it melded to his skin, connecting to his veins and sinking into his being. Fear gave way to calmness. A soothing warmth hugged his heart. The Face's spark was a part of him, and it felt as though it had always belonged there. Because it had melted into him so quickly, thinking that it had been a physical object only a moment before was already strange.

"So if I do this," Adam asked, "how am I gonna get across this huge vessel?"

"Adam Helios, do you not understand?" The entire cavern started spinning in a slow, mechanical circle, and Adam wondered if Phobos was spinning as well. "This entire vessel is powered by one source—*imagination*. Your imagination has created the version of this vessel that you now see, and your imagination will be your vehicle through it. And just as you have created me, now you must create the others."

"So do I just dream up some kind of flying car or something? Seriously?" Adam's voice sped up as the spinning of the room increased in speed. "Imagining my way through space? That's totally not a good exit strategy!"

He clung tighter to the metal orb. He understood the whole imagination business, despite his pleas, but he didn't want to leave the Face behind. Since he'd finally found someone he liked, found a situation he could somewhat grapple with, he trembled at the thought of being flung into space again. He hated being alone and having to figure things out for himself, but the room kept spinning more and more quickly, and he knew he didn't have much longer.

The Face bellowed, like a war cry, "Through the pathway between knowledge and zealousness, from tragedy you will bring light!" The alien's voice deepened further. "From understanding, you shall traverse over the mountain until you are face to face with the darkness itself. All of this will happen to us, and yet it will also occur in your mind. I cannot help you beyond this point. You must proceed from here by your own force of will. It is the only way."

The lights darkened. The spinning was so fast that Adam's feet left the floor. Everything slowly faded to black, and Adam hugged the warm metal orb in the center, clinging to its familiarity.

"Don't leave me," he said. "I don't know what to do without your help. I don't know how to travel with my imagination, whatever that means! Please, please—"

The orb darkened, and its booming voice became a whisper. "Goodbye, Adam Helios. Good luck."

Adam hugged the orb tightly, but then it wasn't there anymore, and he toppled forward in the shadows. Everything was gone. The lights were off, and he couldn't see anything. *Don't freak out.* Adam closed his eyes and reopened them, but the darkness was so total that he could barely tell the difference. He clenched his fists. *Imagination.* He had to find his own way. He had to get out.

His head was dizzy. Constellations reappeared all around him, popping out of the blackness like little pinpricks. Planets rotated around the sun. Mars was beneath him again, and he was floating in the vacuum, devoid of gravity, free but formless. He was in space, inside the vessel, and Phobos was miles behind him.

"Goodbye," he whispered.

Adam was alone again, directionless. He stared outward, trying to understand what to do next. Remembering something Mom had once told him—*the best solutions come when you're not thinking so hard about them*—he forced himself to relax, to mentally step back. He thought about space. He thought about galaxies, about spaceships, about superheroes...

Am I a hero now? Can I become one? Adam felt a warm sensation on the soles of his feet, as if he were stepping on coals. *Heroes. I have to fly somehow. Something like that.* He focused on the heat beneath his feet, and it spread upward to his calves, becoming a fire inside his body. He was imagining it, making it up, but it was real. Somehow, the fire didn't burn his insides. It felt strengthening, empowering, as if he controlled it.

He needed a form of transportation. He couldn't just float across the entirety of the vessel, waiting to bump into anything that crossed him. *Maybe I can dream up a spaceship for myself. A car with wings?* None of those things appeared, but his mind kept concentrating on the heat under his soles, so he focused on that instead. He looked down. A shimmering beam of light burst into life beneath him, brighter than the sun, settling under his feet and jutting ahead of him like a longboard.

No, not quite: a lightboard. It was a shimmering creation of his own mind, powered by the vessel itself. He kicked himself ahead. The board propelled him forward, controlled by his movements. Breathing in deeply, he stared out into the farthest reaches of space, and he pointed ahead.

"I guess I'll go that way?"

The lightboard sprang forward like a slingshot. Adam's feet were safely latched onto its surface. Stars sailed past so quickly that they looked like milky streaks of light. Asteroids blurred at his sides. His heart leapt up his throat. The board twisted between the twin Martian moons, skated across the planet's deserted landscape, then shot back up into the sky like a rocket.

He accidentally swerved toward the metallic form of an Earth-made satellite then ducked underneath it just in time. He angled upward, diving right beneath the rocky surface of a meteoroid, so close that he could smell the dust and ice. He felt like Jupiter Man speeding toward his next adventure.

Adam raised his fist into the air, grinning from ear to ear. He whooped and cheered in uncontrollable joy, letting every star in the galaxy hear his excitement. The lightboard zoomed through space, leaving glowing sparkles in its wake, flowing between the stars. He'd already forgotten the names of the aliens he was supposed to save, but he was ready to meet the next one, wherever it was, and whatever its wacky name might be.

"Get ready, universe!" He laughed at the top of his lungs. "Adam Helios is here!"

Chapter 10: Tangled Memories

Camille raced down the hallway, rushing between two aisles of blinking call bells, scurrying past nurses on their carts, anxious to reach her husband's room. Every sound around her—whether it was nurses chatting, paper being rustled, pills being poured into little plastic cups—ricocheted through her like a bullet. She remembered the metallic screech of her SUV's passenger side buckling inward. She remembered the windows shattering into tiny, sharp pieces and streaks of blackish blood spraying against the dash.

John, please be okay.

She stopped at the doorway to what Dr. Blake had told her would be John's room. She entered just as a young male nurse was replacing the IV on a fleshy, half-naked, vein-covered white man that didn't look like John.

The nurse moved aside, muttering an apology. Camille stared at the bruised, bloated figure before her, trying to recognize the man she loved. His puffy face rendered him unrecognizable, and his arm had been bandaged in a heavy white cast. He was asleep—or drugged, not that it made much difference. The harsh lights made his skin emit an electrical yellow glow.

"Do you need a minute?" the nurse asked.

Camille nodded, her head so heavy it felt as if it would fall from her neck. The nurse dimmed the lights and left the room. Camille inched forward on tiptoes. John, or at least the thing that had replaced John, didn't stir.

His right eye looked glossy, reddened, with mucus stuck in the lashes. A white patch was taped over his left eye socket. Even though

74

Dr. Blake had told her his left eye was gone forever—*damaged beyond repair*, he had said—she couldn't shake the feeling that if she lifted the patch and pried loose the tape, his eye would still be there as it always had been. It seemed utterly surreal that something that always had been there would never be there again.

Right before she'd rushed out of the room and stormed the ICU, Dr. Blake had said something about glass eyes. She wasn't ready for that conversation. A glass eye was just a painted marble in the skull, not the same eye that had always stared into her soul, winked at her, or traced the curve of her hips when they were in the bedroom. *That* eye was gone.

"John?" she whispered.

His big-boned barrel chest heaved in and out with heavy exhalations, but his lips did nothing but sputter bubbles. He seemed awake to an extent but drugged to the point of inebriation. Dr. Blake had said he was on heavy painkillers. Looking at him felt like jabbing a knife into her heart. *He's alive. That's what's important. They fixed the internal bleeding. He's going to live. He's going to be fine.*

"I love you, John," she said. "I love, love, *love* you..."

Or maybe he won't be fine. Camille sat down, grimacing at the sound of the metal-framed chair skidding on the linoleum floor. John's puffy purple brow furrowed. His breathing stopped for a moment... and resumed.

She listened to the sounds of the call bells outside the door: other people in pain, other families, lives saved, lives ruined. Taking care to be as gentle as possible, she held John's bandaged right hand up into the light and looked at it, and the stench was so nauseating she almost dropped it.

His hand was just as gutted as the doctor had said it was. The digits that had previously been known by the names of index finger, middle finger, and ring finger were nothing but bandaged nubs. Peeking between the bandages, she saw that each stump culminated in a mess of stitches. Vomit rose into Camille's throat, and she put the hand down. The smell was too strong. She breathed in and out, focusing on the sensation of air in her nostrils, until the squelching feeling within her stomach died down.

She shuddered. John had always been such a DIY kind of guy, the kind of man who worked with his hands. He loved baseball, backyard carpentry, working on cars, and grilling hot dogs on the barbecue. After losing the hand he used the most, his life would never be the same. Other than his beer belly, he'd always taken a lot of pride in his general health and always told her—in a grave tone rare for him—that if he was ever hurt badly enough to the point where he could no longer enjoy life, to never let him become "Frankenstein's goddamn monster."

And there he was, thanks to the car accident—no hand, no eye, a crazy number of broken bones that might never heal properly. When he did wake up, he was going to hate her, and that was her fault.

He's going to live, Camille. He will *live.* She looked into his open eye. She watched the flesh below his jawline throb with the sign of a heart beating steadily and assuredly. He was alive. *John Helios is alive, that stubborn son of a bitch, and if there's any man I know that can get through this, it's him.* He was going to struggle. The future would be painful, but he'd find a way to make the situation work, and she'd be there for him. Camille lifted his crippled hand again and pressed his bandaged palm against her lips. That time, she didn't feel nauseous.

"I love you, John." She kissed his hand again. "I love you, you tough old bastard."

His lips sputtered, and a thin line of drool flowed down his neck. Remembering her old CNA training, she fumbled for the bed controls and lifted his head so that he wouldn't choke. The sputtering stopped. His eye continued to gaze forward blankly, but his lips opened, and words came tumbling out. "L... lll... love you, honnn... ey."

Camille gasped. She covered her eyes, hiding, and when she peeked out between splayed fingers, a tiny hint of a smile was on John's face.

She kissed his hand over and over again then leaned forward and kissed his chest, his neck, and finally his chapped lips.

"I'm here, baby," she said, breathing unsteadily. "I'm here. I'm here. Don't you worry."

The smile on his face was gone, but Camille stared into his vacuous eye, knowing that the man she loved was still somewhere on the other side of it. She kissed him again.

"I'm sorry that I've been so mean to you," she said. "I've said such awful things. I'm sorry we've been fighting for so long. I take it all back. I'm a bitch. I'm a—"

"Shut up," John said with another almost smile. "You're... amazzz... amazing... a hella lot more... amzzzing... than me. You're the one... that keeps... everything going. I just... help out."

Her heart melted, and she smiled so hard that her cheeks hurt. He was crazy. *He* was the calm one that kept things afloat. She was the lunatic who kept pushing for more, always wanting things to be better, but maybe the balance between the two of them, their great differences, had always been the strength of their relationship. She was the go-getter who pursued things, and he was the one who stabilized her. Looking back, she couldn't believe they'd had so many problems in the last year. John was such a decidedly good man.

She held his hand and gently massaged it. John was smiling from the corner of his lip for a second, but it quickly dropped away. His eye fluttered closed. He was falling asleep. Camille leaned forward on the edge of her hard plastic seat, and she nestled her head in the little dip in his chest.

"Cammm... Camlay... Camille..." he slurred. "Remem... emem... ber the day... we adopted Adam?"

She smiled. Of course she remembered. She remembered when she'd first read the story of that lost little orphan boy in India, a three-year-old with pitch-black eyes, a dimpled chin, and a pinched little mouth. From the moment she saw the sadness in that little boy's face, she'd known she would've killed someone to give him a second chance.

She remembered the background checks, the phone calls, and the forms. She remembered how her mother, John's mother, and everyone she knew had argued against her and told her she was crazy to adopt an orphan from another country—everyone except John. They'd stood there together when that little boy, a kid terribly small and malnourished, first walked up to them. She remembered the moment when he'd first looked up at them with those same giant, dark eyes from the pictures—eyes desperate for love but equally certain no one would ever love him. She'd felt a stirring need deep inside herself to prove to that boy that he *deserved* love, that he could do anything he ever wanted to and be whoever he wanted to be.

They asked the boy if he wanted to keep his old name. *Kavi Kapoor*. She'd thought it was a beautiful name, but the little boy shook his head and refused to answer anytime they called him Kavi. Eventually, he told them with what little English he knew that he wanted a new name, so they'd named him Adam—their wonderful, sparkling little boy, Adam Helios.

Camille sat beside John as he lay in that hospital bed, damaged and torn apart but still as alive as ever. Tears ran down her cheeks as she kissed his hand again.

"I'll always remember that day," she said.

He smiled again. "That was... the best day of my life."

"Me too."

John's heavy eyelid dropped over the glossy sphere it contained, and he quickly fell asleep. Camille continued to hold his hand even as her own body gave way to fatigue and drifted off into unconsciousness. Part of her wanted to remain alert, stressed and high strung. Thinking about Adam only reminded her that the same boy was being operated on in another room of the hospital, that he might be dead, that he might be disabled.

If she could learn one thing from John, though, it was the way he always focused on the positive and let go of what he couldn't control. *That is the key.* That was why he was always so calm.

She couldn't save Adam and had no idea what was happening to him, but John was going to be okay, and even if the next day resulted in tragic news about their son, the miracle of John's life deserved to be celebrated. She held her husband's hand, curled up in her uncomfortable plastic chair, and fell asleep.

Chapter 11: Magnetic Imagination

Clouds of cosmic debris shifted to make way for Adam's light-board. He burned a streak of colorless energy across the galaxy. He didn't know where he was going. He had no map, no compass, no traceable routes to follow. His intuition pulled him deeper into the stars, so he followed that invisible signal, fueled by the positivity beaming within himself.

No wind rushed past, no gravity pulled him down. Though he was somehow contained inside the vessel that the Face had called the Consciousness, the universe that opened up before him seemed limitless. If not for the stakes involved, he would've liked to stop, look around, really take it all in, but he knew he should keep moving. *And it's way too fun racing through it on a lightboard.* Staring out into the Milky Way, he saw flashes of what waited up ahead—aliens he hadn't met yet, worlds he'd never seen—and couldn't determine if those were actual precognitions, his imagination, or both. Somewhere far in the distance was the burning obsidian rock man. Even farther awaited a living mountain of decomposing trash. *Totally not looking forward to that one.*

He'd so far resisted looking down at the Nothing Spot again, but he felt its dark tentacles constantly flickering up at him and drawing him in like a magnet. *I won't look.* He swore that to himself. He had to save those alien weirdos, whatever they were. His falling into the Destroyer would be the death of them. Saving them was what a hero would do.

"Not so heroic when it's your only real option, Earth Boy. Your life on Earth is over. You have nothing to sacrifice."

Adam jolted so hard that he almost toppled from the board. The new voice in his head was foreign—and it wasn't the gentle thudding of the Star Voice but more like a knife to his skull. The voice had sliced away the pride he'd felt at his decision to save the aliens. The creepy new subconscious radio track was an invader from somewhere else, somewhere below, planting dark seeds within his mind. He glanced down at the Nothing Spot, quickly looked away, and—

"Look down at me. Don't be a pussy, Earth Boy."

Adam gave in to the taunt and stared down into the Nothing Spot. The darkness blinded him like a reversed sun, spreading itchy black spores across his eyes. A low, throaty laughing sound emanated from the bottomless hole. The longer Adam stared into it, the more the stars around him died like popped balloons. He looked away.

"I'm still alive. My parents are still on Earth," he whispered in a tone so feeble that a breeze could knock it over. "I'll see them again when I go back."

"No, Earth Boy, the only fate left for you is total brain death, a life of no movement, no love, no feelings other than pain and guilt—helplessly watching as everyone you love rips themselves apart because of your brain-dead flesh.'

Adam accidentally glanced at the Nothing Spot again, and his lightboard swooped downward. He covered his eyes, and it came to a grinding halt, nearly toppling him over the side. Then he shot upward again, getting as far away as he could. When he came to rest, his legs were wobbling beneath him. *I'm safe. I just can't look down again.* Adam shook off the feeling and shot forward through space, painting the stars with his lightboard.

Gotta keep going. Don't look down. Don't look. Don't look. Adam was truly beginning to understand why Mom always looked so uncomfortable around cigarette smoke, especially when she'd first quit smoking—staring into an ashtray and trying not to make excuses for having one last butt. He was like a nail biter with fingers hovering near his mouth. He kept going. Faster, faster, faster. Stars flowed behind him.

Then the lightboard stopped, not at his command but because it had found something.

Two craggy asteroids floated in space, and between them hovered a clear, gelatinous, jelly-textured bubble filled with smoke, roughly the size of a small house. Adam took a deep breath, and warmth circulated through his ribcage. *This must be the next alien.*

It smelled of chlorine. Adam took a deep breath. *Okay, this could be the big test. If this alien jellyfish dude starts talking to me, I've gotta say something that doesn't sound totally stupid.* The closer he came to it, the more the Face's spark within his chest felt warm, comforted, lovingly attached to the odd object bobbing up and down in space like a floating water balloon. *Okay, so the Face is friends with this bubble thing, and since I have the Face inside me, that means it's now my buddy too.*

The smoke inside the bubble was charcoal black and filled with seedy little gray ashes, swirling inside it like a pixelated tornado. Its gelatinous skin swelled and contracted based on inner movements. Though Adam didn't see anything that resembled features, he trusted the intuition of the Face's spark, so he did the only thing he could think to do.

"Um, hi." He smiled. "Nice to meet you. Are you... alive?"

The bubble quivered but didn't respond in any coherent way. Adam narrowed his eyes. *Is this really a lifeform?* It was hard to tell. The gelatinous bubble could be anything.

Adam addressed it again. "Okay, so if you *can* hear me, I'd like to help you guys. The Face told me about, uh, everything."

It didn't *seem* to react to Adam's presence. It didn't suck him in as the Face had, and if it was capable of speaking, then it was choosing not to talk to him. However, the way it throbbed in the starlight was somewhat unsettling, somewhat uncomfortable. It almost seemed to be hiding. Adam moved forward, and the bubble squirmed away.

"It's okay," Adam said. "I'm a friend."

He hesitantly prodded its gooey skin—and his fingertips fused to its surface as if he was touching dry ice. The cold was so intense that it burned like a stovetop. A startled cry escaped his lips.

When he ripped his scalded hand back, three of his fingers—the index, middle, and ring fingers—became engorged with blood, turning a dark purple. They felt heavy and bubbly. *Oh no, oh no, they're going to fall off.* Hives bumped up on his palms. He shook his arm and blew on the fingers. The bumps didn't go away. They grew, inflating into cold white pimples, spreading over his skin like hives.

"Oh my God!" Adam cried. "Oh God, oh God..."

The gelatinous smoke bubble throbbed in the starlight. For the first time, it shifted position as its malleable form expanded outward into long winglike appendages that encircled Adam's sides.

Adam shook his hand. Without gravity holding him down to anything, that action floated him backward, away from the spreading wings.

"What did you do to me?" he asked.

The bubble's gelatinous pseudo wings fell limp, drooping to its sides like the appendages of a dead bird. Smoke funneled more quickly through the creature's crystalline-tinted membrane, but the bubble still did not speak. A brown infection grew in its center, like the x-ray image of a smoker's lungs that his D.A.R.E. instructor had shown him in sixth grade. It looked toxic. It wasn't supposed to be there, but it was, and it seemed to be somehow preventing the bubble from spreading its wings as it wanted to.

The white pimples on Adam's hand popped, leaving tiny little wounds. That stung but felt a lot better than the freakish burning from before. Adam exhaled, smiled, and double-checked his hand. The fingers were still red and throbbing, the tips singed, and they smelled of mucus, but they were no longer so bizarre. *Thank God. I wasn't looking forward to having tiny pimple-born aliens grow out of my right hand.* Adam stared at his hot, swollen fingers and—

Death, death, death. Three fingers sliced off of Dad's hand in one swift motion, nothing but bloody nubs. He's too shocked to cry out in pain. Metal crunches against metal. Window shatters. Crash!

He gasped. His fingers turned from red to charcoal black. *Dad, are you okay?* He blinked. His hand was gone, and in its place was his father's white, hairy, callused hand, with bleeding stumps where those fingers had once been. Adam fell backward onto his lightboard, feeling the numb pain in each fingertip. *I never even thought about Dad.* Adam had been flying around in space, laughing and cheering, while Dad was in the real world missing three fingers, maybe half-dead.

The smoky bubble lunged forward and wrapped around him like a cocoon. Adam screamed as the slick embrace compressed his limbs. The creature tightened like a boa constrictor, burning his flesh as if he were in an oven. He couldn't breathe, gagging on the thick smell of chlorine. His skin itched as if fire ants were crawling up and down his body. The beautiful lightboard shattered into little pieces, and the bubble absorbed Adam through its skin. It drank his sweat. It sucked out his tongue. He couldn't scream. *Let me go! Please let me go!* The bubble's spongy inner muscles twisted and contorted Adam's bones until they could pass through the sieve of its gelatinous skin like pink slime.

Then he was inside, coughing his lungs out but once again with a tongue. His body was reformed, but he was floating in blackness like a doll on strings. Emptiness surrounded him—no sights, no sounds... except a grinding whisper from the Nothing Spot down beneath, a sound reminiscent of glass being stomped against gravel.

"Hate you," the voice whispered from the depths below. "Hate you, *hate you...*"

That time, the voice had spoken out loud instead of inside his mind. It growled like a wild boar that had learned to speak eloquently but hadn't lost its feral edge.

That's not the bubble talking. It's the Destroyer.

The bubble, which seemed to be a different alien altogether—perhaps one working for the Destroyer—slowly pulled Adam down toward the Nothing Spot. As his eyes adjusted to the light, he could see dim gelatinous reflections all around him, showing the round shape of the bubble he was trapped within. *I'm not dead. I'm not in the Nothing Spot yet.*

"Stop, I'm here to help you!" Adam choked.

The bubble said nothing, but the Destroyer snarled a response. "Hate you. Love you. Eat you. Come to me!"

A throaty laugh emanated from far below. Adam tried to feel around, to touch the gelatinous walls reflecting around him. *There's gotta be a way out!* Something sinister crept into his mind, as if a psychic tentacle were wriggling down his eardrum. *Get out, get out!* A violent barrage of images broke into his thoughts like a burglar busting a lock.

The car crash. His body is thrown from the vehicle. He's ejected onto the hard asphalt. The impact cracks his skull open, and—

The Destroyer's guttural call snaked through the flashing memories. "You're trapped inside it, Earth Boy."

As it said that, Adam felt the gelatinous walls compressing even more and gagged.

Dad's eye is impaled by a shard of glass. Mom slumps over the steering wheel. The driver of the other vehicle, a teenage girl, someone's daughter or sister or niece or girlfriend, is also slumped over, her red hair stained redder with blood, her shirt covered in blood. A truck collides with the back end of Mom's SUV. Another vehicle slams into the truck from behind. Fire everywhere.

Adam kicked and punched, but the bubble squeezed him, deflecting his blows, stiffening its gelatinous walls. That was oddly comforting—a signifier that he was at least inside something and not just suspended in nothingness itself. Not yet, anyway. His raw skin throbbed. His throat felt dry and sandy.

The beastly voice of the Destroyer whispered to him from the abyss—still far away but inching a tiny bit closer. "It's your fault."

"It's not—" Adam gasped for air. "Not my—"

"All of their pain is your fault."

He's staring at Joe Sanderson, who is standing over the mutilated remains of Adam's bicycle. Chandra is in tears. Joe is smirking that stupid smirk of his. Adam wants to cry. He spent so long working on that bike. So many hours.

"How d'you like your crappy bike now, bitch?" Joe says.

Joe always calls him a bitch. Joe called him a bitch on the second day of sixth grade, when he slammed Adam's arm in a locker and broke it. It was only a hairline fracture, but Adam remembers the crack, the soreness, and the pain. He remembers how it felt to wear a cast for eight weeks. He remembers how he lied to his parents when they asked how he broke his arm. He told them he fell down the stairs.

No one knew the truth—no one but him and Joe.

"You gonna say anything smart this time?" Joe sneers. "Or maybe ya need your little girlfriend with her ugly lip to speak up for you?"

Joe shoves Adam backward, and Adam trips over a crumpled soda can and falls to the ground. Chandra leaps to his defense.

Joe pushes her aside then leans over Adam and spits in his face. "Don't mess with me again. Go back to your country."

Adam's never fought back before, never even tried. He sees Chandra's tears. A switch flips inside him.

Lying in the dirt, Adam grabs Joe's pasty-white ankle, digs his fingernails into it, and pulls the bully onto the ground with him. As Joe scrambles to get up again, Adam leaps on top of him and slams a knee into Joe's crotch. Adam's hand transforms into a solid rock of knuckles and rage, and he brings that rock down upon Joe's face.

"Yes..." the Destroyer whispered, spinning Adam's flawed memory around him like a tornado. "Closer... closer..."

The bully squirms, and Adam batters his face. Joe's flunkies try to pull Adam off their leader, but Adam doesn't even feel their blows, not even when one of them nails him in the eye. He wants to destroy Joe's stupid smug face.

He grabs Joe by the hair, holds up his head, knees him in the jaw. Purple bruises recolor Joe's normally pale cheeks, brow, and nose. His face is made of silly putty, and Adam is its new sculptor. The skin is broken, but that's not enough. Adam wants to break bone. He smashes Joe's nose. Blood runs down from it. Joe reaches upward for help.

"Adam, don't kill him!" Chandra calls.

Crash.

Metal compacting against itself. A tire goes spinning into the distance. Dad's three fingers get severed, and it's all Adam's fault. He started the fight with Joe.

Don't... don't kill him... don't kill me... don't...

The bubble constricted around Adam. He gasped for air, not wanting to remember any more. He reached upward, clawing at the smoke bubble's gelatinous skin but unable to pierce it. He tried to summon the lightboard, and although he felt a spark inside himself, the spark couldn't seem to light, like a gas stove in need of a match.

He smelled his own blood. He saw himself on the operating table, with doctors cutting open his skull. He was only one step away from being sent back there, and the Nothing Spot seemed to be his portal.

"Come to me, Earth Boy," the Destroyer whispered. "Keep fighting if you want. Keep resisting. It might take hours. Might take days. And the hope you feel now... Every time you fight, every time you fail, that hope will break down just a little bit more. You're mine now, Earth Boy. Eventually, you will be brought down here. Your bubbly friend here will swallow up all your effort. You recognize him, don't you? He's the Courage... or as I call him now, *the Fear.*"

The Courage. The Fear. That made sense. The bubble was a manifestation of the Courage, another alien the Face had mentioned. The Face had also mentioned that some of the aliens had fallen into the Destroyer's clutches. Evidently, the Courage had even been rebranded with a new identity. Adam felt a brief swelling of ambition, knowing that perhaps he could talk to the bubble and convince it to help him.

Yeah right, because I'm so good at talking. Adam tried to beat his way out of the bubble's grasp, but he couldn't escape. The Fear was holding him tightly. When it finally spat him out, once it sank low enough into the darkness, he would tumble down into the Nothing Spot. He had to break out before that happened.

"Stop it!" he cried. "Let me go!"

"Keep fighting." A throaty growl. "Give it all to me. Let me drink your pain. And when you're done... the Fear will bring you down to me."

Chapter 12: Blood Bonds

Camille woke up to pale sunlight oozing in through the window. She'd slept in the hard plastic chair next to John's bed with her neck hanging forward, and the tendons were punishing her with a sore tightness. An obnoxious fly fluttered around in her hair as if wanting a little taste of her all-too-alive flesh.

Eyes clamped shut, she swatted at the ticklish creature buzzing around her head, but her hand didn't brush against an insect. Instead, it landed firmly on John's callused fingers. He'd been playfully teasing her hair.

"John!" she cried.

Camille jumped to her feet. John grinned at her, his one eye gleaming. His face was bristly with stubble, covered in cuts, and his non-eye was still patched over, but his smile was the same as it had ever been. That was the look that always said, *I'm okay. You're okay. We're gonna be okay.* She lunged on top of him, forgetting for a moment that he was injured, and kissed him more passionately and forcefully than she had in years. When she moved off his chest, he inhaled deeply, and she realized she'd been squeezing the air out of him. She was about to apologize, but then he kissed her hand.

"I'm okay," he said in a raspy voice and rubbed her shoulder with his good hand.

She kissed him again and again, though a bit more carefully. "Oh my God, John. John! I love you." Tears poured from her eyes.

"Love you, gorgeous." He chuckled. "Y'didn't think I was down for the count, did ya?"

She sniffled. "I did. I'm sorry, John." She kissed his cheeks, his shoulders, his hairy chest. "This is my fault. This is—"

"Shut up." He clenched her shoulder then let go. "Shit happens, honey, and I'm okay now. Looks like you got off easy though, huh?"

She laughed, wiping her eyes. "Fuck you."

"Ah, gee." He grinned. "Nice thing to say to a guy in a hospital bed."

Camille sat at the bottom of his bed, reached under the blanket, and ran her fingers between his toes. She wanted to curl up in his arms, but he was still too fragile for that, so she settled for squeezing his foot. "I was so scared. I thought you were going to die."

"Me? Hell, I was scared for *you.*" He touched his eye patch and drew back in alarm. When Camille was about to speak, he stopped her with a forced smile. "Don't worry, Camille. Doc already told me about the eye, so I got that shock outta my system. I just keep forgettin'. I'm just not—not used to it yet."

Camille sighed with relief. She bent forward and kissed him again then took his mutilated hand and kissed it, too. Though he looked at her appreciatively, she sensed he was still somewhat in shock, and seeing him so weak and vulnerable made her stomach as shaky as a butterfly in the wind.

"Camille," John said. "Thank you for—wait, how's Adam? Is our boy okay?"

Adam. Camille jolted off the bed and onto her feet as Adam's name passed through her mind like a shot of electricity. *Adam, Adam, Adam.* Even though her legs barely held her, she backed away toward the door. Somehow, deep inside her, she sensed something was wrong with Adam and she had to locate and save him. "Oh God, John, I've got to go. I've got to find him." She flashed John an apologetic look. "I'll be back."

"Is he alive? Camille—"

"I don't know!"

Camille rushed out of the room. He kept calling her name, each bellow weighing on her shoulders like a hunk of iron, but she kept moving. John needed her right then, and she hated walking away from him, but something was wrong with Adam. *I just know it. Mother's intuition.*

She pushed between two nurses, accidentally spilling a bottle of hand sanitizer to the floor. She kept moving. *He's in the darkness.* That was what her mind told her, though she didn't know why. Following her instincts, she raced through the ICU. Normally, she would've been yelling at people, demanding answers, but right then, her heart was leading her somewhere, so she followed.

"Mrs. Helios!" Dr. Blake came running down the hall. "We have news about your son! He's here in the ICU. He's—"

"I'm going to see him now!" Camille screamed. "Right now! Where is he?"

When she stormed up to Dr. Blake's face, he shrank away from her. "You should know," he said, panting beside her, "he's in the first room to the left of the next hallway—"

"Where?"

Dr. Blake pointed and was about to explain more, but Camille left him eating dust. She slid open the door and whipped the curtain away, and behind it was a boy wrapped in so many bandages that he looked like a mummy. Every part of his body was covered in dressings, including most of his head and nose. The few visible parts of his face were so puffy and bruised that he didn't look anything like her son. She knew, though. She felt his heart as if it was inside her chest, and she recognized him. She was looking at Adam, *her* Adam, even if he didn't look like Adam.

Tears welled up in Camille's eyes. Dr. Blake was saying something behind her, but she was too distracted to process any of it. She stepped forward and reached to touch Adam's hand. Before she could, the boy's body erupted in a fit of spasms, wriggling back and forth as if he were being electrocuted.

"He's having a seizure," Dr. Blake gasped. "According to his medical records, there's no history of epilepsy, so this must be—"

"He's not epileptic!" Blood rushed into Camille's cheeks. "You've got to stop this fast, before he—"

"We need to wait a minute," the doctor said. "I'll get ready with the injection if it lasts longer than a few minutes, but—"

"Do whatever you have to!"

Dr. Blake scrambled from the room like a battered minion. Camille stayed beside the bandaged boy, who was shaking frenetically, his every broken limb vibrating within its padded constraints. *Holy crap, holy hell, damn. Thank God I'm here... Thank God I came in here right on time.* Foam drizzled from the side of his mouth, and his eyes were closed. His dark fingers protruded from heavy pads. Camille clutched those cold little fingers, hoping he could feel her. Terror cut holes in her heart. That was her boy, her baby, her only son.

"I'm here, Adam. Don't you die on me."

Chapter 13: Descent

Adam saw a light flash in the darkness for a split second and then disappear. It was external, outside the gelatinous bubble that held him. As the light faded, he heard a voice he could've sworn was his mother's.

"I'm here, Adam. Don't you die on me."

Then it was gone. He was in the shadows again, held aloft above a black hole, with an invisible carnivore pacing in circles beneath him.

His body hung above the abyss like a wet sock pinned to a clothesline. *If I stop fighting, if the Fear lets go of me... I'm a goner.* He knew that. He had to keep struggling.

"M-M-My name is Ad-Adam Helios." He felt the urge to vomit. "I c-come from a place called—"

"I know all about you, Earth Boy." The Destroyer's growl echoed through the gooey chambers inside the Fear and reverberated through Adam's head. "You're the pathetic worm who the Consciousness brought here to stop me. But you can't stop me. I'm inside you. Inside your busted brain."

The gelatinous walls trembled at the Destroyer's whispers, and Adam realized the Fear was just as scared of the Nothing Spot as he was. As if hearing that thought, the chlorine-scented bubble clenched tighter onto Adam.

Adam stifled his tears. "S-S-So is the C-Con-Consciousness."

"The Consciousness belongs to me now." The Destroyer chuckled.

Adam saw flashes of what waited for him below. *Tentacles. Whispers in his ear. A long, forked tongue licking the sweat off his face. Rows of shark-like teeth piercing his flesh.* He didn't know if those were true images of the beast, if his imagination played tricks on him, or if both things were one and the same.

From the depths, the Nothing Spot's whisper once again quivered through the Fear's body. "And you belong to me, as well," it said.

Adam pushed air out of his lungs. "Why are you called the Destroyer?"

"I'm *your* Destroyer."

Tears filled Adam's eyes. "Please don't hurt me."

"I will. You're still in that hospital bed." The Destroyer emitted a low growl.

In response, the Fear shuddered, nearly dropping Adam, who quickly clutched onto its gooey folds as a throaty chuckle rose from the Nothing Spot.

"Out here," the Destroyer said, "you're just *dreaming*, imagining yourself into our vessel. When I'm done with you—"

"You don't have to hurt me." Adam choked. "You don't have to hurt this vessel, either."

"You're mostly dead anyway."

As the Destroyer said that, a light finally appeared in the darkness—a glowing hologram of a human brain, floating far above his head, bumping into the Fear's inner membranes like a ping-pong ball. Adam strained his eyes at its glow. *Am I imagining that, or is the Destroyer creating it?* Then the brain fractured into pieces. Blood oozed between its vessels. One side of it shriveled away into white mold. Adam looked away, staring downward, and his body was shimmering with a sort of x-ray image of his insides—muscles, bones, and veins exposed like drawings from an anatomy book. Suddenly, all his muscles withered away, atrophying, losing all functionality. His bones crumbled to dust. His entire body collapsed into an oozing gray puddle of flesh, glued to the walls of the Fear, with only his head retaining its shape.

His skull struggled to lift itself, fighting against the atrophy breaking it down. "Please let me go!"

"I will," the Destroyer said as the lights cut out.

In the darkness, Adam's sticky body started to pry loose from the Fear's wall. *Oh no, no, no, no.* He pushed back against it as hard as he could, reaffixing himself.

"When I'm done with you, Earth Boy, I'll let you go. Oh, I will. I'll send you back home. On your world, they call it a... a TBI, yes?"

Adam's head sank downward, no longer capable of holding itself aloft. His face splashed down into the hot puddle that was his body. He gagged, trying to push his lips up toward the sky so he wouldn't drown in his own liquefied skin.

"Yes, they call it a traumatic... brain... injury." The Destroyer emitted a low chuckle. "Pathetic."

Adam sees himself in bed, wrapped in bandages, unable to move of his own free will. Occasionally his arm moves, or his eyeballs roll and blink, but that's all the response of neurons firing out of habit, not conscious effort. His mind is broken. He soils his diaper with diarrhea and urine. He can't eat, and yellow fluid is poured into his stomach through a feeding tube. His parents stand beside his bed, on opposite sides, glaring at each other. They've gotten old. His dad is using a walker. They've divorced and gone broke taking care of his medical bills, still hoping in vain that he'll recover someday.

Adam positioned his droopy lips away from the fleshy puddle and gasped in oxygen, sputtering.

"Your body is already destroyed." The Destroyer's voice sounded closer, the closest it had so far. "But I will devour your spirit, Earth Boy. Your fears are my fuel. Your stubbornness is my sustenance. You will make me a *god*, and then the Consciousness will crumble."

A hoarse cough burst from Adam's lungs as they swelled up like balloons. The bones inside his face melted, becoming part of the puddle, and he stared upward, away from the darkness, back to the place where stars might exist if he went high enough. A throbbing, liquefied light pulsed through the Fear's walls, like an electrical current. *What is that?*

The electricity spread further. The walls were shaking. Adam felt the gelatinous material clenching around him again, but not so tight-ly—it was not squeezing him but holding him aloft as though cradling a baby.

Wait, maybe that's the Courage! This must be the Courage, what it was before the Destroyer renamed it the Fear! Adam shouted at the top of his lungs in one final, last-ditch effort to save himself. "Help me!"

Chapter 14: Lifeline

Camille's heart was pounding as Adam's body flailed. Nurses ran into the room. A steady hand punctured his flesh with a needle. Adam's limbs shuddered, jolted... then slumped down.

By that point, Camille had bitten her fingernails into jagged little flecks, a bad old habit she thought she'd dispelled in high school. She started to move toward Adam then glanced down the hall at John's room. She cringed at the thought of John trapped in a hospital bed, having no idea whether or not his son was dead. She couldn't even imagine how scared he was.

Geraldine, the same heavyset nurse who had been there for Camille right after the accident, took Adam's pulse. She then turned to Camille, her eyes crinkled in joy. "He's doing just fine, sweetie. Thank the lord."

"Thank you." Camille gulped. "You're sure he's okay?"

"He's okay."

Camille peered over Geraldine's shoulder at the bandaged boy. "I'm sorry I was such a nervous wreck earlier. God. I'm an asshole."

"Can't blame ya, hon." Geraldine nodded. "If that was my son—"

"Hey," said a slender, dark-haired nurse on the other side of the bed. "Can you pass me a new IV bag?"

Geraldine handed over a bag from the cabinet on her side. Camille moved closer to Adam, examining him closely. His lips were blue. If she remembered correctly, from back in her CNA days, that meant—

Oh no. "He's not getting enough oxygen to his brain!" Camille cried.

"Don't worry, hon. That ain't so abnormal after a seizure. But just for you, I'll take a look." Geraldine touched Camille's arm, and even as Geraldine redirected her attention to the other nurse, her hand lingered there. "You see anything abnormal, Linda?"

Camille pointed at his blue lips. "See?"

The little she could see of the puffy balloon that was her son's face had turned a sickly yellow color. The exposed areas of his arms showed blue veins.

Camille bit on a hangnail, drawing blood. "He looks so—"

"Hold on!" Linda, the dark-haired nurse, suddenly shot bolt upright. "Geraldine, we got a problem. This might be bradycardia—no, no, this is an SCA. Oh God."

Geraldine turned to the heart monitor. "Hell."

Geraldine rushed forward, and Camille followed. Cold tingles danced across Camille's skin as she swallowed the screams threatening to erupt from her lungs. She couldn't take the stress, desperately needing to do something. She hated waiting. She trusted Geraldine—but only to the extent that she trusted *anyone,* which wasn't much. In her fast-moving, stubborn life, the closest Camille had ever come to trusting someone was John, and even that trust was situational.

Geraldine watched Adam's heart monitor and checked his radial pulse. "Ah shit, you're right. It's asystole." She looked up at Camille, and a lump visibly descended down her throat. "Camille, it's a cardiac arrest."

"What? Are you—*what?*" Camille's eyes bulged. *Cardiac arrest. His heart. Oh my God.* "Do whatever you can! Quickly!"

"Okay, let's do this." Geraldine exhaled. "Linda, get the crash cart. Get more nurses in here. Get us some epinephrine. I'll start doing chest compressions."

Chapter 15: The Fear

"Help me!" Adam cried.

The electrical surges running down the Fear's malleable walls darkened, as if the Fear were trying to hide itself.

Adam twisted his face away from the melted puddle of flesh that the Destroyer had turned him into and managed another shout. "You don't have to give up! Please, I can... help you... all of you..."

A spark of electricity sizzled through the Fear's gelatinous shape again. Down below, the Destroyer chuckled, unseen and invincible. Adam's consciousness was fading, and he struggled to stay awake. As his eyeballs tried to drip out of their sockets, the Fear's walls tightened around him. Smoke swirled through the cavern like a tornado. The walls shimmered with light.

"Back off," the Destroyer growled. "The Earth Boy is mine."

Hope leapt into Adam's chest. *It's angry. That means something is going wrong for it. I gotta keep trying to reach the Courage.* Drool sputtered from Adam's broken lips. "Please—" He gagged. "I know that you were once the Courage... before the Destroyer did... this... to you..." Adam moaned. "There's gotta still be... good inside you... who you really are."

As light streaked through the Fear's inner membranes, its skin became translucent. Starlight glimmered through it. The only thing Adam could do anymore was breathe and blink, and even those activities were painful. Every word took tremendous effort.

"You *are*... capable." Adam sucked in air. "Listen, I'm just a kid, but I... Everybody can make choices, that's what the Face said... and I think, really, that's all bravery is. Brave people... They *are* afraid, but they act anyway. And you... you can..."

Adam felt his formless body slide into the cup of two gelatinous hands. The Fear's inner body lit up like a torch. Its shape stretched outward, again forming wings, but the limp, gooey wings of before were replaced by a perfect V shape. Its edges sharpened, becoming crystallized. Unlike the amorphous bubble that had been the Fear, its true form—the Courage—resembled a diamond butterfly.

Adam groaned. "You... can. You *can.*"

Suction lifted Adam's melted body upward. Instead of dropping him, the Fear pushed him against its walls. Adam's shape burst through the Fear's skin, right through its pores. His body disassembled into tiny pieces, each one pushed through a tiny hole. He screamed, and the bellow echoed from every tiny part of his shattered body.

Then he reemerged outside the Fear. He was human again. He had limbs, hands, and feet. He swiveled his head in a circle. He hugged himself, happy to feel ribs again. He ran his fingers down his legs and through his hair.

Stars reappeared in the sky. Galaxies formed around him. Planets popped up like little bubbles. He and the Courage were in the cosmos again, free again, free to be themselves. Adam stared in amazement at the diamond butterfly before him, with its sharp edges and electrified wings, no longer recognizable as the bubble it had been moments before, but it still kept its distance, its wings hunched over like slouched shoulders.

"You saved me," Adam whispered.

The Courage's angular head glanced down at the Nothing Spot then turned to Adam. Its wings fluttered.

It's scared, just like me. Adam stroked the creature's crystalline wings, which were cool to the touch. He felt shudders rising from the Nothing Spot and squeezed the Courage for support. *Don't sink down. Stay strong.*

The Courage's wings wrapped around his body, folding him within its warm embrace. From the creature's wings dripped a golden nectar smelling of honey, which flowed down Adam's skin and seeped into his pores—just as Adam had been inside the Fear, now the Courage was inside him. *It's the Courage's spark. He just gave it to me with that weird nectar stuff, I think.* Inside Adam, the Courage met the Face and shook hands.

Adam smiled. "Thanks, dude." He patted the Courage's wings. "Do you want to come with me? I'd like it if you came. I really would."

A violet-skinned tentacle whipped out of the Nothing Spot like a thrown spear.

"Courage!" Adam cried.

The tentacle's knifelike claw impaled the Courage's chest, and smoke and nectar sprayed out. The knife sliced upward, ripping the Courage in half, sending sizzles of electricity across the stars. Both wings collapsed. The tentacle coiled around the remains and lowered them down into the Nothing Spot.

Adam screamed.

The Destroyer's voice was muted, quiet, but unmistakably there, once again inside Adam's head. *"Hope is brightest before it's snatched away. Once I'm inside you, Earth Boy, there's no getting away."*

A roaring laugh drifted out of the Nothing Spot and slowly faded—no longer a direct threat but no less present. *It's watching me now, just waiting for me to mess up again.* Adam swam away with tears in his eyes, not looking down, trying not to fall. The remains of the Courage's smoke and electricity dissipated. He attempted to summon the lightboard, but the fear inside him was too great, and the lightboard didn't come. He was back in space, back in the vessel. *Alive.* His hope, however, was dead.

Chapter 16: Pump, Pump, Pump

Camille watched the epinephrine drip plugged into Adam's vein. *Wake up, Adam. Please wake up.* Geraldine the nurse pushed down on Adam's chest, hard and steady, her fingers interlaced. Down, up, down, up. The compressions were heavy but fast, and beads of sweat visibly dropped from the nurse's brow. Camille turned away, unwilling to see him like that. She couldn't have him again, know he was alive, then have to watch him die.

Geraldine slumped forward, shaking her arms. "I'm out. Someone else take over."

Linda took Geraldine's place and resumed chest compressions. As Geraldine fell back against the wall, covered in sweat, her exhaustion was clear. The compressions had worn her out. Camille had never done actual CPR, much less restarted a heart, but she remembered how tired her arms had gotten doing it to a dummy in her CPR training course, all those years before.

"What's happening?" Camille pushed up close to Geraldine. "Why is his heart not starting again?"

Geraldine shook her head, eyes lowered. "It most likely *won't* start again, hon." She pointed at Linda, still pumping away at Adam's chest but also starting to get tired—another nurse was in line behind her, ready to take over. "What you gotta ask yourself here, Camille," Geraldine said, "is how long you want us to keep going. Eventually, if his heart is gone too long, even if we *do* wake him up... the brain damage could get pretty dang severe. No oxygen is not a good thing."

Camille tried to breathe. She was shaking. "What about the defibrillator? We need one of those right now!"

"Honey, didn't you say you used to be a CNA? You should know it doesn't work that way."

Camille froze. "Long time ago." *Wait, I'm not thinking clearly. I remember now. The defibrillator is for chaotic heart rates, not a stopped heart. It doesn't—*

"Okay, let me remind you." Geraldine shook her head. "No defib for asystole. Doesn't work like that in real life. This ain't the movies. If we're gonna get your boy's heart going again... this is the way."

Linda the nurse pounded away at Adam's little chest. Up, down. Up, down. Camille came in close, staring at her son's blue lips. *Please, Adam. Don't leave me.*

Then Adam coughed. A cacophony of oxygen burst from his chest, and the sound of his fragile lungs was enough for Camille's own heart to leap toward the skies. His eyelids flipped open. For a moment, Camille even expected him to speak, to react, and to be himself again.

"He's here!" Camille cried.

He was breathing. He was alive. She felt his pulse pounding away in his wrist. *Thump, thump, thump.*

"I love you," she said, kissing his cheek. "I love you, I love you, I love you."

His eyes stared out, dark and wide, but even if his heart was moving again, the real Adam wasn't swimming around in those eyes anymore. His body seemed to have returned to life, but his soul was still somewhere else. The stillness in his eyes pierced through her skull like a poisoned arrow. *That's not my Adam.* Adam's eyes were always moving, flicking around the room. He was intense, observant, holding strong, developed opinions that often intimidated her.

But where? The boy in the hospital bed was breathing, and his eyes were blinking, but he wasn't Adam. The nurses checked vitals then offered Camille words of sympathy that her mind was too distracted to listen to.

When they left, she approached the scrawny, bandage-wrapped creature before her like a freshman approaching the principal's office. "Adam, can you hear me?" She swallowed, and her saliva tasted bitter. "You're alive, Adam. You made it."

She couldn't bear to look at his bruised face. Her stomach twisted into knots at the sight of that blank face. Instead, she stared at his chest. Hoping he wouldn't notice—*if he's actually in there*—she made a half-hearted attempt at a smile. "It's me, Adam. It's Mom. I'm here for you."

His eyes didn't react, didn't even blink. They just started outward as if seeing something on the ceiling that she didn't. His mouth hung open as if he was dead.

"Adam," she said. "Please say something. Please."

Tears ran down her cheeks. She couldn't remember the last time she'd cried as much as she had in the past two days, but she'd never experienced a worse two days in her life. She knelt down at Adam's side and held the boy's bony fingers. Unlike John's hand, which had been warm, Adam's was frigid.

"I'm sorry," she whispered.

Camille had never cried in front of her son, always having been scared of showing him weakness. She didn't know if he could hear her or if any activity still existed within his cerebral cortex, but if he did hear her, then he was hearing her sob for the first time.

"I'm sorry, Adam. God, I'm sorry. Please forgive me."

You don't deserve forgiveness, you stupid, selfish bitch. You destroyed your entire family. Adam, John... they're ruined. Her knees were sore. She wanted to stand, but doing so would tempt her to look into Adam's eyes, and that was the one thing she was most afraid of.

Geraldine poked her head in the door. "Can I get you anything, sweetie? Is your boy okay?"

Camille wiped her eyes and offered a weak smile. "Coffee. No cream, one sugar. Thank you, Geraldine."

"Comin' right up."

Geraldine closed the door. Camille faced her fears and looked into Adam's eyes, which had become shells of glass with no creativity, no warmth, and no opinions. Adam's old friend Theo Schlesinger, after his brain injury, had possessed those exact same eyeless eyes until the day he'd died.

Camille shuddered at the memory of Theo, a nerdy but tough smart aleck, a wannabe rock star with hair so orange it glowed, freckled cheeks, corduroy pants, and the cutest little dance moves. Every time Theo came over, she'd been happy that Adam had finally found a friend. Then one day, Theo's father Mark was vacuuming the living room while listening to loud music. Theo had climbed onto the open window sill to jump onto his dad's shoulders, and Mark accidentally knocked his son out the window. Theo dropped two stories to a concrete sidewalk, smashed his brain, and somehow lived.

He hadn't *really* lived, though. He'd had those glass eyes, the same eyes that Adam now had, and Theo had never been Theo again, not really. Mark committed suicide a few weeks later, and Theo's mother went into bankruptcy. Theo died alone.

I can't let that happen to Adam. A damaged brain, a broken body, and a nonexistent spirit. If Adam is really still in there, trying to bring him back is going to be hell.

Chapter 17: I Do Not Think, Therefore I Am Not

Adam's body floated through space like a sock in a pool of water. Hours disappeared behind him. His encounter with the Destroyer had sucked away all his earlier enchantment, and the loss of the lightboard had left him suspended in the void.

The honeymoon was over, and he was in deep trouble. The alien vessel he'd been brought onto was no cheerful wonderland with mad hatters or grinning cats. It was a dark, scary place filled with dark, scary monsters that wanted to hurt him. The deeper he crawled into the rabbit hole, the more powerless he became.

Adam tried to swim forward, but the atmosphere was not water, and his efforts only flipped him upside down. His stomach collided painfully with the other organs in his body. He pushed forward with a grunt, and the strength of his effort only sent him spiraling in the opposite direction.

His heart pounded again. He forced himself not to look at the Nothing Spot. *Relax. Don't let this get to you. Don't look.* He had to keep moving forward. No matter how scary traversing the Consciousness got, going back to Earth would only plop him into the shattered brain of a half-dead child on an operating table. *If the Destroyer isn't lying to me, that is. Maybe it's full of it? Just trying to scare me? God, I hope so.*

He pushed his weight backward and, that time, was shot forward as from a sling. He flipped upside down, but his momentum stayed in the right direction. Going without the lightboard felt hopeless. Trying to get across outer space that way, flipping and spinning like a buffoon, would take years. *If I have years. If my brain isn't rotted out by then. Crap, I've gotta stop thinking that way!* Adam's rotations came to a halt, and he pushed backward again.

I wish Mom were here. Mom always had a solution for every problem. She never gave up. He hated that the last thing he'd said to her was that she wasn't his mother. *I wish Dad was here too.* Dad always had a way of cutting through the stress, patting Adam's back, and making everything seem okay. Adam teared up at the memory of how he'd snubbed his father whenever Dad had invited him to play baseball on the field with his old college buddies or how callously he'd zoned out whenever Dad tried to give him outdated advice about girls.

I'll never see them again. Adam couldn't stop thinking about how, in the past few years, he'd spent so little time with them. His brain had been filled with thoughts of space, satellites, his bicycle project, and the same girls Dad gave him unwanted advice about. He'd just wanted his parents to go away, to stand in the background, fulfilling their necessary roles without actually interfering in his life. He cringed at the memory of their argument during the car ride.

Dad might be dead. He'd seen Mom, and Mom was okay, but Dad wasn't there in the waiting room with her, and Adam had seen him getting torn apart in the crash. If he *was* dead, that was Adam's fault. If he wasn't, he'd still be missing at least three fingers and would never be able to repair the fence, catch baseballs, or change the oil on Mom's car ever again.

Wiping his tears, Adam somersaulted in space, slowly approaching the glowing rings of Saturn. He admitted to himself, despite his sorrow, that the rings had to be the most mesmerizing sight he'd ever seen. Formed from debris, dust, and ice, appearing still despite their constant movement, the rings formed a cosmic echo. They were cold, lonely, and as beautiful as fresh snowfall glistening in the sunlight. Saturn's huge mass made the exterior of Earth look like a blue pebble in comparison.

Adam floated past Saturn's over one hundred fifty moons and moonlets, trying to remember each of their names. The one with the giant circle on it was Iapetus, and Titan was the big one. Rhea possessed its own circle of orbiting debris, a tiny mirror of the father it orbited.

A sharp jolt took hold of his body and pulled him into Saturn's rings. In his panic, he forgot how useless swimming was and tried to scramble away, which was no good. His strokes sent him spinning like a disc. The force was too powerful. He smashed into a storm of ice particles and covered his face as sharp chunks of ice cut through him. He crashed against a frozen wall. He scurried to the top of it then stood upon the surface of the crystallized pathway circling the entire planet.

"Wow," he whispered.

It almost looked as if he could just walk along the surface of Saturn's rings forever in an infinite loop. Shivering in the cold, he collapsed into a sitting position. *I just need a break from this, to catch my breath. Figure out what I'm going to do.* He pulled his legs up to his chest and wrapped his arms around them.

In the distance was a tiny blue dot that he knew to be Earth, and he broke down in tears. *I'm never going back. My brain is broken, my parents can't save me, and I've been abducted by aliens.* He inhaled, and his breath was ragged and choked up. His tears drifted out into the atmosphere, floating around his head in icy droplets. Sobbing so pathetically while sitting on Saturn's rings and gazing at the most beautiful thing he'd ever seen felt like a terrible waste, but he couldn't help it. *I feel so alone.*

Adam wanted to punch himself for not asking the Face what would happen to him if he *did* save their precious Consciousness, provided the Destroyer didn't kill him first. He saw only two possibilities: one, he would stay in the vessel forever. Two, he would get sent back home.

If he stayed in the vessel, he'd still have freedom to move, to live, and to experience things. He'd be the first Earthling to learn all about this strange alien species, but he'd also never see his parents again or his hometown or anything on Earth.

He buried his head in his chest. That possibility seemed so remote that he could barely conceive of it. More likely, the aliens would send him back to Earth afterward, where he'd get back his ruined old body but not his old life. *Traumatic brain injury—that's what the Destroyer said—if it wasn't lying to me.* He'd become the same immobile puddle of flesh that the Nothing Spot's dark energies turned him into, but this time he had no crystalline alien savior to rescue him.

His teacher Ms. Stafford had once talked in class about a book called *Johnny Got His Gun*, about a soldier who got his face and limbs blown off, so he had to live the rest of his life with no senses and no independence.

"Oh my God," Adam whimpered. "Please, God, don't do that to me. Please. Please."

Adam kept thinking about Theo Schlesinger, his first—and last—friend back in second grade. Theo had been so cocky, so brave, and so much better at talking to people than Adam was, but Theo had broken his brain too. About a month after the accident, Adam's mom brought him to see Theo. Before going, Adam had been relieved that his friend had lived, excited to see him again.

However, the Theo trapped in that wheelchair wasn't the same Theo from before. The new Theo left puddles of drool on his shirt, made noises that weren't English, and constantly hit himself in the head, leaving dark bruises all over his brow. Adam had run from the room screaming, too young to understand, too young to process. Theo had become the monster under Adam's bed, the recurring nightmare he had on his scariest nights. He'd gone to see Theo a few more times at Dad's insistence, but Theo had only lived another year before choking to death on a pizza crust.

Adam was shaking. *Now, I'm just like Theo.* The lives of his parents would be ruined, all because they'd adopted some stupid little kid from

India who'd gotten in a stupid fight. He would never ride a bicycle again, never look at the stars. He imagined a long life stuck in a hospital bed or wheelchair, with everyone staring down at him, talking to him only in baby voices, talking *about* him even when he was in the room. Other people would have to change his diapers, feed him, and wash him. If he lived another thirteen years, only the first half of his life would have been spent doing the things he cared about. If his life stretched on longer than that, twenty years longer, thirty years...

He crossed his legs, leaned down, and buried his face in his lap. Sobbing like a baby, he wondered if anyone back on Earth would ever bother to wipe his eyes or if they'd make fun of the little brain-damaged boy for crying.

He closed his eyes, and inside his head, he saw a man sculpted from black rocks, flickering blue-and-white flames emanating from his shoulders. He knew the figure, the same one that had guided him from the beginning. Adam inhaled, and the blue flames entered him, but they were soothing, like breaking through a snowstorm and stepping into a house with a fireplace. The medicinal fire opened his lungs with a crackling warmth, and he expelled cool air.

"Is someone there?" He opened his eyes and stared down the length of Saturn's crystalline rings.

A jagged crack was open on one side of the ring he was perched on, revealing a blue cavern down below. He crawled inside, taking care not to be swept out into space.

The icy walls inside the cavern were like bulletproof glass, and his breath was frosted. He rapped on a jagged section, and an echoing chime echoed down the tunnel. Stepping around sharp stalagmites and slippery slopes, he followed the cavern around the circumference of Saturn until it ended in a flat, snow-covered wall. He wiped a section of it clean and stared through to the other side.

He jumped back. On the other side of the glassy ice was a jagged, vaguely human shape. Submerged there was a man with a head, two arms, and two legs, his entire body carved from shiny black obsidian.

The rock man's lower half was buried inside the ice. Adam tapped on the ice. The obsidian man turned to face him and then tapped back.

Chapter 18: Battery

The obsidian man had no face, just a smooth, flat black plane with no features and no contours. His square neck spread out into jagged shoulder blades wider than two bodybuilders standing side by side. His arms were twisted columns of spiky rock terminating in five squared-off fingertips. His obsidian surface shimmered in the light of Saturn's rings but was covered in places by a fine layer of frost. The icy sheen crackled as he twisted to face Adam, his movements restrained by his trapped legs.

"You." The obsidian man's voice crunched as if he had gravel in his throat, but his tone was flat. "You have come." His rocky arms bent inward like those of a praying mantis.

Adam's exhalations had fogged up the icy wall, so he wiped them away. He peered through the cracked ice, trying to see how the obsidian man's legs had gotten buried in the ice. *Okay, so there's some kinda dark blur beneath him. It's pulling him down through the ice—if he breaks free, he'll drop right into the darkness. I can kinda see it through the ice. It's... oh crap. He's falling into the Nothing Spot.* The ice was holding the obsidian man in place over the abyss just as the Courage had held Adam.

Adam tried to speak, but the words caught in his throat. "Hello... um... ah..."

The icy wall was marked by etched words that looked as though they'd been carved by a sharp utensil: "The end of the Optimist."

Adam touched the letters then pulled back. "So you're... the Optimist?"

The rocky figure's shoulders slumped. "I am that which you perceive me to be."

The Optimist drooped over on the ice, revealing a line of black protrusions along his spine, reminiscent of a stegosaurus.

Okay, this dude is totally the coolest-looking alien so far. Adam pressed his forehead to the cold, glassy wall, trying to spy a mouth on the figure's face and not seeing one. "Have you always been here? Like this?"

The Optimist shook his head, and the humanness of the gesture almost gave Adam a heart attack. "I have not."

"Oh, yeah." Adam smiled. "I guess you wouldn't have been named an optimist, then."

The Optimist did not smile back at him—it couldn't, of course.

Adam looked down at his feet, digging one beneath the other. "Sorry."

"Tell me, human of Earth." The obsidian man tilted his head. "What is life like on your world? I am so curious. Do you find it worth living?"

Adam snaked his hands into his pockets, feeling as though he was in the principal's office again. He swayed from side to side. "Dude, you're asking a kid who just had his head cracked open."

"I suppose it is not, then?" The Optimist pressed his flat hands against the icy floor and stared between his splayed fingers. "That is a shame."

"I don't... I dunno." Adam pushed back tears, thinking of his parents again. "I'm not the right person to ask. You aliens picked the wrong person to help you."

"Your days on Earth," the alien said in its monotone. "What are they like?"

"Me? Heh. Every day of my life is just so—"

"Painful?" The Optimist brought a slated fist to his chin. "I suppose that no matter where one exists in the universe or in what form life might be shaped, pain will always exist. It is a necessary consequence of consciousness. Of course, so is happiness"—the Optimist looked up to the ceiling of the cave, grasping at the strands of Saturnian light that cut through the ice and shone down on him—"but happiness is always a prelude to more pain."

"I just don't get this whole thing." Adam took a deep breath. "Who are you, really?"

"The Face and you discussed this, yes?"

"Yeah. Sure, man. But crap, I dunno." Adam shook his head. "Why do all of you look so different from each other? I mean, you kinda even look humanoid. The other two sure didn't."

"I do not look anything like you, Adam." As the Optimist pressed his hands against his chest, his frosty overcoat crackled. "I do not *look* like anything because your human sense of sight is not something we possess nor can be perceived by. I also do not have a name, a body, or a voice. None of these traits can be used to describe any of us."

"But I *see* you. I hear you too. And the Courage smelled a lot like chlorine."

"Adam." The Optimist's monotone voice rose just a trace. "Were any of us to encounter you in a physical way, you would not be able to process us—your eyesight would not capture us, your ears would not hear us. It would be as if we were not there. Your brain is not wired for beings such as us, and perhaps, one might also say that we're not wired for such mechanical beings such as yourself."

The Optimist grasped at the light again, his neck craned backward. "And thus, Adam Helios, when we travel the cosmos, we do not use the flying saucers of your world's mythologies. As the Face told you, our vessel is built of imagination. As I'm certain the Face informed you, that is why you were the candidate we chose."

"Yeah, I know. I daydream too much. And I have a brain injury. Perfect combo—*great*."

Adam could almost swear the Optimist smiled. Maybe that was just a trick of the light, a mirage on the icy wall standing between them, but something was different about the alien when he talked about that subject.

"One can never daydream too much," the alien said. "We've explored the entire universe by daydreaming, and it's daydreaming that has brought us here. And now, through your imagination, we have painted our vessel with the colors that you see outer space in. We have shaped ourselves into physical beings. We speak your language, reflect your own understanding of the universe, and—"

"Yeah, yeah, the Face told me all that. This whole thing is just an illusion. I still don't quite know how to take that. I know you guys are real, but then the way I *see* you isn't real or... something."

"Adam Helios, if you understand nothing else, then remember this: perception itself is nothing more than an illusion that sentient beings use as a tool to interact with a universe that is impossible to perceive."

"Whoa." Adam stepped back.

"Everyone, even on your tiny blue planet, lives in a different universe from their fellow humans despite the fact that all of you use the same five senses. We on this vessel use not senses, but something else, something your language has no words to describe. The way that you perceive yourself, Adam Helios, is not how *I* perceive you."

Adam smiled. "Wow, so what do I look like to you guys? I mean... Ah crap, I guess you can't explain that."

A tiny flicker of blue flames lit up along the Optimist's spine then died out. The obsidian man collapsed forward.

Adam knocked on the glass again. "Hey, are you okay?"

"I thought you could save us." The alien's voice sounded broken. "Your mind fit the profile. You fit *us*." The floor around the Optimist cracked, black veins spreading along the ice. "But I do not anymore. We have already lost."

After another crack, the Optimist slid farther into the ice. His abdomen descended into the floor, his thick barrel chest caught tight in the ice holding him up, but the ice around him was cracking into tinier and tinier pieces.

Adam banged on the wall, trying to break it. *If this guy lifts his arms, he's a goner.* "Hey!" Adam cried. "Hey, do something!"

"It's too late," the alien whispered.

The sliding motion had halted, at least for a moment, but the Optimist didn't try to save himself or try to crawl out. He seemed to be resigned to his fate. Adam couldn't see beneath the ice, but he imagined that somewhere below, a violet tentacle was wrapped around the Optimist's feet and was pulling him down into the Nothing Spot. *He's going to go down the same way that the Courage did.* Trembling at the memory of the Destroyer, Adam knocked on the ice again. The Optimist turned to face Adam, revealing his front side. A massive chunk of the obsidian man's chest had been torn out, completely removed. A gaping hole yawned in the place his heart was supposed to be.

Sensing Adam's gaze, the Optimist gestured at the hole. "My spark was here."

Adam's feet twitched as though he was standing at the edge of a perilous cliff. "The Destroyer did this to you, didn't he?"

"Yes." The Optimist fingered the hole then withdrew his hand. "All of this is my fault, for I am the battery that powers this entire vessel, the leader that steers it through space. I am its defender... and I failed. This"—the Optimist gestured toward the ice that had submerged him and continued to swallow his upper half—"is a consequence of our great vessel's infection. The Destroyer found me when I was at my weakest, sensed my lack of hope, and stole my spark. That is how vessels such as this become infected, Adam Helios—when their brightest selves are reduced to depression and beings like him seize the reins."

Adam remembered the tentacle that had impaled the Courage, the raspy voice, the power of a creature that had turned him into a goopy puddle. He stepped back. "He's not here, is he?"

"He is everywhere." The Optimist slipped as the ice cracked again. "Once he unites the other sparks with mine, the Consciousness shall die."

"But I thought—"

"Yes, uniting them is the only way that the infection could be cured... *if* the Consciousness is the one that unites them. But if the Destroyer does it first—and, trust my judgment, he will..."

"Then he'll win?" Adam whispered.

"I'm sorry." The obsidian man shook his head. "Your entire journey here is hopeless. The Destroyer is making you do his work for him. I apologize for taking you away from your world."

With another crack and a whoosh of air, the Optimist was brought down to his upper arms. Adam gasped, raced to the frosted wall, and banged on it. His fist bounced off, and he slipped to the floor.

On the other side of the ice, the Optimist's rocky surface became coated with crackling ice crystals. "Leave me." His voice creaked as if it was rusty. "Leave this place. There is nothing for you here. You shall simply die with all of us."

Adam banged on the wall again. "I don't have anything to go back to!"

"You have family. More friends than you realize. People who love you. And your condition still fluctuates with every moment. There is still a small chance that your brain may survive the car crash."

Adam bit his lip. "How would I get back?"

Ice caked the Optimist's rocky skin, and his voice was increasingly strained. "Just think... about... home. No place... like..."

"But then, if I went back, all of you—"

"Death... for us all..."

Adam closed his eyes, and for a moment, he imagined the Earth—ground level, a landscape of trees and mountains. "So there's a chance for me if I go back." He inhaled deeply. "But if I stay here, there's a chance that I can save all of you. And if I go, all of you will die. Seriously, is that what you're saying?"

Adam looked again at the inscription carved into the ice: "The end of the Optimist." He thought about the Face, the Fear, and this Optimist, who was slowly being torn apart by the Destroyer. He thought about how the sun looked back on Earth and how it reflected so beautifully in that blue sky, surrounded by clouds, overlooking his little town.

"I can't." Adam shook his head. "I'm staying here with you guys."

The Optimist's arms were sinking.

As sadness welled up in Adam's chest, he pounded his fists against the ice. "Get out of there, Optimist!" he cried. "Listen, I know that life is painful and all that crap. I get it! But my dad, he always says—"

"Says... hope... no..."

"My dad, he always says that happiness is what we make for ourselves!" Adam banged his fists again. "Listen, we can do this. We can save the vessel, the Consciousness, the whatever-it-is... and we'll do it together!"

"Together?" The Optimist leaned his blank face backward, peering at the dim outlines of stars that shimmered through the icy cavern.

Then the stars shook. The universe bulged and receded. The ice rattled. An earthquake shuddered along Saturn's rings, knocking Adam off his feet. Stars swirled around like a tornado.

The voice of the Consciousness shuddered through the ice. *"Listen to the boy."*

Stalactites crashed downward, breaking into pieces. Adam crawled away, barely avoiding impalement. Cracks spread across the walls and glowed orange. The Optimist turned to Adam with a tilted head, as if asking the Consciousness, *"This boy?"* and Adam's heart pitter-pattered.

"Is it possible?" the Optimist shouted to the sky above the roar of explosions.

Adam jumped left, barely dodging a crashing chunk of ice. He looked up at the hole through which he'd crawled into the cavern. He had to get out. The ice was going to crush him.

"Is it true?" the Optimist asked the universe, arms spread.

Blue flames lit up along the Optimist's spiny back and erupted from his hands. The obsidian man tore away the chunks of ice holding him prisoner. A white fire burned along his shoulders and swirled over his chest. The Optimist lifted himself out of the hole.

Adam stood up, legs wavering as the earthquake came to a shuddering halt. The Optimist's flames were so bright that Adam shielded his eyes.

"It's possible!" the Optimist cried out as he strode before Adam and stood upright, about seven feet of black rock. White and blue flames coiled around his body.

The cavern shook again, and chunks of the wall broke open, hurling Adam into space, spinning him toward Saturn. He screamed, trying to regain control over his momentum. A warm, rocky hand seized him by the wrist.

"I have you," the Optimist said.

Then Adam was floating in space again, between Saturn and its rings, face to face with the fiery man of rock. Adam gasped in awe at the Optimist's smooth, shiny surfaces and the constant flowing motion of the fires emanating from his granite shape. *Yeah, this guy is totally the coolest alien ever.*

"Thank you, my friend," the Optimist said. "I owe you my life."

As Adam spun backward again, he took hold of the rocky figure's arm for leverage. The flames did not burn him, but the Optimist's skin was warm and hard. Adam looked into the slate face above him with slack-jawed wonder.

"This is the real you. With all the fire and stuff, I mean," Adam whispered. "You're the one I saw back on Earth."

"This"—the Optimist touched Adam's chest—"is the real *you*. And the fire is inside you."

The Optimist pressed down, and an electrical warmth throbbed through Adam's ribs and pulsed into his heart. Static shocks trickled down his spine and flowed down his calves and into his soles.

"Oh my God!" Adam laughed as the lightboard burst like a lightning bolt beneath his feet. He knelt down and touched the lightboard's surface. It was like a metal slab radiating heat. Then he looked up at the Optimist, noticing the obsidian man's flames were composed of the same ethereal light source as the board. "Man, I missed this thing."

"You are the Galaxy Seeker." The Optimist clapped Adam's shoulder. "This board is yours, and it is also *you*."

The Optimist stepped onto the lightboard right behind Adam, as if they were riding a horse together.

Adam laughed again then looked out into the endless expanse of stars. "Are you coming with me? I won't have to be alone anymore?"

"Never again, my friend."

Adam turned around, and the Optimist embraced him in a tight, hard hug that sent blue flames rippling through both of them.

"Where to?" Adam asked.

"Follow the guidance of your heart, Galaxy Seeker. It shall never lead you astray if you listen to what it's saying."

Adam turned to face the galaxy again. The Optimist rested his hands on Adam's shoulders, both of them facing forward. The lightboard shot into the universe like a slingshot, leaving a streak of glowing white atop the blackness of space.

Chapter 19: Respite

Only the morning before, Camille had last driven through the suburban cul-de-sac where her home was, but she felt as though she'd been gone for years.

Nothing had changed. The yards were still square and green grassed. The apple orchard was blooming with its sweet aroma. Little kids were still bicycling down the sidewalk, and Old Man Thomas was sitting on his porch, drinking his breakfast beer through yellowed teeth. He lifted the can toward her as her taxi drove past, and she waved.

She nudged the cab driver. "It's coming right up."

The previous morning, back before her car had been turned into scrap metal, she'd left for work after a tense argument with John that was supposedly about him breaking all the eggs though that was really just an excuse to cycle around the same wheel of grudges that neither of them had given up on for a decade. She'd stormed out to work so angrily that she hadn't even bothered to say goodbye to Adam.

The Camille Campton-Helios that she'd been the day before was completely different from the Camille who had just spent the day and night in the hospital waiting room. Coming home felt like pretending to be someone else.

"That one." She pointed. "The house with the red door and the red porch."

She got out of the car, paid the driver, and waved at the Watsons as they walked their three collies down the sidewalk. She glanced at John's dirty old hatchback, parked in the driveway, which she would probably be driving for the time being, considering that her car was beyond totaled and John would have no depth perception. Her nerves sizzled at being out of the hospital. Her fingers clenched into fists. *I need to get back there, ASAP.* If she was planning on staying there overnight again, though, she had to collect insurance papers, legal documents, state IDs, and anything else that might prove necessary. *Grabbing a change of clothes probably isn't a bad idea, either.*

She marched up the red stairs, stomping so hard that the loose boards rattled, and stopped at the front door to catch her breath. Two of the windows were wide open, sprinkled with morning dew—a token sign that the house's residents hadn't expected to be gone overnight. The mailbox at the bottom of the door was stuffed with junk mail.

She opened the door. "Hello?"

She said it out of habit, and her heart dropped once it left her mouth. The only response was the hum of the television set, where a CNN broadcaster was talking about war overseas. Normally, John's habit of forgetting to turn off the TV irritated her. She hated the energy waste. But for once, it was a beacon of nostalgia that brought her back to the better, simpler time that had existed less than twenty-four hours before.

The house seemed as distant as a childhood home. The scented candles still left a nutty almond aroma in the main hall. She passed by her framed stamp collection, a relic handed down from her deceased stepfather. Normally, the stamps brought back good memories, but that day, they just reminded her of his death. What did make her smile, oddly enough, were the cookie crumbs on the coffee table. *Adam never listens. I always tell him to use a plate or the ants will infest everything.* Normally, that also would irritate her, but thinking about Adam sitting there, munching on cookies, calmed her hectic heart. That was a foreign feeling. The house was full of perfectly white plates, cups, and bowls, with white tablecloths and white towels in the bathroom—a neat tidiness she cared so much about—but all that felt so much less real and human than a teenage boy's cookie crumbs.

"Just one day later," she whispered, shaking her head. "One fucking day."

The grocery bags on the kitchen counter were sopping wet. A bucket of melted vanilla ice cream clung onto warm hamburger beef. *Oh, that's terrific. I must have forgotten to put everything away when I got the call from Adam's school.* Though the Camille of yesterday would have obsessively checked every item and scrubbed the counter with bleach, the Camille of today had other priorities to worry about, like a son and husband in the hospital. For the time, she ignored the grocery catastrophe.

She opened the top drawer under the microwave and flicked through the folders containing all their insurance information. The words on the pages faded into blurs, and she rubbed her eyes, slumping over the counter with a long, painful yawn. Her legs felt wobbly, so she pulled up a stool and sat down. She'd barely slept the night before and hadn't eaten, either. She needed protein, but the bacon on the counter didn't seem appealing.

She also needed coffee. Coffee was easy. Coffee would wake her up. As she dumped out the old grounds and fired up the coffee machine, she peeked up at the spiral staircase connecting the kitchen to Adam's room on the second floor. She imagined him walking down those steps in a black hoodie, hands in his pockets. *That was one of the last times I saw him, before...*

Before *it* happened, yes. She'd seen him come down those stairs the previous Sunday at about eleven, maybe even noon. She'd been hunched over a pile of papers on the counter, just like now, stressed out over bills, credit-card debt, and anything else with a dollar sign in it. Then Adam had walked downstairs in that black hoodie, hands pocketed, slowly shifting from side to side like the troubled adolescent stereotype most teenagers became at one point or another.

She remembered thinking it strange to see him move so slowly, so deliberately, almost as quiet as he had been when he'd first come to the States. She still expected him to come bounding down the stairs as he had when he was younger, full of smiles and positivity, full of great ideas about how to change the world. The colder, intellectual, self-conscious Adam that had sprung out of puberty still unsettled her.

"Hi, Adam," she'd said.

As a young boy, he used to race up to her and give her a big hug then tell her about how he'd spent all night drawing up plans for time machines that ran on fire and could go backward in time about five minutes before new fires were needed to charge their batteries. The thirteen-year-old Adam, however, didn't even lift his gaze to meet hers. "Morning, Mom."

He poured himself a bowl of cereal—*breakfast at lunchtime,* she remembered thinking—and was about to take it into the TV room. Then he caught her glance, hesitated, and instead ate it in the kitchen. Seeing the guilt in that gesture made Camille feel like an old woman that Adam took care of out of obligation, but not love.

Stuffing a heaping spoonful of cereal into his mouth, he looked up at her. "You okay?"

"I'm great," she said. "Why?"

He shrugged. Hunched over the counter, he still looked so small and fragile. "You're worried," he said. "I can tell."

"I'm... yeah, I guess." She sighed, overemphasizing her exasperation. "These bills. I don't know. I have so many places asking for money, but I don't have money. Credit... God. Adulthood drives a person crazy, Adam."

"Heh." Adam smiled at that—an actual smile, not a smirk. "I don't get the whole credit thing."

"What about it?"

He looked into his cereal bowl. "Seems like, I dunno, if a person doesn't have money to pay for things, then they shouldn't buy them on a loan. Just pay for what you can afford. That's what I'm gonna do when I move out, anyway."

They both burst out laughing. A moment of warmth passed between them there, a moment when they were mother and son again—not the same mother and son they had been before, but a remodeled version, maybe even a better one.

"Yeah, okay." Camille grinned. "And all you're going to eat is cereal, right? Isn't that what you said last week?"

He shrugged. "Cereal, spinach, grapes, and chicken salad. Get all the core food groups in there. No reason to eat anything else."

They both laughed again. That was the best morning they'd had in months. After Adam finished his cereal, he went down to the basement to put some new additions to his precious homemade bicycle, and Camille went to see her mother. Once the work week started, they hadn't really spoken again until the afternoon when everything changed.

Camille's phone vibrated, reminding her of the calls she'd missed that morning from Joe Sanderson's father—she didn't listen, for the reminder that two lawyers wanted to sue her wasn't making anything better. That was another catastrophe they were going to have to deal with soon, once this medical emergency was over. *If it's ever over.*

The coffee machine was done dripping. *Dripping away, just like my life.* She shook that thought away. She couldn't let herself think so negatively, not yet—not while Adam still had a chance. She needed to keep fighting for him. No one else would if she didn't.

Her cell vibrated. She dug it out of her purse, pushing through a tangled mess of vitamins, ibuprofen, her checkbook, and scraps of notebook paper. When she answered the call, she was greeted by the fretful voice of Dr. Blake.

"Mrs. Helios, um, how are you?"

"Just dandy." She bit her lip before a swear could slip out.

Dr. Blake seemed like a nice guy, and so far, he'd been a good doctor. If she ended up having to bite his head off later, that should only be for a good reason.

"Let's hear it, Doctor," she said.

"Are you, well... still in the hospital?"

Her stomach churned. "At home. Five-minute drive. Can run back. Is now a good time to meet?"

"Yes." Heavy breathing. "We need to discuss your options in regard to Adam. Can we meet in my office in about one hour, perhaps?"

"No, John's hospital room. His father deserves as much of a say as I do, yes?"

"Um, yes, my apologies. Certainly, we can meet there. Is one hour from now okay? If you need any longer—"

"Make it the next thirty minutes. See ya." Camille hung up the phone. She reopened the folder of insurance information and got back to work.

Chapter 20: Searching for a Search

The lightboard streaked through the stars, and Adam stood at its center with the Optimist riding shotgun. Like an illuminated knife, its blazing surface cut across the heavens faster and faster until the stars dotting the backdrop of the Milky Way galaxy actually began to resemble Milky Ways themselves, little white spirals circling an enormous ball of fire.

Neptune, a blue eyeball in space, disappeared behind them. *Bye-bye, Neptune. See ya later!* They rushed past Pluto so quickly that Adam could barely glimpse it. *Bye-bye, planet that isn't really a planet.* Just a little farther out, moving in a distant orbit, was another blue-tinted sphere, cloudy and dark, that Adam had never seen before. He gasped, grabbed the Optimist's craggy shoulder, and pointed to the new planet.

"It's real!" He stopped the lightboard to get a better look. "We just discovered Planet Nine. It's the planet that Mike Brown and Konstantin Batygin were talking about. There it is!"

The flames circling the Optimist's torso flickered white, and he wrapped his heavy obsidian arm around Adam's shoulders. After an awestruck pause, Adam launched the lightboard forward again. The sparks inside him didn't feel any curiosity in the new planet. As they tunneled deeper into space and the planet faded from view, only then did he realize that if the vessel was really just built from his imagination, that meant he hadn't discovered Planet Nine at all—he'd just imagined it because he'd *like* to think it was real.

Oh well. I guess it's not a big deal. He stared back at the white streaks of Earth's solar system, disappearing behind him. *Jeez, compared to what's ahead, everything behind seems so... small.* He felt less connected to his five senses, his knowledge of the universe, and his personal history—as if the farther out he went and the more his mind expanded, the less focus he could put on personal life details. Even his entire galaxy was just a tiny speck in a universe more enormous than he'd ever realized.

"I'm not really a kid anymore," he whispered. "Am I?"

"You are not," the Optimist said.

"Am I still... y'know, a human being?"

The Optimist shrugged. "What *is* a human being?"

As Adam moved through the vessel's membranes, new senses opened up within him. He perceived distant voices ahead but not through his ears or through language. A hum, a distant murmur, grew inside him. He could not quite see but rather *sense* the enormous mountain of trash that waited for him far ahead, like a reverse memory from tomorrow. Something dark was inside that mountain. He didn't want to go there, but he knew he had to.

"I know what's ahead, somewhere in the stars, past what I can..." Adam bit his lip. "Past what I can actually see with my eyes. It's like I'm looking into the future. Is that... destiny?"

The Optimist pulled Adam closer to him, a hug somewhere between fatherly and brotherly. As he let go, residual blue flames danced across both of them. "It is not destiny," the rocky man said. "Destiny does not exist."

"It doesn't?"

"Choices define direction, not fate. Consciousness is the bow, and time is an arrow."

The lightboard swooped beneath an asteroid, and Adam jokingly punched him in the arm. "I gotta say, dude, I still think it's weird that I'm talking to an alien and that the alien is making metaphors based on my planet's medieval weapons."

The Optimist stared at him with its eyeless brow. "The metaphors that you hear me say are based upon your perception of—"

"I know, I know," Adam said. "Just kidding with you."

Looking back, he no longer saw Earth's sun or even planet nine. Everything he'd ever known, even through the eye of a telescope, would be meaningless trivia compared to anything he encountered ahead. "So destiny doesn't exist, huh?"

The Optimist's faceless face was still pointed at Adam, and Adam tried to imagine it making an expression. The rock man's head, chest, and shoulders reflected the stars upon their glossy black surface. "No. And neither does time."

Adam looked around, rubbing his hands together, trying to remember that the hands attached to his arms were not real, nothing but pictures created by imagination. The stars sailing past them weren't real, either. Neither was the lightboard beneath them.

"Huh." He shook his head. "Give me a few hours to figure that one out."

The obsidian man extended an arm, and blue flames rippled down his bicep then floated over his palm in a fiery depiction of the infinity symbol. "There is no such thing as a before. No such thing as an after. The illusion of these things only exists within human perception, which has also created the even greater deception that you know as the present."

"But the present is happening right now."

"Is it?" The Optimist looked at Adam with something that almost looked like a smile. He snapped his jagged fingers, and the blue flaming infinity symbol danced down the length of his arms and across his shoulder blades until it settled over the other hand. "You perceive the reality of this present through your human eyes, and your eyes can only perceive the universe through light—"

"Right, and light moves at a certain speed. So yeah, between the moment that something occurs and when light enters our eyes—"

"I do not have eyes." The Optimist left the infinity symbol dangling in midair and drew two flaming dots on his flat face with an upturned half circle beneath them—a smiley face.

Adam laughed. *I guess he makes jokes too.* The fiery cartoon smile silently laughed with him. After a few moments, it disappeared, and the Optimist reclaimed the infinity symbol, spinning it around in his hand like a top.

"Okay, whatever, dude." Adam wiped his eyes, still grinning. "But seriously, so when light enters *my* eyes... I think what you're saying is that my people can't actually perceive reality in the present because of the time it takes light to transmit images to them, so they can only see what occurred a million, billion, trillionth of a second ago—"

"And piece it together. Yes, Galaxy Seeker. So this present that you speak of is an illusion. Of course, all of this is based on the assumption that your human framework of time is accurate to begin with, which it is not. My species certainly does not use such a limited system. Most of the multiverse does not, either. In a few centuries, your species shall not bother with this *time* concept, either." The Optimist clasped his hand, snuffing out the infinity symbol he had been playing with.

"You can see that?"

"I don't know how to answer that." Optimist shrugged. "So much of the way you describe things is based on your sense of sight, which I confess is something I don't truly understand though I'm trying to. It actually sounds rather peculiar to me—the idea of light reflections creating shapes and colors, and you having two squishy spheres in your skull that tell stories to the brain. Quite odd."

"Okay, okay." Adam pointed forward. "Well, you know what, I want to use my odd little sense of sight to get a closer look at those purple things."

Violet-tinted clouds encircled the next galaxy like Aurora Borealis, emitting holographic projections on the planets, moons, and asteroids. Something flickered in those projections, some sort of creatures, and laughter throbbed within them. Adam moved to ask the Optimist what he was looking at and then decided not to. Curious though he was, he found something wonderful in not knowing what the purple streaks were, about creating translations through his imagination instead of trying to enforce the rigid doctrine of explanation upon them. *It's more fun this way, at least for a little bit.*

Above them, the violet streaks pulsed and throbbed with light and happiness, but below, down in the Nothing Spot, a thin voice screamed. A colorless shadow blanketed an entire solar system beneath them, obscuring it in darkness.

Adam winced and hid behind the Optimist's bulk. "I'm scared, Optimist. I know we need to go to some kind of mountain, and it's gonna be bad when we get there."

"That mountain you are speaking of is a being known as the Rage." The Optimist's white flames went dark blue, almost indigo. "We will get there, but first we must encounter another being. I am dreading this one in particular, for he is close to my heart."

Adam couldn't determine whether that statement meant the Optimist's love for the next alien was fraternal, compassionate, or romantic, then decided it was probably none of those things but was instead some alien emotion he would never relate to. *Who the heck knows?* "Okay," he said. "So what's this one's name?"

"You shall know him as the Mad Glee," the Optimist said, "for the Destroyer's insanity has poisoned him in deeper, darker ways than any of the others. He is not what he once was."

Adam repressed an urge to smile at the name. The Optimist pointed ahead, his finger burning like a candle, at a wooden door floating in space. The door was fixed to the front of what looked like a concrete cube about the size of a hotel room.

"Okay, that's weird." Adam felt as if ants were crawling down his spine.

"He is in there."

The lightboard slowed as they approached the door, which was hanging loosely from the jamb as if someone had broken in. The door looked like any regular door on Earth—an unsettling juxtaposition, considering they weren't even in Earth's solar system anymore—and the sides of the concrete cube had the same sort of sliding windows as were in Adam's living room though these were tinted black. *Something about it gives me the creeps.*

"Do we have to go in?" Adam shuddered.

"It is your decision if we proceed."

Adam inhaled deeply. "Okay."

The brass handle was marred by fingerprints and had been mostly unscrewed from the door. When Adam touched it, it fell off and drifted away into space, where it might one day circle around a nearby planet and become part of its ring.

The door creaked open. Adam and the Optimist stepped inside, leaving the lightboard hovering outside the door like a warmed-up car. A moldy carpet squished beneath their feet, and the room reeked of urine.

The normalcy of the surroundings was stranger than anything Adam had seen yet. The inside of the concrete box reminded him of the tiny studio apartment that Adam's creepy uncle Fred had lived in a few years before—dirty, squashed, but terribly bland. Adam's foot slid on something, and the Optimist caught him just in time. It was a pile of yellowed porno magazines, spread across the floor like a collage. Adam covered his mouth, repressing the urge to vomit.

"Nobody's in here," Adam said.

He peeked at the twin-size bed, which was pushed up the wall. The sheets were dirty with stains and crumbs, and the pillow was matted down, but no alien was in sight. The only picture on the wall was one of Adam and his parents. *Nope, can't get much creepier than that.* Liquid splashed behind him, and Adam spun around. A coffeemaker was dripping into a pot, spewing a substance that resembled oil more than coffee.

"I don't like this, Optimist." Adam crossed his arms, clenching his chest. "There's something really weird about this place."

"He is here." The Optimist pointed at a television set.

Adam stood beside him. *That TV looks like it came from the stone age.* It was the sort of insanely heavy box that Adam vaguely remembered from his early childhood, back before flat screens took over. As he stepped toward the TV, a neon sign tacked to the wall behind it flickered to life, with green neon letters spelling out "Welcome, Earthboy!"

The television turned on, and the screen rustled with white noise. A piercing whine blared through its dusty speakers.

The Optimist whispered in Adam's ear, "We are in the Mad Glee's domain. Proceed carefully."

Chapter 21: The Mad Glee

The television set switched channels, and the white noise switched to the image of a pink cartoon hand waving hello, with pop music playing in the background. Adam jumped back, staring downward at a rectangle of pink light reflecting on the moldy carpet. He looked up at the screen again. The station switched to footage of what he assumed was an old president—*I think that's Kennedy, isn't it?*—waving hello as he stepped off an airplane. The station switched to a fireworks show blasting over a harbor then changed back to the waving pink hand.

Adam whispered into the pinhole that he assumed to be the Optimist's ear. "So you and this guy were close?"

"We still are. My energies created his." The Optimist's voice sounded heavier, as if two boulders were being crunched together.

The TV screeched again. The station switched to a grayscale close-up of an Earthling man's perfect grin, packed full of shining enamel teeth. The smile was painfully forced, as if his mouth had been pinned up on each side, with glistening gums. *Those teeth look way too perfect, like dentures or something.* Even when the man spoke, his voice muffled by the TV's speakers, those teeth never disappeared behind the man's lips.

"Hello, *hello,* hello, Earth Boy." The Mad Glee's voice was like the most grating music ever composed. Between every word, his pitch changed dramatically, veering from squeaky to deep and grizzled to falsetto.

Adam moved closer, but the Optimist pulled him back.

"Hello there," Adam said.

"Ah yes, oooh *yes*." The grin pulled wider, showing more teeth than any normal human mouth. "It's a pleasure to *meet* you, Earth Boy, to *see* you. Welcome."

"My name is Adam, not Earth Boy."

"Why yes, you are!" The station changed to documentary footage of a yellow snake coiling around a tree then switched back to the perfect smiling teeth. "And *I* am the Mad Glee, the one of gleeful madness, yes I *am*."

"It's, uh, great to meet you." Adam hesitated, looking at the Optimist. "You already know my friend the Optimist, right?"

"Optimist himself is here to stay, here with you"—the screen showed another explosion of fireworks then went back to the mouth—"and here with *me*. Yay!"

"Mad Glee," the Optimist said. "We have important things to discuss."

"Important things, oh my, oh dear." The TV face screen ran his tongue along those shimmering teeth. "Maybe we can talk about how all of you, yes you, my dear friends, *trapped* me in this nasty little concrete box in space, yes?"

"You allowed the sickness to corrupt you. You were risking the vessel's—"

"It doesn't matter, Optimimmy." Mad Glee chuckled. "We both know that when Mr. Earth Boy and Mr. Destroyer team up, they're going to set my corrupted little self *free*."

Adam stepped back to the door, but it was closed and locked. *Oh man, I got a crazy bad feeling about this.* The TV screen flickered with the golden lights of yet another fireworks show, that one playing out over a desert.

The Optimist's flames died down to a dull gray. "Galaxy Seeker, are you okay?"

"I'm not on the Destroyer's side," Adam said, frantically looking at the Optimist for confirmation. "Am I?"

The Optimist shook his head. "Mad Glee, the Galaxy Seeker needs your spark."

"Oh, how nice of you." The mouth cackled through the TV speakers, emitting dust. "First, you lock me into this oh-so-boring existence in this dreadful little apartment, and now you want to steal the one thing that makes *me...* me?" The smile dropped into a grimace for the briefest of seconds then pulled back again. "No can do, Optimimmy."

"Imagination is important," the Optimist said. "Hope is important. But—"

"Oh?" The TV flickered to white noise and then showed documentary footage from a prison. A guard beat an inmate then slammed the inmate's face into the bars. "Then why did you take mine away?"

"Because every being in the universe deserves autonomy," the Optimist said. "One being's dreams cannot be followed when they come at the cost of another's freedom."

"Oh, shush! Those peons on Earth would have loved to have me as their benevolent ruler! They'd be happier with me—"

"There's no happiness in slavery."

An Olympic gymnast cartwheeled across the screen. "Quiet, you! My domination would make everyone there *so* happy, *so* delighted!"

"You were... what?" Adam sat down on the bed, felt something squishy beneath him, and quickly stood up. "You were going to...?"

"Mad Glee." Optimist redirected Adam's attention, drawing a plus sign in blue flames. "At this very moment, the Destroyer continues to pump poison into the veins of our vessel. He is marching toward the Consciousness's heart, and he will destroy everything that we have."

"Oh, pish-posh talleywag nonsense bag." An elaborate fireworks show came on TV again, showering light upon what was recognizably New York City. "You've always tried to hold me back," the Mad Glee said in a Cockney accent. "It's such a drag." The station switched to a cigarette commercial. When the butt was lit, the screen flashed back to the fireworks show.

This Mad Glee dude keeps showing fireworks, big things, exciting things. He must seriously hate this dingy apartment.

The toothy smile flickered back onto the screen. "Earth Boy," the TV speakers muttered, "have you just been listening to lil' boring ol' Optimimmy there, or do you want a different perspective on your journey? It doesn't have to be about *us*, you know. It can be about *you*, your future, your dreams. I can help you."

As the Mad Glee laughed, electrical sparks sizzled from the outlet the TV was plugged into. The neon wall fixture burned out.

Adam ducked under the Optimist's arm and crouched before the television, its flickering screen only inches from his face. "What are you talking about?"

The Mad Glee chuckled then displayed footage of a boy in a wheelchair.

Oh my God, it's Theo. Theo drooled into his lap, his eyes glazed over. A long surgical scar glistened on his forehead. Adam bit down on a scream. *Please no, please don't be me, please not that.*

"Adam, don't—" the Optimist said.

"Earth Boy!" the Mad Glee sang. "I can save you from your brain-damaged destiny if you trust me."

Adam grabbed the sides of the TV. "How?"

"Break me out of this stupid little box." The Mad Glee's screen became a growling tiger. "And together, we'll take over the galaxy."

Adam looked down. "But the Destroyer..."

"Oh yes, your slimy purple friend has nasty dirty breath." The TV switched to clips of bedbugs crawling beneath someone's mattress. "But your comrade the Destroyer has given us freedom from the burn of fictitious morality, and for that, we *owe* the bastard. We don't need to *serve* that creepy little octopus creature, but we can *use* him as *our* launching pad."

"Galaxy Seeker!" The Optimist pulled Adam away from the television. "Do not fall into the trap. Do not—"

The TV screen sizzled. "Back off!"

Electricity blasted from the television into Optimist's body, shooting him back across the room. The Optimist collapsed onto the moldy carpet as the smell of burnt rock filled the room.

Adam hurried to his friend's side. "Optimist!" Adam shook his shoulders, his obsidian skin charred with ashes.

The obsidian man groaned but did not wake.

The television switched to another fireworks show.

"He's my friend," Adam said.

"He's holding *you* back," Mad Glee said. "You are just clinging to him because you don't have friends in your regular life. But I can be a *real* friend to you, Earth Boy. Your new *best* friend."

Adam breathed in heavily. "But... I don't..."

"He can't save you. But I can. Optimist will just send you back to Earth, where you can spend the rest of your life eating through a tube in your stomach." On the screen, a different brain-damaged boy rolled off the side of a bed then lay helpless on the floor, on his stomach, his nose crushed and bleeding. "But if you and I get together, we'll be gods."

A superhero flew across the TV screen, the first Indian superhero Adam had ever seen, and he needed a moment to realize the hero was him.

"Adam, my boy," the Super-Adam said, facing the camera with a wink, "I can promise you an unlimited field of discovery, adventure, thrills, and knowledge. No responsibilities to worry about, no consequences. No one holding you back. Just follow me, and achieve anything you've ever wanted!"

Adam moved toward the television. "Thanks, but..." *I could be independent. Travel through space, know everything, see everything.*

"You deserve the power I offer you. Your dreams *can* come true!"

The Mad Glee's glowing screen showed a weird cartoon of a small boy kicking a football, over and over, like an animated GIF. The screen zoomed in, showing the boy was a cartoon depiction of Adam and the football was actually the severed head of Joe Sanderson.

"I don't want that," Adam whispered, closing his eyes.

When he looked back, the TV screen was showing him kissing Chandra Goswami. He lifted her into his arms and carried her to a mountaintop, and they lay beside each other, looking up at the stars.

"But I want—" Adam started.

Then the TV changed, and he was again flying across the screen as a superhero. His cape rustled behind him as he burst through Earth's atmosphere and tore apart a flying saucer with his bare hands. Then he used the wreckage to construct his own spaceship in midair.

"With my help, Earth Boy, nothing can hold you back." The Mad Glee's voice fizzled through the TV speakers. The station switched to a red carpet in space, being unrolled toward the screen. Above the red carpet was a field of thousands of asteroids and a whirling tornado of fireworks blasting through the cosmos. "You can be a god in this world, perhaps even the god of your namesake. We'll call you Helios the Great."

Adam stared at the fireworks on the screen, thinking of all the times he'd stared up into the night sky, wanting to be a limitless figure, a powerful figure, a great man that the bullies could never mock again.

"Join me," the Mad Glee said.

However, as he watched black-and-white images of Helios the Great being worshipped by the denizens of alien planets and having statues created to honor him, Adam thought about his parents. He remembered the car crash. He remembered the last time he'd seen his mother in that waiting room. *They could have left me in India. They could have been happier that way.* Because of him, Mom had been forced to sacrifice some of the things she wanted to do and to work long hours—all for him, all so he could be happy.

Adam shook his head and looked away from the TV. "I can't. I'm sorry."

The televised fireworks continued blasting through the asteroid field, burning the surface of the red carpet. "Why not?"

"Because I have to do what's right." Adam folded his arms. "I can't do anything for the people I know on Earth, but I'm the only one who can save this weirdo vessel. I gotta do that. It's the right thing to do even if it means that when I go back home, I'm gonna be brain damaged. I'm sorry, Mad Glee."

"Well that's a *shame*." The Mad Glee purred like a cat. "That means I'm just going to have to kill you."

A muscular white arm broke through the screen, shattering the glass. Five meaty fingers grabbed Adam by the throat and dragged him into the television.

Chapter 22: Gleeful Reckoning

Adam fell through the television screen as if it were a trapdoor and somersaulted through the center of an exploding firework. The hand tightened around his throat. Choking and gagging, Adam ripped the hand away from himself, and it flew backward. He collapsed onto the same red carpet he'd seen on the TV screen, hovering before a fireworks show in space, but the supposed asteroid field that had been on the screen was a watered-down version of the Mad Glee's reality. As fireworks scattered across the cosmic landscape, a field of human body parts floated among the lights.

The hand that he'd fought off was lost among a sea of shrunken heads, hairy legs, pale, splotchy feet, arms, eyeballs, stomachs, and ribcages. All those parts were cauterized and bloodless but unmistakably human.

Adam vomited then almost vomited again when he saw his puke drifting weightlessly before him. The TV set floated in the air behind him. The Optimist was trapped inside it, beating on the glass.

"The screen won't break!" the Optimist said. "Go toward the Mad Glee's center. Find his spark!"

Adam tried to kick through the screen, but the glass held. A tangled mess of cold fingers smelling of puke yanked him back down to the red carpet. A disembodied fist punched him in the face, and he spat blood.

"Oh my, dear little Earth Boy!" A giggle trembled down the red carpet, wrinkling it. "Come *play* with me. You want my precious little spark, doncha?"

Fireworks blasted from some mysterious center point, obscured in a cloud of rainbow-colored smoke. Adam leapt into the air, and the lightboard appeared beneath him. *Gonna give this my best shot.*

"I'll come back for you!" he cried toward the TV set as the Optimist's obsidian fists continued banging against the glass.

Flipping the lightboard around, Adam rushed toward the fireworks, dodging decapitated heads, toes, and a dangling fence of chalk-white spines. His stomach shrank into itself as he tried not to vomit again.

The Mad Glee chortled as a blast of explosive lights launched from the sky, streaming toward Adam. They burst at the front of his lightboard, sending him flying backward. A school of hands grabbed him like hungry piranhas, holding him hostage and pushing him down in the direction of the Nothing Spot. Adam screamed at the top of his lungs and shoved the hands away from him. Before they could grab on again, he blasted away on the lightboard.

Another explosive missile of lights swooped toward him. He cut upward on his illuminated board. The lights exploded far beneath him. He sliced through the jumble of arms and legs blocking his path, cutting into the tornado of rainbow smoke that was the Mad Glee's center.

"You can still join me!" the Mad Glee cried in its shifting cadence. "We can take over the universe *together*!"

Adam coughed as kaleidoscopic mist pushed down his lungs, tasting like what he'd imagined of cigarette smoke. *I'm almost there. Gotta keep going!* He pushed the lightboard forward, entangling himself deeper within rainbow-refracted snakes of gas.

The Mad Glee spoke again, and sparkles of light sizzled in the clouds. "Don't you dare try to hold me back."

Adam cut through the cloud until he came upon a stark, charred asteroid. *This has to be it. Man, I hope.* The fireworks were shooting out from natural jets embedded within the asteroid's surface. *It all comes from here. Okay, good sign.* The asteroid cracked open, and out of it came a planet-sized tornado, swirling with body parts.

Adam jumped back, legs wobbling. *The spark is inside him, inside my imagination. I gotta go deeper.* He leaned forward, and the lightboard rushed into the tornado's center. The winds swept him away. Hands grabbed at his face. Feet kicked him. Teeth bit down on his skin. He cried out in pain but closed his eyes. *Focus, Adam. Focus like you've never focused before.*

"I'll find you," Adam said.

In the darkness behind his eyelids, he broke away from the sounds of the crashing rocks and the sparkling electricity. He focused on the faces of his mother and father, imagining them there in the hospital, waiting for him to come alive again. He'd neglected them. He knew that now. Children all over the world didn't have parents, and he was the selfish boy who had never appreciated his for everything they did. *I'm sorry, Mom. Sorry, Dad.*

"What are you doing, Earth Boy?" the Mad Glee's shriek bounced off the storm of body parts. "Come play with me!"

Adam held his eyes shut. He kept his feet planted firmly upon the lightboard. *Responsibility.*

"No!" The Mad Glee shrieked, sending spiked amplifications into Adam's eardrums.

Eyes closed, heart beating steadily, Adam reached out into the darkness, farther than his hands could possibly stretch. He clasped onto something cold, damp, and soggy.

"Responsibility," Adam whispered.

He pushed the squishy object to his chest, and it seeped into his pores, joining with him like one piece of clay molding to another. Coldness ran down his intestines. The Mad Glee screamed... then stopped.

When Adam opened his eyes, the tornado of lights had faded. The cauterized body parts were gone. The asteroid's remains floated through space, but all that was left of the Mad Glee's insanity was a soft, smoky pink blur—beautiful but haunting. Adam's body absorbed its spark.

The damaged TV set containing the Optimist floated nearby. Adam shot toward it on the lightboard and kicked the screen. It broke open easily, no longer protected by the Mad Glee's power. The obsidian man climbed out of a box too small to possibly hold him, his flat surfaces reflecting the pink smoke.

"You did it, Galaxy Seeker!" He hugged Adam.

Adam gulped. "I did. Yeah."

"We are nearing the end of your journey," the Optimist said. "Only a few sparks remain."

Adam stumbled, feeling the weight of the Mad Glee's spark in his chest as if a stone had been placed beside his heart. *I can't even remember what home feels like. What kinda person was I before this? I don't remember.*

"Let's go," Adam said.

He stared ahead, and the lightboard propelled him and the Optimist further forward into the stars. As he soared though the cosmos, though, Adam realized that his body—his unearthly body, so identical to his physical one yet so different—was losing weight. Particles separated from his mass, drifting behind him. His mind had evolved, and the constraints within which his imagination had initially contained itself with were no longer applicable.

He and the lightboard merged into a single bolt of energy, a shooting star. The weight and tangibility that had previously held him back no longer existed. Positive energy flowed through every atom of his shape. He no longer had to look ahead to see anything as he had completely panoramic sight. The universe's power throbbed within him. The Optimist flew alongside him, body lengthwise, arms held forward. They laughed together, sound waves bouncing between them like a thousand ping-pong balls.

Then a white hole opened within Adam's ethereal shape, and in that hole, he felt a rush of cold air as the portal expanded. Streaks of glowing energy stretched from his sides like beckoning hands. He felt a rush of frigid wind, a harsh dryness. *I swear to god, something's growing inside me.*

Then, the white hole in space that had once been a human being named Adam Helios opened up like a door, and Adam's all-too-human consciousness separated itself from the star he had briefly become. A clunky human shape fell inside the hole, and Adam's mind dropped back into the confines of a skull. The bumbling body crashed down upon the surface of a pale desert, spread flatter than a pancake beneath a blinking fractal sky.

The sand was as white as snow and totally undisturbed by footprints, plant growth, or anything but wind. The Optimist lifted Adam to his once-again-corporeal feet, and they stared out at the distant horizon. Adam stepped back and forth, trying to get used to his body again. *Whatever the heck just happened was super freakin' weird. I can't even... Wow.* Everything had occurred so quickly that he could barely keep track of it. The exuberance he'd experienced a few moments before already seemed like a dream.

"Jeez," Adam said, scooping up a handful of cool, silky sand. "What just happened?"

"We have gone deeper inside your mind and thus deeper into the Consciousness's core." The Optimist wrapped an arm around Adam's shoulders, squeezed, then let go.

No sun shone in the fractal sky, and in its place was the black hole of the Nothing Spot, leering at them from above instead of below. The Destroyer had eaten its way into the center of the vessel.

"We must continue," the Optimist said.

Adam couldn't summon the lightboard anymore—at least, not as an external object. *It kinda feels like the lightboard is inside me now, actually.* The Optimist walked ahead in the desert. Adam took a step forward and felt something hard below his foot. He lifted his sole. Nine little marbles lay in the sand, each colored in a different pattern. Peering closer, he recognized them as the nine planets of Earth's solar system, including the newly discovered Planet Nine. He examined the blue-and-green Earth-painted marble for a moment then dropped it back into the sand. *Okay, now that's too weird.*

"Galaxy Seeker?" the Optimist called back.

The Optimist's black silhouette had walked far ahead, his blue flames flickering between the sand-sweeping winds. *Oh crap, I'm falling behind. Stupid marbles.* Adam raced to catch up, following the Optimist's enormous footsteps.

Chapter 23: Measuring the Consequences

Camille lifted John's mangled hands to her lips and kissed them. He stared at her from his hospital bed, his eyes heavily lidded by pain medication, then turned to face the foggy horizon outside the window. The sun peeked through the clouds as if teasing the potential for afternoon sunlight but not fully committing to it. Camille glanced at the door, waiting for Dr. Blake to emerge. *Bastard is running late.*

"I'm useless now," John muttered, his words slurred by the drugs. "A friggin' invalid."

"You're not. I love you." Camille kissed his hand again. "I'm sorry that this happened. It's my fault, but I'm going to make up for it."

"Not your fault." John shook his head, tears in his eyes. "Accidents happen."

Camille swallowed. "I'll make up for it. I promise."

The glass door slid open, bouncing wimpy gray reflections of sunlight across the room. Dr. Blake stepped in, holding his clipboard up like a mask. He shifted his weight back and forth from one foot to the other, and Camille reminded herself to be friendlier to him. The last thing she wanted was to give her son's doctor a stress disorder.

"Mr. and Mrs. Helios." He seemed to consider lowering the clipboard-mask but raised it again. "I hope this afternoon finds you well."

"Fresh as a spring chicken." John coughed. "What's goin' on, Doctor?"

Camille squeezed John's hand. "You said you wanted to discuss something, Dr. Blake?"

Dr. Blake sighed and flipped through some papers on his clipboard, though Camille suspected he just wanted to avoid eye contact with them. "The news is both good and bad," Dr. Blake mumbled.

"Good and bad always means bad in my book," John said, doing his usual shtick of joking around when he was nervous.

"The operations on your son," Dr. Blake said, "have been successful for the most part. No body parts were severed, and we've completed a posterior lumbar infusion—"

"What's that?" John asked.

"Metal rod in the spine," Camille whispered to him, remembering the websites she'd researched earlier that day.

"Yes," Dr. Blake said. "We've done similar operations to his ankle and wrist."

"Will he be able to walk again?" she asked.

Dr. Blake looked down. "Hard to say. But we have a more important concern right now."

Camille bit her tongue. *You got that right, mister.* "Oh yeah?"

"Yes, we need to discuss your son's traumatic brain injury." Dr. Blake rubbed his eyes. "We're still looking into it, but you two will need to have reasonable expectations about what's going to happen."

Camille glanced at John, trying to remember if she'd told him about Adam's brain injury. She didn't think so, based on the way John's lips had shrunk inside his mouth, as if he'd bitten a lemon.

He moved his hand away from her. "What's gonna happen?"

"We don't yet know the extent of the damage," the doctor said. "We've done x-rays, but until Adam becomes somewhat more cognizant... that is, *if* he becomes cognizant..." Dr. Blake looked up at them then shook his head. "I'm sorry. I'm doing a terrible job at explaining this. I know that if this were my son in there, I'd be ripping myself apart."

Camille wanted to climb into bed with John, curl up under the blankets, and shrivel up beneath him. *I can't stop thinking about Theo.*

"You said the word *if*," Camille replied. "Not *when* he becomes more cognizant, but if."

"I'm sorry." The doctor put down the clipboard, and his soft hands disappeared inside his pockets. "What I'm trying to say is that your son might not be the same boy you knew before. The brain is a highly delicate organ, and the slightest damage to it can change everything about who a person is. He might have a radical personality shift. He might lose abilities he had before or perhaps even gain them. Or he might—"

"Might be a goddamn zombie." John reached for Camille. "A brain-dead zombie. That's the most likely thing, ain't it?"

Dr. Blake closed his eyes, inhaling through his nostrils and exhaling through his mouth in a way that signified he was familiar with meditation techniques. "I'm sorry." He gazed into Camille's eyes. "I recommend that both of you discuss a plan of action now. Your son is currently on life support, and... there are options if we are unable to restore his regular functions. There are a couple of group homes in the next town over. There's also a nursing home down on Central Street with a unit that specializes in his kind of care. There are also plenty of agencies that will provide caregiver services right at home, and I personally believe that home care is the best option if you can afford it... but it's not always possible financially, depending on what kind of budget you have to work with. Let me know if there's any information I can provide."

Camille wanted to lunge forward, sink her claws into the doctor's throat, and rip his head off. Blood boiled through her veins. *I can't let myself shout at him. It's not his fault.* She wanted a target, someone to blame, some*thing* to blame. "There must be something you can do." She exhaled through gritted teeth.

"I'm sorry, Mrs. Helios."

"There must be *something!*" She leapt upright, knocking her chair down behind her. "This is my son, Doctor! Do *not* tell me there are no options. Give me a list. Give me a number to call. Give me a sledgehammer to take on anyone who stands in my way. But I'm not putting him in a fucking nursing home and... and..." Tears welled in her eyes. "There must be something. Some one-in-a-million chance to—"

"There is... something. A one-in-a-million chance." Dr. Blake backed up against the door. "Maybe."

Camille lunged toward the door, blocking him in. "Tell me."

"There's an experimental procedure, created specifically for this kind of TBI. It's a synthetic reconstruction of the beta-amyloid proteins, the same kind that cause Alzheimer's. Those proteins are... sticky, and so this procedure injects a modified version of them into the brain, to promote the reverse effect, ideally healing the brain instead of destroying it with plaques and tangles. It involves rewiring the connections, using the proteins as a sort of glue, bringing everything back together to essentially recreate the person—based on the idea that consciousness is essentially, well, a code... a code that can be reproduced—and bring the person back. Ideally. If it works."

"Has it been done?" Camille gasped. "Where? When? Who did it?"

"This procedure, well... um..." Dr. Blake filled a plastic cup with tap water and took a drink, his grip so shaky that water speckled down on his coat. "I was one of the ones who helped develop it. Back when I was a student."

"Let's *do* it, then. For fuck's sake." Camille looked at John for affirmation then back at Dr. Blake. "Has it ever been tested?"

"Yes, but—"

"Wait." Camille moved toward him. "You mean to tell me that you actually helped create some experimental procedure for *exactly* this kind of brain injury, and you've been hiding it from us?"

"No one's ever come out of this procedure alive, Mrs. Helios." Dr. Blake stared into his plastic cup then glanced up at her.

Camille couldn't hold his gaze. *No one's ever come out of this procedure alive.* She backed away, beads of sweat rolling down her forehead, and the doctor audibly sighed in relief.

She picked up her chair and sat on the edge of it. "No one?"

"It's never been performed successfully." Dr. Blake refilled his cup from the tap but only swished it around instead of taking a drink. "That's why I dropped out of the project. Every test subject died. It was deemed a failure." He shook his head. "I would be risking my license if I were to have this procedure performed on your son. I'd need to get approval from the hospital, first. Then you'd need to sign extensive waivers, releasing the hospital from all liability if things went wrong. And you'd need to understand that the chances are that this procedure would kill the boy, just as it killed the prior test subjects, or potentially render him *completely* brain-dead. It doesn't take much to decimate the human brain. It's delicate."

"So you're telling me," Camille snapped, "that we have two options. Either we give up, accept that Adam's beyond saving, and put my pre-teen son in a nursing home or group home or whatever, or we bank it all on some one-in-a-million-chance science project that *might* bring Adam back but will probably kill him?"

Dr. Blake nodded.

John stared out the window with his teeth locked together, his heart visibly pulsing in his throat. Looking at him, Camille knew she was the one who had to make the call. *John is too stressed as it is, too drugged, too distracted to think straight.* The decision was hers. Her son's fate rested in her hands, and if she made the wrong choice, she'd be the one forever responsible.

"Give me the night to think about it," she said.

Chapter 24: Drawing Closer

Adam and the Optimist walked toward the flat line of the horizon, and the Nothing Spot glared down at them like an angry black eye. Bone-white sand shuffled beneath their feet. An evolving array of fractal patterns blinked in the pale gray sky. Cold winds rustled Adam's bones, plastering sand against him. His throat felt lined with moldy newspaper. Particles of sand kept getting inside his mouth and nostrils, biting into the soft flesh of his inner cheeks. His eyes stung, and he had to keep brushing sand from his lashes. His calves burned, his feet begging for a hard, solid surface to step on.

"This sucks." Adam stopped, panting for air.

The Optimist waited for him, always several paces ahead. No matter how far they walked, nothing changed. The horizon was flat and the air foggy, and the desert possessed no dunes, no canyons, no plant life—nothing but that terrible flat whiteness. Adam collapsed to his knees. "Water," he panted. "Need... water."

The Optimist walked back and tried to help him up, but Adam shook his head. He didn't want to stand up anymore. "Can't," he repeated. "Need water. Or, crap, even a Coke. Don't care. Something."

The winds howled, piercing Adam's eardrums. The Optimist tugged on his arm. "Galaxy Seeker, you must not give up."

Processing his friend's words took Adam a moment, for neither of them had spoken in hours. Adam's face fell into the sand, and his chin smacked into the same planet-colored marbles that he encountered every time he'd fallen. Every time he stopped, every time he considered giving up, he'd found those nine worlds again and again.

"We're going in circles," Adam panted. "Same stupid marbles... every time..."

"We are not going in circles." The Optimist crouched down. "I do not know why those nine worlds keep appearing. Perhaps you should take them with you."

"No." Adam swallowed a mouthful of saliva mixed with sand and instantly regretted it. "Creepy. Not putting tiny planets in my pocket."

God, I just want some water. Ice cold. Soda. Juice. Milk. Anything wet, as long as it doesn't have crappy sand in it. Adam covered the marbles with sand. He stood up, his legs shaking. The Optimist's flames flickered dark blue, and the two of them continued walking through the desert. *This is worse than when Mr. Jenkins had us run laps in gym class last month.*

"Are we going to make it out of here?" Adam asked.

"Perhaps. That is up to you. We must try, regardless."

"Dude." Adam coughed out sand. "You really are the most cynical optimist I've ever met."

"True optimism is neither naïve nor stupid." The obsidian man stopped and drew a flaming heart over the hole in his chest. "Optimism is not about pretending the darkness is not there or pretending that monsters do not lurk in the shadows. It is about knowing the monsters are there, taking a chance, and turning the lights on."

"Okay." Adam stopped to catch his breath then nodded. "I'll try." He stopped walking and looked down at the marbles, which had once again appeared at his feet. "Okay, I'll pick up these dumb things. Let's just be *optimistic* that picking them up doesn't drown my solar system in pocket lint or some crap. Stupid marbles."

Adam picked up the marbles. *I seriously hate how creepy this feels.* Nothing happened. As they continued walking, Adam pressed the marbles together, and when he did so, his legs felt a little less tired. His heart slowed to a steady beat. Strangest of all, the mist started to clear.

"Galaxy Seeker." The Optimist turned to face him, his flames flashing yellow. "I believe that you may have made an excellent decision."

Adam clasped the marbles. The mist continued to fade as the wind rustled harder. The desert floor rumbled, and sand shifted beneath their feet. The Optimist held Adam back with his arm then pointed down at where the sand beneath their feet had hardened into rock. A sand-covered pedestal pushed upward from the earth, like the turret of a sand-castle, and grew to a height equal to Adam's waist. Nine marble-sized slots were sliced into its face, like a coin-operated machine.

"Jeez." Adam shook his head. "If I someday make it home, I'm going to throw out any marbles I ever see again."

"I think you know what you must do," the Optimist said.

Adam moved to drop the marbles in but stopped. "What if it's wrong? What if I'm, like..." He pulled back. "What if I'm dropping all of the planets in my own solar system into some kind of alien trap? I dunno."

"Does it feel wrong?"

Adam looked at the obsidian's man blank face and shook his head. "No. It doesn't."

He dropped each marble into one of the holes, and the pedestal whirred with approval. It dropped back beneath the sand. Adam glanced at the Optimist with a shrug.

Then the desert growled. The sand flowed like liquid, rushing ahead of them. The ground rumbled. Adam and the Optimist toppled backward as a statuesque figure rose up from the earth. When they looked up, a feminine silhouette made purely of sand stood over them, her mermaidlike tail connected to the ground.

"It's her," the Optimist said.

"Who?" Adam shielded his eyes from the blinding sky behind her. "Who are you?"

The feminine sand sculpture slid closer to them, lifting her six arms into the sky as if beckoning for the sun. Her crocodilian mouth stretched around both sides of her head, all the way to her ears. Dozens of sand-carved eyes blinked open from the sandy surface of her face, neck, and shoulders.

She's like the best sandcastle ever.

She helped Adam and Optimist back onto their feet then turned away from them as if ashamed of having done so.

"Who are you?" Adam repeated. "And, uh, thank you."

"She is the Motherboard." The Optimist dusted sand off his shiny legs. "And she deserves to be heard."

The Motherboard's wide mouth opened like a toothed beak. "I am what I am," she said in a voice so silky that Adam immediately felt comfortable around her. "But perhaps I am not what I am."

Adam approached her. "Hi, Motherboard. My name is Adam Helios, and I'm—"

"Perhaps you are," she whispered, the gaze of her many eyes descending to the desert floor. "But perhaps you are not."

Adam twitched backward. "What?"

"You think you are." The Motherboard's six insectoid arms fell slack. "But perhaps you are nothing more than a thought."

"I'm a real person," Adam said. *I am, aren't I?* "Yeah, I'm totally a real person. Like you."

"Perhaps." She made a clicking sound then turned to face them again.

Something about her many eyes was fragile, as if all of them were on the verge of tears. The feminine sandcastle rested on the hardened desert crust, seating herself. Adam sat next to her and noticed she was shuddering.

"I'm a person," he repeated. "My name is Adam."

"Perhaps not," the Motherboard whispered. "Perhaps you may be nothing but the creation of a traumatic brain injury. The brain's response to trauma. The brain's inability to accept its new state of being, resulting in delusion. You may merely be a flawed perception, an extension of the psyche's preferred form, what it wishes it could be instead of what it *is.*"

Adam darkened. "No." His words didn't ring true anymore, but he kept going. He pointed at himself. "This is real. I'm real. And if what you're saying is true, then it would mean that you're not real either."

"Indeed."

The sands flowed across the desert, flowing over the Motherboard's figure and dripping from her hands. When he looked at her face again, a giant chunk of her head had fallen away—a gaping hole where her brain should have been. He cried out and stumbled backward, bumping into another sandy figure behind him—that one similarly female but with a different face, broader shoulders, and a pregnant belly.

"Hallucinations," she whispered. "Delusions. Fantasies."

Adam jumped to his feet, running to the Optimist's side. He shook his friend, and Optimist's flames turned indigo.

"Am I real?" Adam cried. "Please tell me that I'm real."

"I believe in you, Galaxy Seeker," the Optimist said. "Do you believe in yourself?"

"I don't know."

An array of sandy figures erupted from the desert floor, all sand-sculpted women with the same massive hole in their heads. All of them had dozens of eyes.

"Perception is flawed," the Motherboard said, the original sand-woman approaching Adam. "This name that you are using, *Adam Helios,* is a creation of language. It is merely a framing device that your parents created when they adopted you."

"Then maybe I'm not Adam Helios," he said. "Maybe I'm Kavi Kapoor. Maybe—"

"Kavi Kapoor is also a framing device that was replaced by the Adam Helios framing device. Both are false." Tears broke free from her eyes.

The pregnant sand-woman took Adam into her arms. She hugged him, pushing his head into her bosom.

For a moment, he held her... then pushed away. "You're wrong," he said. "I'm real."

"Adam, Kavi... these are just names." She shook her many heads. "Names are but a combination of grunts created by the human mouth in order to define something that exists. The names themselves are imaginary. That is Earthling language."

"Believe in yourself." The Optimist grabbed his shoulder.

Adam strained to keep a hold of his thoughts before they dispersed to the wind. "Then there's also no Motherboard," Adam said. "No Optimist. No Earth. No cats and dogs, no—"

"No, Adam-Kavi, none of these things exist. Language is inherently inaccurate," the Motherboard said. "It creates false meaning. There is no Adam-Kavi. No Earth. No *you* and no *I*. Nothing really exists, not in the way we perceive it."

"Nothing exists," Adam said.

The black hole in the sky overtook the fractals blinking beside it. Adam stared at the Motherboard's sympathetic expression. His feet sank into the sand. Then something occurred to him.

"Hold on." He clawed at the sand, held it in front of her face, then cast it aside. "This sand is real. My perception might not be. But the sand is, in some way, real."

"It is not."

"Just because my perception is messed up and whatever," Adam said, "maybe our descriptions are flawed, but we're still describing *something*. That means that something exists behind the lies that language creates." He looked at Optimist. "Right?"

"I agree," Optimist said.

The Motherboard hummed but did not speak. Her many sandy bodies moved closer, listening intently to his every word.

Adam took a deep breath and said, "And I exist too. I think; therefore, I am."

"Yes." The Optimist strode up beside him and put an arm around Adam's shoulders. "*We* are."

The Motherboard opened her many mouths, and water gushed out of them. Holes opened in the desert, and geysers erupted, blasting bubbling hot water across the desert. Water pooled around Adam's ankles, warm and jet filled as a Jacuzzi. Adam dipped his head beneath the water to drink from it. As it flowed down his throat, it became cool and nourishing. He stood up. The water rose to the height of Adam's knees and stopped. Only one of the sand-women remained. She smiled at him with tears of water flowing down her cracked cheeks.

"Thank you," she said. "You're right, Adam-Kavi. We are all real."

The sand-woman melted into the water, delightedly splashing her arms in it until she dissolved. The warm, bubbling ocean replaced the desert. *No more sand.* Beneath the surface, dozens of tiny mermaid figures swam around his legs like fish, guiding him forward.

Adam leaned forward to drink again. The water rushed down his throat and heated in his chest. His heart slowed, a smile came to his face, and he felt the Motherboard's spark meet those of the other aliens inside him. *I've got almost all of them, now.* When he stood up, the Optimist splashed him with water, soaking him from head to toe.

"Hey!" Adam cried. "Why did you do that?"

Though he had no mouth, the Optimist burst with laughter. "Why not?"

After a few more drinks of water, they walked forward again, occasionally splashing each other as they went. Adam looked at the sharp hole in the obsidian man's chest, where the spark had once been—the spark that was in the Destroyer's hands.

"The Rage is next, right?" Adam asked. "The trash-mountain thing."

The Optimist looked down. "Yes."

They silently agreed not to discuss the Rage for the time being, but as they went, the sky darkened, and the Nothing Spot cast long shadows upon their path.

Chapter 25: Decision Point

Camille had asked Dr. Blake for one night to consider his experimental, one-in-a-million procedure, but as the hours creaked by, she wondered if she'd be able to make a decision at all. By two in the morning, she was still wandering the halls of the hospital, checking in on Adam, and reading numerous TBI blogs on her phone. None of that made her choice any easier.

Camille crept past the nursing station, where the nurses of the eleven-to-seven shift were preparing a fresh pot of coffee, trading gossip, and pouring meds. The lights were darkened in Adam's room, and when she slid the door shut, the blinking blue glow of his vitals machine stared at her like an angry robotic eye.

The bandaged boy on the bed, the not-Adam that *was* Adam, slept soundly. Not-Adam's exhalations were calm and steady, so unlike the restless sleep of the little boy she remembered. When he had been young, Adam always slept badly, always afraid of monsters sneaking into his room at night.

They want to stick my Adam into a nursing home. My baby. My little optimist. She took her shoes off so that the tapping of her heels wouldn't disturb him and slumped down in the chair next to his bed. He smelled of sweat and blood.

"Hi, Adam," she whispered in a voice so feeble that she wanted to punch herself for being a wuss. "It's me. It's Mom."

The blue robot eye illuminated her son's features. Though many of the bandages had come off, what lay underneath was no easier to take. All his hair had been shaved off, and future scars ran down his scalp.

Surgical stitches decorated his torso. A deep slash had mutilated his chin, and others adorned his cheeks and brow.

"You look so skinny." Camille swallowed. "Have you *been* this skinny, and I just didn't notice?"

He resembled a display of bones with skin and veins wrapped over them. *It's like he's already dead.* His mouth hung open, revealing missing teeth and bruised gums. A guttural moan escaped from his lips, getting Camille's hackles up—but it quickly died down, revealing itself to be nothing more than the same diarrhea of the larynx that he'd been groaning throughout the day. Camille wanted to believe he was trying to form words, even in his sleep, but she had no way to know.

"I love you, Adam," she said.

"Gunngh..." Adam moaned, rolling his head onto one side.

He's still asleep. Camille hadn't smoked a cigarette in over a decade, but she suddenly craved one. *My boy.* His eyes were clamped shut, but Camille couldn't break the notion that if she shook him awake, he would revert to his old self.

They want to put my boy in a nursing home.

"Adam, it's gonna be A-okay, it's going to..."

She stopped herself because it *wasn't* A-okay, just like it hadn't been A-okay the last time she said those same words, just moments before starting the car ride that destroyed their lives.

The new Adam groaned again. "Glnngh."

The robotic blue eye sped up with Adam's heart rate. His knuckles rubbed frantically against the bedrail. When Camille moved his hand, she saw his knuckles were bruised. He'd been rubbing them against the rail for a long time, maybe hours. If she hadn't noticed, he probably would have kept at it for so long that he would have bled all over his sheets. Remembering her younger days working as a CNA, she realized that even *she* might have not caught that in time. *Especially in a nursing home.* The CNAs in those places had to scramble between thirty or more different residents, many in constant need of care, and that meant that little things like Adam's knuckles might not be saved.

A nursing home.

She could picture the scene as if it were in a movie. She imagined a slightly older Adam in a wheelchair or in a bed, transferred only via the mechanical Hoyer Lift that carried people in a V-shaped sling, dangling them from little hooks. Taking care of him would be a lot of work, and the staff would try their best but would still have too much to do. They'd put him in front of a television set all day, wetting and defecating himself, until it was time to either change him or put him to bed. His wrists would eventually turn inward like paper cranes. His head would drop into his chest, his scarred chin nothing but a memory. His eyes would never focus on another person again—they'd just blink and look away, like Theo's had.

"God." Camille squeezed Adam's hand.

Adam, her Adam, would be there in that future nursing home, trapped in that future wheelchair, for decades. She saw it vividly. She and John would visit him there, decorate his room, talk to him, make the bed for him...

Then the nursing staff would mess up the bed so they could get him in it with the Hoyer, then roll him back and forth to wipe his ass... Camille shook her head. At first, she knew, both she and John would visit Adam every day, if the situation came to that, but if Adam were in that state for ten years, twenty years... She didn't know if any parents, even she, could put themselves through such agony on a daily basis. Even sitting in the room with him right then, directly after the accident, was ripping her heart to shreds.

I'd be a terrible mother to a disabled kid. I know it. She was always so busy, so caught up in the moment, working like hell, fighting people at every turn. If that was the future, she knew she'd end up being one of those neglectful parents she'd always hated. She would be too busy to visit, too scared to visit. She wouldn't —

She swallowed her fears. *Oh, bullshit. I'd never be too busy for Adam.*
Yes, she was a fiery workaholic, but if she were ever to be the primary
guardian for a disabled child, she'd be fighting for that child every day,
at every turn, fighting to ensure that he got the best life possible. That
was who Camille Campton-Helios was.

"Ung," Adam said.

The door slid open behind her. Camille turned, expecting to see a
nurse, but John was there, clad in a hospital gown and standing precari-
ously between two crutches. With his slouched stance, she was shocked
at how much he looked like a weathered old man instead of the strong
teddy bear he usually was.

"John, you're not supposed to be out like this," she said. "Go to—"

She stopped when she saw tears welling up in his one good eye.
She'd only seen him cry once before, just one time over the entire
course of their marriage, and that had been when his mother died, but
that was nothing compared to the crumbling figure standing before
her, his mouth sputtering.

"I can't... I... won't." He shook his head.

Camille leaped up and helped him into the chair. "I'm sorry." She
poured him a cup of water from the sink.

"I ain't even been in here yet. Not until now." John took a drink.
"Ain't even seen him since it all went down."

Camille gasped, realizing that was true. The whole time, as Camille
had gotten constant updates about Adam's condition and stopped in
to see him every few hours, John had been injured, trapped in bed, unable to see or hear from his son. John put the cup down, his breathing
strained. He buckled forward, burying his face in his son's lap, and wept
from his one eye like a cyclopean infant.

"Adam... son..." he whimpered. "I'm so friggin' sorry. So sorry.
Hell."

Camille laid her hand on his shaking back, guilt resting on her
tongue like acid. John sat upright again and wiped his eyes—wiping

the nonexistent one out of habit, she supposed—and then stared dead center at Camille. "I can't believe this happened. Just a few days ago he was... y'know, and now he's..."

Camille nodded and squeezed John's mangled hand. *Say something, Camille, say something that makes him feel better.* She bit her lip, afraid of putting her foot in her mouth. "Yeah."

John's brow furrowed. "You want to do it, I'll bet. This crazy experimental operation, I mean. You want to do it, don't you?"

Camille dropped her face into her hands. "I guess I do."

"Well." John smiled from the corner of his mouth. "I'm right on board with ya. I trust your opinion a hella lot more than my own."

Camille nodded again. "Adam matters too," she whispered. "And *you* matter. I've always prioritized myself, my career, my goals, and just acted like family was supposed to fall in place with my vision, or whatever. I've been an egotistical monster. But my family *matters*. And now—"

"Bullshit. You're a stubborn go-getter, Camille, not a monster. And you're the *center* of this goddamn family, not an outsider. Adam and I, we ain't much for talking. You keep us all together." John stared at the blinking blue mechanical eye then looked away. "You're the kind of strong person who gets things done, stronger than I could ever be. I love you for who you are. Don't forget it."

John looked up at her and kissed her lips. Their mouths met and connected like two shy teenagers'. Camille slid into his arms.

"I love you," she said.

"I love you too." John nodded. "So does Adam."

"I'm going to make up for my mistakes." She squeezed her fists. "If I have to risk it all, I'm going to do whatever it takes to bring our boy back until he's staring up into the night sky again."

"I'm with ya, hon."

"We'll do it." As she said the words, Camille shuddered with fear. *I'm risking his life.* However, if the choice was between a one-in-a-million chance, or a pained life of no communication, she was sure that it was a risk he would want her to take. She bent over Adam's body and planted a kiss on his stitched cheek. "Love you, my little optimist."

Chapter 26: Shroud

The sky darkened. The water became ice cold. Adam stopped walking as chills whispered profanities into the marrow of his bones.

"It's watching us." Adam's voice shuddered.

"It is always watching," Optimist replied.

Adam continued sloshing forward, his feet getting stuck in mud. *Yeah, okay, definitely not liking this.* As they moved toward the next alien, the Motherboard's watery surface became increasingly swampy and congested. The blinking white sky deepened to a cloudy maroon. Lightning cracked open the clouds. Rain poured down on them with such torrential fury that Adam burst out laughing.

"We're gonna need an ark for this one!" he shouted, his voice drowned out by the storm's roar.

"What was that?" the Optimist shouted back.

"Just something my dad always says when it rains!"

"What?"

"Never mind!"

The rain continued to wage war upon them, slaughtering whatever humor could've been found in the situation. The Optimist's white flames swirled at the impact of the raindrops but were otherwise immune, so he walked ahead of Adam and acted as a torch for the both of them. They trudged forward, rainwater streaking down Adam's body. A monstrous black outline of a mountain rose from the horizon, obscured by distance, fog, and rain. *Great, looks like the worst hike ever.*

Adam's chest tightened. "Well, there's the Rage." He gulped his fears down then pushed forward through the mud.

The sparks fluttering inside him became more afraid with every step he took. He felt a terrible sureness that whatever awaited him ahead was going to hurt him worse than he'd ever been hurt before. The car crash had destroyed his body, but facing the Rage would destroy his soul.

The water had become a total swamp, full of disgusting mucus that reeked of sewage. *Kinda reminds me of the toilet that one time Dad had to fix the plumbing last year.* The rainbow reflections of oil trails snaked around his legs. Tangled vines had sprouted up from the swamp's floor and clawed out of the water, their leaves coated in fuzzy gray mold. A cardboard sign had been impaled upon a stake, and a flash of lightning revealed the words "Brain Death" written on it.

A light appeared beneath the water's surface. Adam expected the Motherboard's multi-eyed visage to appear within it, but instead he saw the face of his own mother, Camille Campton-Helios, rising from the swamp. Her lavender perfume cut through the noxious odors. Tears were in her eyes, but she was smiling.

"I love you, my little optimist," she said.

"Mom!"

Adam dove toward the illuminated patch of water, but it faded before he could reach it. Mom had disappeared, drowned out by the pouring rainfall. He felt warm moisture on his cheek, as if he had been kissed there. The comforting feeling was quickly driven away by the rain.

"Come back!" he cried.

He splashed the patch of water where her face had been. He ducked underneath, digging through the mud to find her. *Please come back. I miss you.* When he rose to the surface, gasping for air, black sewage was clustered beneath his fingernails. The Optimist's rain-streaked obsidian shell was standing before him.

"That was my mom!" Adam shouted. "She spoke to me. Did you hear her? It was real, wasn't it? It must've—"

"I heard." The Optimist put a hand on Adam's back. "She loves you, Adam. But we must keep moving."

Adam couldn't tell if the wetness on his face was tears or rainwater. The swamp water thickened to the consistency of applesauce. *Okay, guess I'm never going to eat that again.* Adam touched the hole in Optimist's chest, and the obsidian man moved back as if Adam had stabbed him. The hole had felt as smooth as the rest of his body but as cold as a flagpole in winter.

"It must've really hurt, right?" Adam asked, wanting to touch the hole again but knowing he shouldn't. "When the Destroyer took your spark?"

The Optimist moved Adam's hand away. "Imagine that for all of your life, you had pursued a dream. Then imagine that someone took that dream, stomped on it, and then twisted it to hurt everyone you cared about. That is what it felt like to lose my spark."

Adam breathed in heavily.

The Optimist turned around, his flames darkening to a violet color then turning blue again. "For your sake, Galaxy Seeker, I truly hope you never have to suffer such pain."

The Optimist's words were sincere, but Adam heard remorse in them. *He feels guilty because I will have to suffer exactly the pain he's talking about. Whether it's the Rage or the Destroyer, one of them will get me.* In the swamp, scraps of Earthling trash floated past them—familiar soda cans, grocery bags, and a paper-towel roll. *It's so weird to see human trash out here in a place like this.* Adam followed the Optimist's glow into the shadow of the enormous mountain only a few miles ahead.

Chapter 27: The Rage

Piles of trash rose from the swamp's muddy surface like tumors spewing out the compacted remains of broken windows, tires, beer bottles, and other human relics. Adam gagged on the rancid stench of the pollution. He and the Optimist passed a brick wall with a gaping hole in its center, followed by a line of broken houses that mirrored Adam's home neighborhood. *Like everything has fallen apart since I left Earth... like it's all my fault. Is it?* The whole trashed neighborhood was covered in the same fuzzy gray mold, cobwebs, and vines.

The mountain rose above everything, its muddy surface glistening with raindrops. At its base lay a towering landfill of broken refrigerators, totaled cars, bicycles, and washing machines. Above that, the mountain itself possessed a moldy skin of green slime, boiling with sticky bubbles, heaving in and out as if breathing.

"Maybe we can just go around the whole thing." Adam clasped himself tightly.

"We can't skip stages," the Optimist said. "To access the Consciousness, we must seize the Rage's spark. We must either go to the top or be dragged inside it."

"Awesome." Adam gulped. "There's no other way?"

The Optimist shook his head. His flames had darkened to an indigo color that struggled to survive the rainy downpour. Adam took the Optimist's enormous palm, which emitted heat like a marble statue that had been sitting out in the sun. The Optimist's rocky fingers squeezed Adam's hand.

He's scared too. Both of us are. "Feels good not to be alone," Adam said quietly.

The Optimist squeezed again.

So glad he's here. Blue flames spiraled up and down Adam's arm like a glowing corkscrew.

Hands clasped, they walked together to the mountain's base. The swamp rumbled. A nearby house collapsed inward, its dusty frame emitting one last scream as it spilled into the muddy water. An elephantine groan vibrated from the mountain. Adam fell backward, but Optimist caught him.

"How will we get its spark?" Adam asked.

"I do not know, Galaxy Seeker."

"Oh. Wow. Man, oh man." Adam wiped sweat from his brow. "Joe Sanderson doesn't seem so tough anymore."

They scurried over the hill of bicycles, cars, and washing machines. Moldy porcelain dolls looked up from the trash pile with dead eyes. Gears protruded upward like knives. Once they had traversed to the mountain itself, Adam stepped onto the Rage's boiling green skin, and his foot sank into its sticky surface as if it were a vat of cement. He ripped it out, and his next step sank inward as well. *This is worse than walking in sand.*

The hike began, one gluey step at a time, leaving a trail of footprints in the slime. Rain continued beating down upon them. They avoided hunks of metal, wood, and plastic that occasionally punctured the green skin from beneath, trying to stab at their feet. A sticky bubble burst at Adam's side, and he toppled backward into a broken window frame.

"Ow." His head spun as his vision blurred. "Crap."

The Optimist ran to his side. "Galaxy Seeker?"

Adam climbed out of the frame, cutting his fingertips on broken shards of glass. His shin was slashed open, and blood oozed down his leg, the rain washing the wound. He climbed back to his feet, and as the skin on his leg pulled taut, it felt like hundreds of hot needles stabbing right into the muscle. "Hard to stand." He winced. "Hurts."

"I see." Optimist pressed his hands to the bloody opening, and warm flames wrapped around Adam's leg like a blanket. When the Optimist removed his hands, the wound was cauterized. Adam stepped forward, still wincing, but with no more bleeding. They continued their hike.

Lightning flashed in the sky, and the slope became increasingly vertical. They were forced to climb on all fours, cosmic creatures reduced to groveling dogs. The mountain rumbled again, and that time, the groan sounded more human, as if words were there but drowned out by phlegm. The broken-down houses below them appeared smaller than his fingernails. *Theo's drop wasn't even half of this. If I fall now, I'm a goner.*

Adam grunted, poking his fingers through the gunk and pushing himself up the mountain. What had been hiking was veering closer and closer to rock climbing. He could smell his own perspiration. They still had a few miles to go, most of them straight up. The mountain swayed back and forth in the wind. Adam clung to a busted lamp protruding from the surface, and the lamp ripped out. Adam screamed as he fell backward off the side of the mountain.

The Optimist caught him and pulled him back to the mountain's surface. Even with his obsidian friend cradling him like a stuffed animal, Adam didn't stop screaming. *Falling, falling, falling!* His heart crashed down from his chest, plummeting through his stomach. His feet tingled, as if feeling the drop. *The fall. Falling, falling, falling.* When he finally came back to his senses, he wrapped his arms around the Optimist's heated bulk then cautiously stepped back onto the mountain.

"I'm gonna die," Adam said. "This is it."

"Do not give up. You've made it farther than you ever expected to. I trust in your ability to win this battle."

"You shouldn't." As the mountain swayed again, Adam nearly dissolved into a sputtering mess of tears at the thought of being thrown from it again. "Oh God."

"Adam—"

"I'm just a boy." His toes curled, trying to cling to the ground. "A stupid kid."

"You are the Galaxy Seeker," the Optimist said, "and I believe in you."

The peak of the mountain was still painfully far ahead, its curved tip coiling around itself like a beckoning finger. They continued climbing its surface. A violent rumble passed through the mountain, and Adam squeezed Optimist's arm for support, wishing the shaking would stop. Only a few yards ahead of them, the slime ripped open, revealing a gaping hole in their path. The stench of rotten eggs blasted from the hole in hot waves. The mountain shook, sending a broken microwave toppling past Adam's head.

Adam's vision blurred in shock. *If the microwave had been just a few inches to the side...* He recovered, breathing in and out. Within the slimy hole before them, a female corpse was pushed to the surface. The dead woman was clothed in shredded rags, her head hanging sideways from a broken neck.

"Optimist, is she..." *Dead. Yes, she's obviously dead.*

Matted black hair fell over her face and chest, obscuring her features. She'd been in the slime so long that her flesh was moldy, withered, stretched tight over broken bones. Pus oozed from gaping wounds in her dark skin. Snot-colored tendrils wrapped around her limbs, plugging her veins and throat.

"She's dead." Adam gulped. *Don't throw up.* "Oh my God, that's a dead woman. I've never seen a dead woman before."

The piercing wail of an infant shattered the air. Hiding beneath the dead woman's hair was a baby, its skin smeared with grime, wearing a soiled diaper. Adam pushed closer, fighting off the Optimist's attempts to hold him back. The baby's face was buried in its mother's moldy breast, still desperately trying to suckle milk.

The dead woman's neck jerked upright. "Leave," she growled.

Adam jumped. The hair spilled away from the dead woman's face, revealing skinless cheekbones and pus-dripping wounds. Her eyes had been partially swallowed inside dark holes, but they looked terribly familiar.

"You have... my eyes." Adam moved back, sweat beading on his forehead. "My mouth, too. You're my—"

"You are not wanted here." The dead woman hissed through blackened teeth. "Leave my mountain."

Adam fell onto his tailbone and sank inside the mountain's wet surface. Bubbles inflated and popped all around him. The baby in the dead woman's arms continued sucking on her moldy breast and then squalled. *Is it laughing, crying? It must be crying because if it's laughing... Stop looking, Adam.* He tried to stand, but his hands were suctioned inside the slime.

"You don't need to be afraid of me," Adam said. "We're not here to hurt you. My friend and I here, both of us, can help you."

"You?" The dead woman's eyes burned with loathing. "All of this is *your* fault."

The rain poured. The baby screeched. Adam sank slightly deeper into the mountain's slime. The Rage shook so violently that scraps of metal burst from above Adam's head, and a trash bag tumbled down beside him. He looked over at the Optimist, whose head was lowered, then faced the dead woman with a lump in his throat.

"No, Mrs. Rage. I didn't do any of this. The Destroyer did. Let me have your spark, so I can save you from him."

"You orphaned idiot." The woman rocked her baby. "Your fears and resentments are the force that *created* the Destroyer."

"What?" Adam looked at Optimist, but the obsidian man would not look back at him. As the baby screamed, the woman's sharp fingernails dug into its soft flesh.

"It was you!" she screamed. "The sickness existed before you, but your petty jealousies gave it shape. Your weaknesses turned it into a living creature. Your fixation on your past, your fear and hatred of people like Joe Sanderson, your anger at your parents, your childish self-pity because your classmates don't like you—"

"That's not true!" Adam cried, rain dripping down his body as his legs sank knee-deep into the muck. "I'm not afraid! I don't hate people! I'm not angry at—"

"Your Destroyer has murdered us all!"

Boulders crashed down the mountain's side. Car engines, chairs, and file cabinets stabbed through its slimy surface. Slime bubbles exploded all around them.

"Tell me it isn't true, Optimist." Adam's face reddened with anger.

The Optimist stared at his feet, and Adam quivered. *Please tell me you didn't lie to me.*

The Optimist spoke hesitantly. "Your imagination shaped all of our present forms." He looked up. "But this Destroyer is *yours*, not ours. The sickness came from Earth, and when we brought you here, what was merely a sickness became your Destroyer within."

"You never told me!" Adam's fists hardened with rage. He remembered beating Joe Sanderson's face in. He remembered how good it felt.

A giant bubble rose from beside Adam, burst, and covered him in toxic filth. He struggled to breathe, slime seeping into his pores. The mountain started dragging him under its surface.

The Optimist tried to pull him out of the muck, but even the obsidian man wasn't strong enough. Blue flames circled down his shiny black arms, burning away at the slime. "Fight the darkness within you, Galaxy Seeker!"

Another explosion rocked the mountain. The Optimist flew off the side, and Adam could not break from the slime to save him. The obsidian man became a flaming dot, descending to the ground below. He smashed down into the pile of trash at the mountain's base, shattering into a sparkling array of little black rocks. Tears stung Adam's eyes as he watched the obsidian stones roll between the refrigerators and washing machines. A final puff of flames went up from the trash pile and then faded away in the rainstorm.

"Optimist." Adam choked up. "No, please don't be dead. Please."

"He is crippled," the dead woman hissed. "Like you."

"But he was my friend," Adam whimpered.

The dead woman's rotted teeth ground together. "You were right when you said that Kavi Kapoor should have died in India," she said, her claws digging into the baby. "Then maybe the Destroyer known as Adam Helios would have never existed."

The baby in her arms bit down on her breast so hard that Adam heard the chomp. Blood pooled inside her shirt, staining it scarlet. The woman screamed, shattering Adam's eardrums, letting the entire universe know of her pain. The baby turned to face Adam with a mouthful of sharp teeth, blood dripping from its chin. It spat out the remains of her nipple.

"You're mine, Earth Boy," the infant muttered. It pointed up at the Nothing Spot with its chubby little hand. The dead woman crumpled into the mountain, taking the baby with her.

Adam wailed to the sky, hoping the Consciousness would save him. *I can't get out!* His chin disappeared beneath the slime. *I'm sorry.* As he sank into the Rage's body, his musculature atrophied. His limbs became veiny sticks. His ribs protruded from the slender flesh of his chest. His hair burned off, leaving nothing a but a fuzzy skullcap in its place. His legs knotted and twisted around each other, and his spine buckled forward. Lard-tasting slime poured down into his lungs.

The boy that was Adam Helios sank into the Rage's body.

Chapter 28: The Dotted Line

The coffee was too hot and too grainy. The fiery grounds jabbed at Camille's tongue like a tattoo gun. She put the cup aside, trying not to let on that she was in pain. "These are all the papers, Doctor?"

Dr. Blake nodded. "Yes."

Camille and John sat together on John's hospital bed as Dr. Blake leaned back against the door, his fidgeting gestures and furrowed brow drawing a perfect portrait of anxiety. The sky was cloudy but not quite dark enough to justify turning on the hospital room's blaring overhead bulbs, which left the room filled with shadows. *It's that uneasy, not-light-not-dark ambiance. Hate it.* The stack of papers on Camille's lap was smaller than she'd expected—a basic agreement, a minimal explanation of the procedure, and two lines centered on the bottom, awaiting their signatures.

Camille sipped on her coffee again, letting it burn her tongue, proving to the universe that pain would not hold her back. "I expected a longer document," she said. "Short ones worry me."

John scanned through the papers, his shoulder pressing into her back. He was supposed to be lying down, and normally he did whatever the doctors told him, but he seemed too wrapped up in the moment to care about his own health. "Yeah," he said. "That's it?"

Dr. Blake sighed. "Basically, this is just about liability. If we're going to do this experimental operation, these papers release the hospital from all responsibility, should something go wrong."

John frowned. "And it'll probably get all frigged up, right? That's what ya kinda implied last time."

"It's never gone... right." Dr. Blake looked at the floor. "We have no proof it'll ever work, as I explained before. But I'd *like* for it to work, yes."

"Because then you'd get credit for the whole thing," Camille said. "Because then you'd—"

"Mrs. Helios, I'd like to ask you to stop speaking to me so disrespectfully, please." Dr. Blake's lips pinched into a thin line. "Listen, I know that both of you are at the end of your ropes. I understand, and I can't imagine how painful it must be. I have a son myself, you know." He took out his phone, scrolled through, and flashed a little kid's photo at them so quickly that they didn't have a chance to take it in. "But what happened to your son Adam isn't my fault. Do you know that I've been putting my life on hold to take care of your son to the best of my ability? Do you realize that I've slept here in the hospital the last three nights, Mrs. Helios, going through file after file in search of possibilities? That my wife and son are eating dinner alone, without me, as I work night and day to take care of your boy?"

Dr. Blake crossed his arms. He was shaking, a tightly-wound man who had finally come unspooled.

Prickles spiked up Camille's spine. Her fingers clenched tightly around her pen. "No. I didn't... I didn't realize."

"It's my job." Dr. Blake exhaled. "I got into this field because I wanted to take care of people. Including your boy. But please, stop punishing me for what I can't do, what I can't promise." He paced across the room. "Let me level with you. Just last year, I put a bicycle up for sale on Craigslist. It was the same bike I'd always ridden as a teenager, you know—it was special to me, my getaway whenever my parents were fighting, whenever I wanted to sneak out and see my first girlfriend. I brought that rusty old bicycle to med school, rode it to every class. But one day, after I'd been working as a doctor for a few years, I put it aside. Forgot to take care of it. It fell apart. It was a piece of complete junk, worthless, hadn't worked properly in years."

Camille covered her mouth. All she could think of was Adam working on his bicycle, night and day, then riding it to school with that proud smile on his face. "Adam loved bicycles," she said, looking at John and then back to the doctor. "Listen, Doctor, I'm sorry I—"

"Wait." Dr. Blake raised his hand. "Like I said, I put my old bike up on the Internet. I was so frustrated with the damn thing that I put it in the free stuff section, a curb alert. I just threw it right out there on the sidewalk. The next day, this scrawny kid came over to my house in this black hoodie and with a backpack slung over one shoulder—"

Camille's heart leapt into her throat, and a gasp escaped her lips.

Dr. Blake sat down and folded his hands into his lap. "Your boy, Mr. and Mrs. Helios, answered my ad. But he didn't just take the bike and go, like anyone else would, even though it was just a curb alert. He knocked on the door quite respectfully, told me he was collecting scrap parts for a bicycle he was making. *Smart kid*, I thought."

John gulped. "Yeah."

"I told him to grab it, said I wanted to move on from it. He asked why. I told him the story of my old bike. I said how I wished I'd taken better care of it, that I'd once wanted to pass it on to my own son one day, but it was too late now. I told him to take the whole thing back home with him and throw away whatever parts he didn't need. Then, as he grabbed the bike, I went back inside to have some coffee. But then I went back outside an hour later, and the bike was back. It was just sitting on my front porch, leaned up against the window... and he'd fixed it. Seriously, he'd fixed the bike. He'd put brand-new parts on it. New gears. New pedals."

"Wow," Camille whispered.

"And he was gone. I didn't even get to thank him," Dr. Blake continued. "I don't know if he brought the bike home and fixed it or if he had parts somewhere or what. But he was gone, so I couldn't ask him. I wanted to get money to pay him something, to thank him, but I had no idea who he was. Until the day the ambulance brought him, I didn't know his name."

Camille stared at the floor, imagining the scene that Dr. Blake had described, picturing how Adam had probably walked away with that little dimpled smile on his face that he had when he thought no one was looking. She thought about all the times she had snapped at Dr. Blake since this whole nightmare had begun. She imagined his wife and son sitting at home, eating dinner alone.

"So yes, I know that your boy is a wonderful person," Dr. Blake said. "And I'm going to do everything I can to bring him back."

"I'm sorry." Camille walked over to Dr. Blake and hugged him.

When she stepped back, he fidgeted with his name badge, but his features had softened. "Mr. and Mrs. Helios, I—"

"Camille," she said.

"John," John said in quick succession. "No more of this formality business."

"Camille, John... you may call me Ben." The doctor blushed. "You know full well that this whole procedure is probably going to fail. But I swear to both of you, I'm willing to do whatever it takes."

Camille gulped. "How soon can it start?"

"In two hours. We have to move fast if we have any hope of full recovery."

Camille picked up the papers and looked at them. Two hours was such a short time. Outside the window, the sun was peeking out from the clouds, but the moon was also visible on the horizon. *It's almost like we're between two time periods, the time when Adam is alive and the time when Adam is dead. No, no, don't think that. Stop.*

"That's so soon, Ben," she said.

"Are you sure you want to do this?" Ben asked.

Camille popped open the cap of her pen and signed. She handed the papers to John, and he did the same. Then she snatched them from John's hand and stuffed them into Ben's coat pocket, crumpled, rushing to get the decision away from her before she could have any second thoughts.

"It's our only chance," she said. "Let's get this operation started."

Ben left the room, and they watched him through the glass door as he signaled to another doctor that the procedure was a go. Camille and John looked at each other. *I hope we made the right choice.*

ACT III of III:
THE DESTROYER WITHIN

"There is no coming to consciousness without pain. People will do any-thing, no matter how absurd, in order to avoid facing their own soul. One does not become enlightened by imagining figures of light, but by making the darkness conscious."
Carl Jung

Chapter 29: Endgame

Camille stood over Adam's bed, feeling every stroke of the clock breathing down upon her back like an unfed lion. She stroked the unstitched section of his forehead and listened to his heart rate beeping from the machines.

John stood beside her. Camille moved her hand, and John kissed the boy's forehead.

"You'll be fine, kid," he said, his voice choked up. "I'm proud of ya, and you'll be good cuz you've made it this far, so you're about the toughest son of a gun I ever knew. See ya when you come back, son."

John hovered over Adam for another moment then stood up and gave Camille a strained smile. Seeing him so vulnerable, so shaky, pained her.

He clasped Camille's shoulder then whispered in her ear. "He's gonna be fine. Trust me. I got a feeling about this." Holding his stomach, he stumbled out of the room, wincing with every step.

John softly closed the door behind him, but Camille could hear him sobbing through the glass. She lingered at Adam's bedside, unable to wrench herself away, knowing she was rushing into a future where Adam might or might not be dead. Ben had sworn to give the operation everything he had, but he didn't have much hope of it going well—and really, neither did she. *Even if he survives, if the operation doesn't work, it means total brain death. That's what Ben said. He'll be brain-dead forever.* All she could do was hope that the procedure was what her boy would've wanted, but she couldn't know for sure. Thirteen-year-old kids didn't tend to sign advance directives.

Adam squirmed in the bed, rubbing his knuckles against the side rail again. Drool spilled from a corner of his mouth and ran down his cheek. Camille dabbed it away with her sleeve. His eyes were open, but their blankness made them hard to stare into. His gaze flicked around the room, never lingering on a single object, never focusing. His heart rate kept speeding up, only slowing a bit whenever she squeezed his hand.

He's scared of something. She could tell—mother's intuition. Though Ben had explained how scans showed that the brain damage was too severe for him to accurately process anything going on around him, she could feel the emotions stirring within him, the terror that had clenched his heart. *What is he scared of? Maybe he knows there's an operation happening.*

His eyes rolled back and forth across the room. His legs kicked. Camille squeezed his hand, but his heart rate was only going up, not down. Seeing him like that, wracked with pain, terrified of something he couldn't express... *I hope this is the right choice. I know it's what I would want if that were me in his place, so I just have to believe that it's what he would want too.* The operation was the only chance he had for recovery, no matter how slim it was. Brains didn't recover by miracles. *But I'll never forgive myself if he dies or goes brain-dead.*

"Am I making the right decision for you, Adam?"

She stroked a vein in Adam's hand. His tongue, dry and cracked, rolled out of his mouth. Saliva ran down his neck, and she wiped it away.

"Adam, I love you. I wish you could tell me if this procedure is a good choice. But I guess I don't get to know that. All I can do is cross my fingers and hope that... that this chance is worth it. To have you back. To give you your old mind back, maybe."

For a second, she thought she saw Adam smile. *Don't be stupid, that's just confirmation bias, my mind digging for clues that aren't really there.* Her heart ached at the memory of his real smile, the one with the dimple she would never see again.

"I'm sorry it took me so long to accept you. The *older* you, I mean." She kissed his forehead. "I guess I always missed the little boy you used to be, back when you'd dance in circles, sing songs, jump on the counter, and pretend to swing a lightsaber. It was hard to see you become an older Adam, more cynical, more introverted. I missed my little optimist."

Camille swallowed back tears, trying not to choke up. *Not yet. I have to get it all out there. This might be my last chance.* "But just because I missed the little kid, it wasn't fair for me to be so angry at the older kid for replacing him. That was wrong. I was wrong." She wiped his drool away again. "Dr. Blake told me about how you fixed his bicycle. That was really nice of you. Teachers always have told me about how smart you are. You grew up into this amazing little person, and I should have recognized that. Accepted you for who you were. Tried to understand you instead of getting angry. We argued too much in the last few years. We did. It's my fault."

Camille rested her head on Adam's chest and listened to his heartbeat. *After today, it might never beat again.* She had to hope that it would, though. She had to have faith. "You're going to make it through this." Her tears dropped onto Adam's face, and she dabbed them away. "You will. And when you do, I promise I'll get to know you, the *real* you, because it sounds like you're a wonderful young man who all of us could learn something from."

The glass door slid open. Two nurses stood there, holding a stretcher, watching her with uncomfortable expressions, waiting for her to move away. Camille stood up, kissed Adam on the forehead one more time, then stepped back. The nurses transferred him to the stretcher and wheeled it out of the room. Camille waved goodbye, swallowed her fear, and—

Brain death.

A kaleidoscope of mental images spun through her mind like a wheel. She saw Adam stretched out with a hole drilled into his head, blood pouring out of it. His eyes popped. His ears bled. His skin rotted, his bones contracted, his muscles atrophied. Then, standing over her son's corpse was a tall, wiry creature of tendrils, spines, and sharp teeth. The violet-skinned animal broke open Adam's skull and started eating his brain.

Brain death.

It had no eyes, but it knew she was there. It smelled her. It reared its head at her, licking flecks of Adam's brain from its teeth with a forked black tongue. Its shark-like mouth pulled back into a grin.

Then it was gone when reality reasserted itself. Camille fell back into a chair. *It's just my imagination. Too many horror movies. Too much trauma in such a short time. Just a thought in my head, nothing more.* She couldn't breathe. A panic attack was setting in, and she inhaled deeply to make the fear go away. The vision dissipated, but even though she was back in the hospital room, back in real life—even though she knew she'd escaped from a panic attack and should relax—the memory of her strange vision had poisoned her mind.

"Hang in there, Little Optimist," she said to the open door.

Chapter 30: Drowning

Adam's shrunken remains sank deeper into the Rage's slimy body. The sparks within him emitted a gentle glow, as if a handful of lightbulbs were shining inside his chest. The sparks illuminated his environment just enough to make visible the endless array of trash surrounding him. His body crunched between the remains of broken-down appliances. Feces floated past him. Batteries leaked acid. Everything was covered in gray mold.

His limbs were like limp noodles. What remained of his lungs were clogged with slime, and he could barely breathe. The lack of oxygen to his brain made it hard to put together clear thoughts, as if his mind were a disassembled jigsaw puzzle and the most important pieces weren't in the box. *Drowning. Sinking. Brain death.* He coughed out a gooey substance that tasted of spoiled milk, but that only opened his airways for more slime to seep in. *Drowning. Breathe. Can't. Live... Why? Why.* Fuzzy mold grew on the sagging remnants of his body.

Can't breathe.

The glow within him darkened, and the universe faded to black. He felt a needle sticking into his spine. *Inject. Sharp. Ow. Me?* He heard muffled voices discussing an operation that was going to be performed on "the boy." The boy. *Yes, we're going to drill here. This is the part of his brain we need to operate on first.* On his hairless head, a dull, wet marker pressed against his temple and drew a circle. Adam tried to scream, but mucus poured down his throat and drowned him out.

The sparks within him glowed more brightly again, illuminating the gelatinous folds of slime. He floated between junked cars. The mold on his skin had spread from his chest to his shoulders and hardened into a crust.

He choked on vomit. His body floated down among a spiderweb of broken, bleeding veins. He tried to grab one, to keep from sinking farther into the Rage's bowels, but his arm was too weak. One of the veins burst open and spewed blood in a gushing waterfall.

Can't think. Can't breathe. He couldn't remember his name. *I'm just the boy. Not a name anymore. Not a person anymore.* He heard voices again but couldn't understand them. Language was losing meaning, becoming little more than strange guttural sounds. He was just a throbbing ball of emotion, sick with sadness, craving love he would never receive. The slime thickened, and he could barely move. *There is no love. No one should love me. I'm just the boy.*

The boy.

The boy with the bad brain.

Despair filled his being. His muscles were sacks of sand. He was a skeleton coated in diseased, molding flesh, covered by stitches and gaping wounds. His vision went dark. Blood gushed from his eyes, nose, and mouth. *Everything is fake. My mind is a Nothing Spot. The Nothing Spot is what I am.*

A female voice broke through the darkness, awakening his synapses. "Hang in there, Little Optimist."

I know that voice. His vision returned to him. A burst of oxygen punched out of his chest, exhaling from his lungs. He didn't know who or what *she* was, but he knew her voice was something that mattered to him, something important. Vomit again filled his throat, and he gagged on it. *Don't give up.* He looked up through the caking of slime, mold, and trash, and an incandescent pearl floated above his head. A word occurred to him—*spark*—and he reached upward.

His arm was too weak. It flopped back to his side. Holding the female voice at the forefront of his thoughts, he gritted his teeth and tried again, but his shoulder wouldn't twist upward. In his mind, he saw a burning obsidian rock man, a friend. Beside that man, he saw a woman made of sand, a woman who was many women at the same time.

She said, *"You're right, Adam-Kavi. We are all real."*

Adam reached up again with his twig arm, aches rippling through him, his mouth full of salty sludge. He seized the glowing pearl then jolted back in pain. The skin of his palm was scalded. *The spark burns the Nothing Boy.* He reached for it again, his skin melting, but he didn't let go. He instinctively pushed the pearl into his mouth and swallowed it, which left an acid trail down his throat.

He could breathe again.

The lights went dark, and Adam shot downward as if he'd been propelled by a jet. He hurtled down into the Rage's bottommost pits. His muscles, flesh, and internal organs inflated like water balloons, and he felt human again. He could move and think. He burst through the bottom of the slime and dropped into a cave. He crashed down against an icy floor.

His scraped knees bled onto the ice. He panted for air—cool, clean, wonderful air—his brain still foggy, and his vision swirling with bright colors. When he finally regained his senses, the first things he saw were the stalagmites that had sprouted from the icy floor and the stalactites hanging from the ceiling. *I guess I'm in a cave now or something?* Before he could ponder it further, slime erupted from his throat.

He wiped his lip. Shaky with dehydration, he stood up. His feet slid on the ice, but he caught his balance on a nearby boulder. The floor of the cave was flat as an ice-skating rink. The frosted walls emitted a blue glow.

Keep moving. Don't think. Don't look back. Just keep moving.

He walked through the cave, grabbing any protrusions he could find to keep his balance. He maneuvered down a long tunnel, avoiding any turns, terrified that at any moment the floor might open up and swallow him, and he would be digested in the Rage's intestines.

He walked through the cavern. In the next big room was a fifteen-foot ice sculpture of the Optimist. A fountain of what looked and smelled like car radiator fluid spewed from the hole in the Optimist's chest, and the coolant bubbled into a circular pool in the cavern's center. Adam crossed his arms. *I don't like it. It seems like an insult to my friend.* He glared at the ice sculpture, trying not to remember what the real Optimist's body had looked like when it shattered into obsidian fragments. *Little black rocks. Puff of flames. Crippled, like me.*

On the other side of the pool, the floor opened up into a spiral staircase—steep steps, icy, cracked. The spiral dropped so far down into the ground that the only doorway waiting at its base could have been the gates of Hades, where Adam's personal Lucifer was no doubt licking its violet lips. A whispering voice blew up from the bottom, step by step, and tickled Adam's ear canal like a feather.

"Bring me my sparks," it crackled softly.

Adam would happily have spent a million lifetimes getting tortured by a million Mad Glees rather than walk down that spiral staircase, but he didn't see any way out of it. *This is the whole reason I came here. Kinda late to have second thoughts. But what the heck am I gonna do?* He had no plan, no idea how he was going to beat the Destroyer, or if his victory was even possible. Like a mythological hero, he had come to slay the dragon—but he'd forgotten to bring a sword. Another whisper rattled the spiral staircase. Adam moved down onto the first step then jumped back. *I can't do it, I just can't.* He forced himself to take the step again, almost slipped on its frosted surface, and took the next step more carefully. His blood ran cold.

"I'm coming for you, jerk," Adam said.

Chapter 31: Panic

Camille and John held hands in the waiting room, their widened eyes and bowed heads reminding her of two children awaiting confession. The TV was off. The lights had been dimmed. A police siren buzzed past the window, the swoosh of traffic a grim reminder of the outside world and its asphalt underbelly, which had plunged them into their mess in the first place.

John's crutches were lying next to his seat, and the sight of him sitting in the waiting room wearing a johnny gown would've been comical if the circumstances weren't so dire. The nurses wanted him to stay in bed, but Camille had demanded that they let him sit with her in the waiting room, so they'd allowed it. Camille stared at his sewed-up finger stumps, trying to forget the vision she'd experienced when they'd taken Adam away.

Brain death.

The smiling sharp teeth—the violet tentacles. *Was it real?* It couldn't have been real. It had felt almost like a religious experience, but not of the modern Christian variety. The entity she'd encountered resembled something from a more ancient, more barbaric mythology, the sort of cruel god that would have demanded human sacrifices at its altar.

Shaking at the thought of it, she got up and made herself a coffee from the Keurig. "I'm scared, John." Her voice cracked. *I'm seeing monsters, and I don't know if you'll believe me.* "Do you think he's okay?"

"I got a good feelin', hon."

He smiled at her, but in her panicked state, she didn't know whether his optimism was the sort of idealism she should admire or a ludicrous denial that required therapy. John used the remote to turn on the TV, but the soap opera that lit up the screen didn't interest him, and his one good eye gazed at it blankly.

He's lost in thought. He's scared too.

Anxiety always made him scuttle into his shell like a hermit crab. For years, she had tried to force him to talk more, to beat him into opening up when he was stressed, but she was beginning to realize that maybe nothing was wrong with the way John handled anxiety. He just handled it differently than she did, and she had to accept that.

Well, maybe it's me that needs to talk to someone. However, Camille was scared of turning on her phone and facing a stampede of texts. Instead, she watched the minute hand spiral around the clock's face, ticking until Adam either woke up, died, or ended up brain-dead. Ben had said they wouldn't know anything for a few hours, at least.

Hours. She gulped down some coffee, trying not to think of her little boy's head being chopped open and rewired.

A herd of footsteps pounded through the hallway, along with a flurry of voices, young voices—a crowd. Then, as the rolling ball of sound approached the waiting room, the voices became whispers.

The door opened like a floodgate as over twenty preteen kids spilled into the room with bowed heads and hands in their pockets. Camille dropped her coffee cup to the floor. *It's Adam's class.* She recognized most of them as the same kids she would see on the playground, back when she'd dropped her son off at elementary school. She sometimes spotted the same kids wandering the cul-de-sac or buying candy bars at the gas station. Camille couldn't understand. *How do all of them know? Why are they all here?*

Though most of them kept their heads lowered, a few couldn't resist nervously peeking up at Camille. *They know who I am.* The kids took their seats, but the tap kept pouring as a group of adults followed the kids inside. Principal Hamer walked in beside Mrs. Hamer, Adam's math teacher. His other teachers followed, including his old third-grade teacher, Ms. Clark. As Camille stared at the open door, slack-jawed and mute, a young boy in a baggy hoodie walked up to her, biting a fingernail.

"Hi, Mr. and Mrs. Helios," the kid in the hoodie said. "I hope Adam's okay."

"Thanks," Camille sputtered out. *How did you all make it here?*

"Hey, yeah, me too," said a kid across the room. "Real sorry to hear what happened. He's a good guy."

More kids followed, along with more adults, dozens of them. Camille's eyes were like globes. *This doesn't seem real. Doesn't make sense.* Her spilled coffee cup still lay on the floor. Principal Hamer shook John's hand, and the two men exchanged the weird silent nod that men only do with other men.

"Is this really happening?" Camille whispered in John's ear, clutching him with her nails.

"Heck yeah, it is." He grinned. "What a weird coincidence, huh?"

John kissed her cheek, beaming with pride. Drawing on his positive energy, Camille finally relaxed into a smile. *I can't believe it.* Adam had always been an outcast, but people *did* like him. They *did* care, deep down. A young girl with jet-black hair and a round face walked up to Camille and shook her hand. A scar ran from the girl's upper lip to her nose, the remaining signature of what had been a cleft lip.

"Hi, Mrs. Helios," the girl said. "My name's Chandra. I'm Adam's... uh, Adam's friend."

As the young girl said that, she brushed the hair from her face and looked away. Camille caught something in the girl's glance—something about the soft way she said "Adam's friend"—and smiled to herself. *This girl totally has a crush on my Adam!*

Camille swallowed her delight, ridiculously worried that it might embarrass Adam, and she nodded to Chandra. "Pleased to meet you, Chandra. Just call me Camille."

When Chandra smiled, she covered her mouth—revealing a shyness about her lip scar that was no doubt the result of too many mean comments on the playground. Despite the smile, Chandra's bloodshot eyes betrayed that she'd been doing plenty of crying. "Have they started the operation yet?"

"Yes," she said, and everyone quieted to listen to her. Camille fumbled under the attention. "You, all of you... How do all of you know about the operation?"

John nudged her, smiled, and made a telephone symbol with his good hand. "They got a little wake-up call this morning," he said. "A real *quiet* call."

Camille kissed him. "You're wonderful." She turned to the crowd and cleared her throat, getting ready to explain everything about the operation, to fill them in on the details. Before she could, a shock of red blocked her vision. She fell backward in her seat. Noise blurred. Everything went static.

The vision—it was happening again.

"Hon," John said, "is everything okay? Or—"

A violet tendril whipped past her vision. "Adam!" she cried.

She scrambled to force the vision out of her mind. *I can't hallucinate like this. Not now. Not in front of everyone.* She bolted toward the waiting room's exit, and as she turned the handle, the vision reappeared in her head. *Brain death.* The spiny monster was still chewing on her son's gray matter, its tendrils wrapped around his broken little body. Camille closed her eyes, trying to force herself back to reality.

She threw open the door of the waiting room and ran down the corridor. She slipped on a wet patch that had just been mopped, slamming hard onto the floor. When she looked up, the spiny monster was grinning at her. The remaining skin of Adam's face dripped from its blood-soaked chin.

"You," it growled, its lips pulling back to reveal glistening black gums.

"Get away from my boy!" Camille shrieked.

"Too late." The monster licked its teeth. "You failed as a mother. Now, he's mine."

Camille screamed at the top of her lungs. The vision shattered, and she lay curled up on the hospital floor, a cringing, crying mess of frayed nerves. She shouted Adam's name over and over again until she saw John standing over her, his face red with terror.

"Honey—" he started.

"Adam!" she screamed. "Adam! Adam!"

Tears gushed from her eyes. The waiting room door was open, and all the schoolchildren crowded around it to watch the madwoman shriek. John tried to reach down for her, but the crutches stopped him, and he winced in pain. Mrs. Hamer bolted out, grabbed Camille under the arms, and lifted her back to her feet.

Camille collapsed into John's embrace. "Don't take him away from me, you monster!"

Camille fell apart in John's arms, sobbing like a lunatic. *You failed as a mother. Now, he's mine.* She inhaled deeply, steadying herself until she could breathe normally again. With her head nestled on her husband's shoulder, they walked back to the waiting room. Nobody made eye contact with her, and she blushed with hot embarrassment. *They think I'm crazy.*

The vision had felt so real, though. *So real.* The little girl that had a crush on Adam, Chandra, brought Camille a new cup of coffee. Camille ran her fingers through the girl's soft, silky hair and mouthed the words *thank you*. John wrapped his arm around Camille's shoulders, and she poured the caffeinated black nourishment down her throat, scalding her insides and hoping to scald the hideous creature inside her as well.

Or maybe it's inside Adam, not me. She dropped her cup... again. Coffee splattered all over the floor. No one laughed. No one said a word. John sighed then mumbled an apology, pretending he had mistakenly bumped her. But he hadn't. She knew it. Everyone knew it. It was her fault.

Just like Adam's brain death was going to be her fault.

Chapter 32: Here I Am

Every step of the spiral staircase was coated in frost. Adam had slipped multiple times and couldn't believe he hadn't crashed to the bottom yet. *Yeah, well, assuming there is a bottom, anyway, and that this crazy Tim Burton ride doesn't just keep circling down forever.* The icy walls seemed to contain watery innards as the shadows of fishlike creatures swam within them, each one possessing glowing blue eyes that reflected off the ice. Adam couldn't see their faces, but he imagined each fish was looking at him with a terrible little smirk.

"Adam," said the Star Voice.

The Consciousness hadn't spoken in so long that Adam barely recognized it. He almost slipped down the stairs. "Consciousness, is that you?" he asked, his voice straining not to break. "Please be you."

"You have made it far, Adam Helios."

A red glow appeared in the icy wall, and the smirking fish scattered away from it. Perspiration dripped from the wall's icy surface. Adam touched the red glow, and warmth radiated outward. Tears stung his eyes. "Please don't leave me alone again, Mr. Consciousness." Adam's throat was choked up.

"I have never left you." The warmth throbbed with his heartbeat. *"I am the Consciousness. You have been inside me since I brought you here, and you have done well. You have much to be proud of."*

Adam pressed his face against the red warmth like a puppy nuzzling its mother. He closed his eyes, letting the heat soothe his fear. "I know, Mr. Consciousness. But I'm really scared to keep going. I need your help."

"You are afraid."

196

"Um, yeah." *I just told you that.* "I feel like I'm gonna pee my pants any second." A weak smile spread across his lips. "If that's even possible in this spaceship, I dunno."

"There is nothing wrong with fear."

"Easy for you to say."

"The Fear and the Courage are the same entity," the Consciousness said. *"Do not forget that."*

"I don't know what's going to happen. I have literally no clue what I'm gonna do when I reach this monster."

Adam hugged the wall, wanting to be inside it, wanting to hug the red warmth that had saved him from the car crash, saved him from the Destroyer, and loved him like a third parent. The warmth swelled in and out to the beat of Adam's heart.

"The Destroyer is going to kill me."

"He may."

"Cool." Adam swallowed. "Not quite what I was hoping to hear."

"But you may be victorious, as well. That's up to you, Adam Helios. But I have faith in your abilities. I hope to see you on the other side of this."

"Me too."

The warmth of the Consciousness flowed out of Adam's body, the red glow disappeared, and he was alone again. *Except I'm not really alone because I'm inside the Consciousness. The Star Voice is with me.*

Adam straightened his back. "I'll make you proud, dude."

The spiral staircase finally ended in a crystal-walled tunnel with an icy floor. At the very bottom was a crumpled heap of wood, painted red. A torn, dusty sheet hung from one blunted corner. After a few moments, he recognized the pile as the remains of the little red racecar bed his dad had made for him when he was a kid. *I guess I never appreciated it the way he hoped I would.* He remembered how sad his father had been when he disassembled that little bed, replacing it with the queen-size one Adam slept in.

"Sorry, Dad." He stroked the edge of the broken wood, pulling out splinters.

The words "Brain Death" were spray-painted on the red wood in black letters. Adam moved away, swallowing a lump in his throat.

Gripping onto stalagmites for balance, he carefully maneuvered down the crystal tunnel. *Gotta stay calm. Calm. Yeah, right.* The icy floor crackled under him like snow exposed to sunlight. The metallic stench of blood drifted to his nostrils. He started to hyperventilate then took a deep breath to keep himself from collapsing into a sputtering mess and continued onward. *I can be brave, like the Consciousness said. I can. I have to.*

In the darkness ahead, a guttural moan echoed back and forth between the cave's two walls. The shadows of two enormous spinning circles flitted past on the wall, like Plato's shadow representations, and disappeared. As Adam turned a corner, moving into a smaller cavern, he realized the moan wasn't actually echoing. It was multiple moans, colluding together in a strangled mess of noise.

Six of them, to be exact.

Six creatures sat in six wheelchairs lined up against the wall, their wheels gently rolling back and forth. Inside each cushioned seat was a pink blob, shiny and wet, with two human eyes floating on its surface and a drooping mouth. A tube was plugged into each one's stomach, feeding each a yellow fluid that smelled so much of vanilla that it forever spoiled all the memories of the vanilla cookies Dad used to bake every New Year's Day.

As the blobs breathed in and out, loose skin fell between the slats of broken ribcages. Arms and legs hung from their sides like paper straw wrappers. Adam fought the urge to run away in tears. *Gotta keep going. I can acknowledge them, but I shouldn't look.* The wheelchairs rolled back and forth with their exhalations.

"Galaxy Seeker... please..." one of the blobs gasped.

"Adam... help us."

"Too late, the Destroyer has him. We are dead."

Each of the wheelchairs was labeled with a dollar-store nametag and a permanent marker, but otherwise, they each looked almost identical. The Face. The Courage. The Optimist. The Mad Glee. The Motherboard. The Rage. Their eyes were red with tears and their mouths so dry that flecks of lip were torn loose like snakeskin.

Adam kept his head down. "I'm so sorry, guys."

"He calls us *guys*... as if we're his friends..."

"We are."

"*You* are."

"I'm sorry," Adam repeated then rushed onward. He had all their sparks inside himself—*yeah, except the Optimist's spark, which is probably the most important, and the Destroyer's holding onto it*—and he wanted to remove each spark from his chest, to stuff it into their disabled bodies so they could be themselves again. That wouldn't work, though. The aliens had told him that all the sparks had to be united, and that meant facing the monster holding the last one.

"Save us," one of the aliens groaned, its voice so far behind him that if he wanted to pretend he hadn't heard it, he could.

Adam almost broke down crying. "I will." *If I don't get destroyed.*

Adam kept walking until the cavern ended at a wooden door with a poster of the Milky Way galaxy tacked to it. *Is that really my bedroom door? Yeah, it totally is. Creepy.* He turned the handle, his palm slick with sweat, and opened the door to a room that looked exactly like the one he had slept in every night since he could remember. Faded Jupiter Man posters decorated the walls. Glow-in-the-dark stars were pinned to the high ceiling. His old telescope, the special one he'd gotten on his seventh birthday, was resting in the window. The queen-size bed was unmade, blankets pulled back on the side Adam always got out of.

Outside the windows, the night sky glowed with the illuminated spheres of Earth, the moon, Mars, and other planets. *So we're back in outer space.* Adam stepped forward then jerked back when his foot landed on something squishy. The hardwood laminate flooring had been replaced by a spongy pinkish-gray substance that looked like a pit of giant earthworms. Almost as if it was—

No, it was a brain. *My brain.* Adam swallowed bile. *Oh God, I can't take this. Just can't... can't do it.* The seam in his enormous brain ran straight to the center of his bed like a pathway. Over by the window, the squelchy floor was damaged. Dangling strings of loose matter hung from burned wounds, dripping clear fluid. *My brain injury.* Within that gaping hole was the Nothing Spot—swirling, empty blackness. The pitiful finale. The place where all his memories, identity, and logic were fated to meet their end.

"Here I am," Adam said. He stepped forward, and when the gray matter wriggled beneath his feet, it took everything he had not to run back, screaming.

He flipped on the light switch.

A whirl of tentacles, claws, and cactus-like prickles uncoiled itself from the ceiling and scurried down the wall like a man-sized spider. The violet-skinned creature crawled to the center of Adam's bed, breathing loudly, drool spilling from the lips of its crocodilian jaw. Its nostrils flared in his direction.

The door slammed shut behind Adam. The creature had no eyeballs, nothing but scarred sockets where they should've been.

Adam pushed back against the door. The hissing animal sat on the edge of the bed, its vaguely humanoid body revealing itself beneath a mass of violet tendrils sprouting from its abdomen in the place of arms. It licked its lower lip with a forked black tongue.

"I've been waiting for you, Earth Boy."

Chapter 33: The Destroyer

The Destroyer's violet skin glistened with oily sweat. Rows of porcupine spines decorated its backside and shoulders. Its tentacles wriggled beneath it with delirious excitement, some of them sliding between the covers of Adam's bed.

Adam backed up hard against the closed door, his heart going *boom, boom, boom* as brain matter squished beneath his feet. *This is the end.* The door was locked. The Destroyer cocked its eyeless head to one side and grinned with a mouthful of jagged sharp teeth.

"You're afraid of me." It growled.

"Because you come from me," Adam whispered.

"Yes." Drool spilled from the Destroyer's lips. "You created me to destroy you. Me. Your Destroyer. Just as I have ravaged this extraterrestrial vessel. I broke them. All of them. In your name. With your fears."

The Destroyer crawled forward, leaving a steaming puddle of sweat on the sheets. A low rumble purred from its chest, fluttering through the spines on its back as if it were having an orgasm. Adam anxiously tried to force the doorknob open. *Please, please, please open. Can't do this.* It wouldn't budge. The Destroyer inched toward him, its clawed toes digging into the brain-celled floor. It pointed one hooked tendril out the window.

"The accident was your fault," it said. "Our fault."

Outside the window, a blast of smoke darkened the glass as a car pummeled Mom's SUV. It flipped off the road. Dad's severed fingers splattered against the glass. The stench of burning oil blasted into the room.

Adam looked away. "That wasn't my fault."

"You caused it," the Destroyer sneered.

Adam tried to ignore the window, but he heard the sound of fists smacking flesh outside. *Stop it, stop listening, stop.* He heard Joe Sanderson grunting in pain, and he remembered those were the same grunts the bully had uttered when Adam's rage had turned Joe's white face into purple silly putty.

"*You're* the Destroyer," the spiny creature said, its tendrils coiling around Adam's neck and stomach like a predatory squid—vicious, *hungry.* Its hot exhalations blasted against the side of Adam's face, and as tears stung Adam's eyes, the Destroyer licked them from his lashes with its forked tongue.

Adam tried to pull away, but he wasn't strong enough. "No," he whimpered. "I'm not you."

"Stupid little Earth Boy." The creature gripped him tighter. "So afraid. So *weak.* You've destroyed the lives of the people you care about. Take credit for your hard work."

Adam lowered his head. *I can't look out the window. I shouldn't. I have to look away.*

The Destroyer propped his chin up with a hooked tendril and forced him to stare outside the glass at the sight of his earthly body spread out on an operating table. His skull was chopped open. Bleeding. Broken. Grey matter oozed from the wound. The doctors were taking notes.

"I'm not dead yet," Adam gasped.

He tried to close his eyes, but the Destroyer lifted the lids with its little hooks, pinching them so tightly that Adam cried out in pain. Outside the window, the doctor was informing his parents about the operation. They looked horribly pale and drained, bloodshot eyes swimming with hope... then their faces fell. *It failed.* They separated to opposite sides of the room. When they got home, they signed divorce papers.

"Please stop," Adam begged.

Though he pushed and kicked, the tentacles tightened around him. The Destroyer pressed its gnarled lips against his neck, sucking the sweat from his skin, leaving hickeys. Outside the window, his father walked down a bridge at night, stepped onto the railing, and jumped from the side.

"No!" Adam screamed.

As the wails left his lips, energy escaped from him. His vision blurred. His muscles slackened. His legs felt weaker. Sweat poured down the Destroyer's body, and the creature shuddered with perverse delight. Muscles expanded within its tentacles, and the creature swelled up like a balloon until it was nearly double the height of Adam.

"Yes." It growled. "Keep feeding me."

Adam struggled to control his mind, to block out the Destroyer's influence, but the creature's increase in size had also increased its power over him. *I'm on a vessel powered by my imagination, for Christ's sake, I've gotta take control of my own mind!*

The Destroyer scooped him up like an infant. He tried to fight back, but he was like a floppy fish on a hook. Every movement exhausted him. The creature, whose body had grown so massive that the room shook with its steps, carried Adam over to the window and pressed his face to the glass.

Outside, Mom was sitting in a dark little apartment, flipping through old photos of Adam when he was young. The table was sticky with spilled wine. Pill bottles were lost in the couch. She took a gulp of wine straight from the bottle, her movements sluggish, as she spread an unemployment check out on the table.

Then she vomited all over herself. She raced to the toilet, where she threw up again. Gunk poured from her mouth. She vomited a third time and swung backward, and her eyes rolled to the backs of their sockets. Then her head pitched forward, and her skull cracked against the toilet seat, breaking skin, breaking bone. No one was around to see it, no one to call for help.

"The future of your parents." The Destroyer hissed. "Miserable. Divorced. Dead. Your fault."

"I know it's my fault!" Adam cried, tears pouring down his cheeks. "I know that! Stop hurting me!"

The Destroyer's stomach rumbled. Its shoulders expanded, and its chest broadened, revealing veins the size of tree trunks. Adam became nauseous as more of his energy was drained from him. His skin shrank, becoming as wrinkly as a paper bag, while the Destroyer's tentacles became stronger, faster, and more massive. Adam's mouth tasted salty.

"More!" the creature screamed, throwing back its neck and revealing an upper jaw loaded with multiple rows of serrated teeth.

The Destroyer threw Adam onto the bed, where he landed like a human hacky sack. He was cold, shuddering. He nuzzled up in the covers, craving warmth. *I'm just a kid. Please stop hurting me. I'm not the Destroyer. I'm not.* The room quaked as the Destroyer marched across it. The massive creature stopped at the foot of the bed, toes piercing the brain-matter floor. It peered down at the cringing Earth Boy it had dumped there.

"You human idiot," the Destroyer said. "You brain-dead piss-and-shitting *animal.*"

Adam squirmed, his wrists curling inward, his toes clenching together. He gasped for air as more energy expelled itself from his lungs, inflating the Destroyer's jacked muscles. From beneath the bed, the Destroyer pulled out a tiny hunk of obsidian rock and dangled it in Adam's face. *The Optimist's spark.* Adam tried to grab it, but his arm swung forward and drooped down like a wet sock. The Destroyer had grown so tall that it had to buckle forward to not crash into the ceiling.

Sweat poured from the monster's skin, dripping into Adam's mouth and eyes. Adam struggled to grasp at the obsidian rock the Destroyer was dangling before him. The creature pulled it away then scooped Adam off the bed with its tentacles.

"Now, with your help"—its chest purred—"the Consciousness will die."

The Destroyer bent Adam over its knee then slammed his back as though burping a newborn. It clapped Adam's back again, knocking the wind out of him. Again. A fourth time. Five little glowing lights, like fireflies, buzzed out of Adam's open mouth and dangled in the air.

"Oh no!" Adam cried. "No, you can't—"

"We *will*."

The Destroyer snatched the lights and squeezed them together with the obsidian rock. When he let go, a perfect glowing triangle of stars appeared before them, the same triangle the Face had once shown Adam, which felt like a long time before. *The Consciousness is united again.* The Destroyer dropped the lights into its mouth and swallowed. The protrusions of six little wormlike veins scurried down the monster's throat and then bulged in its chest, trying to escape but trapped within.

"The Consciousness is dead!" the Destroyer roared, its voice blasting the room like a grenade. "Now, I *am* the Consciousness!"

Tendrils coiled around Adam's body like a boa constrictor. Adam cried out, feeling the emptiness inside himself. *My friends are dead. I failed them. I killed them.* The Destroyer brought Adam back to the windows, back to where his favorite old telescope stared out into his failures on Earth, and then lowered him over the swirling blackness of the Nothing Spot.

"I'm sorry!" Adam cried. "I tried to save all of you! I tried to—"

"You *failed*."

Adam swung his useless limbs. *Maybe there's a chance still. Maybe I can get inside the Destroyer's chest and... and... no.* As the Destroyer lowered Adam into the Nothing Spot, its black waters seeped into his skin and stained it like ink. His hands vanished inside the hole. His face vanished. His mind became increasingly fuzzy. His body and his soul—if it was his soul... he couldn't tell—became translucent and meaningless.

Life would not continue after that moment—only a terrible Nothing-ness. *I don't exist. I'm not real. I don't matter.*

"You no longer exist," the Destroyer whispered. "You are Nothing."

I am the Nothing Boy.

The Destroyer dropped Adam into the black hole, and the lights went out.

Chapter 34: Brain Death

When Adam's eyes opened, nothing looked the way it was supposed to. All the artificial lights were red instead of yellow, and everything was fuzzy. No lines were clear—no clear shapes. His eyes kept rolling around in their sockets, and focusing on anything visual suddenly required enormous effort. Every part of his body felt heavy, some limbs heavier than others, as if his blood were filled with lead. Everything hurt—his head, his legs, and his neck.

He cried out for help, but his throat just gargled. "Hlllggggh... gunh." He tried again. "Unnngh."

Oh no. Please no. His heart sank into his compressed chest, which felt broken, cracked, and suffocated, as if his ribcage were bolted into a metal vest. His blurry vision didn't clear up, but he started to piece together the vague shapes of furniture, windows, and a television set beneath the red glow of the overhead bulbs. *It's my house.* Two floating heads sat in front of the television set. Somewhere above, he saw the black hole of the Nothing Spot, getting smaller and smaller. *I'm still sinking into it. I can still escape. Maybe I can get the floating heads to help me, to lift me up.*

"Gnnnaaauuggh!" he screamed.

He tried to move his arms, but they flopped to his sides. His legs couldn't kick. Something plastic stabbed into his gut, dripping mucus onto his stomach. One of the floating heads, the one with red curls, turned to face him.

"Oh look," Mom said, "he's awake."

Tears of happiness rushed from Adam's eyes at the sound of his mother's voice, but the tears quickly went cold. He tried to move, failed again, and reality set in. *Oh no. Please no.* His heart stopped. *This can't be happening. I can't live this way. This is no way for someone to live.* His broken brain had been placed inside a broken body.

Mom's floating head rushed up to him. "Hey honey," she said. "Bad dreams?"

Adam tried to touch her, but his hand had become hopelessly tangled in the rubber wheel of his chair. *Oh God, oh God, oh God.* The floating red-haired head that was Mom kissed his cheek. *No, no, no, Mom, please just kill me, I can't do this, I can't live for years like this just waiting and waiting and waiting to die, I can't...*

The other floating head approached, and that head breathed heavily, as Dad did when he was stressed.

"Little guy is crying," Dad said, wiping Adam's eyes.

"Blsssshh... ung... ggnnaaah..."

Adam's blurry, bobbing vision flicked to the ceiling, up to the Nothing Spot, which was only a pinprick. With grinning teeth, the Destroyer looked down on him through the hole. Its hideous face was the only thing that was clear. *I'll never see a person's real face again.*

"This is the rest of your life, Earth Boy." The Destroyer purred. "A life of blurs. Bobbles. Emptiness. Nothing but *me*. We'll always be together."

Adam swerved away, straining against the seat belt in his chair. *No, no, no, anything but you, anything but that!* He squirmed in his seat, his bladder tightened and then opened like a shaken soda bottle. Warm urine formed a puddle in his paper underwear. "Plssshh gahhh!" His eyes couldn't focus on the blurry shapes that were his parents.

"He's trying to say something," Mom said.

"He's just making sounds with his throat." Dad stroked Adam's arm. "Camille, hon... you can't keep getting your hopes up."

"You're right." She sighed.

"Disrrryyyerrrr!" Adam cried. *Des-troy-er, say it. Destroyer.* "Disss... rooyy... unngh."

But then focusing was too hard. A deep coldness danced across Adam's temple, and his vision went dark. He was too heavy. Staying awake was too hard. He was too tired. He collapsed into his wheelchair, falling like a weight. *Don't fall asleep.* He strained to keep his eyes open, but he wasn't strong enough.

When the darkness overtook him, the nightmare began. He heard voices, clear voices. Even though he knew he was sleeping, even though he knew that when he woke up, he'd be in his wheelchair again, none of that knowledge helped. *I can't escape the nightmare. I can only wait for it to end.*

"Loser," said Joe Sanderson, his bruised face floating past in the darkness. "My parents are gonna sue yours into the homeless shelter because of what you've done."

"Pllggghhh... ung..." *None of this is real, none of it matters, none of it is—*

He tried to pinch himself, but he couldn't feel his hand.

Chandra Goswami's face floated into his vision, her lips puckered. Then she drew away, giggling. "I only kissed your cheek because I felt bad for you." She laughed. "I don't want to be your friend. Seriously? You're going to be a virgin forever. You're going to... going to..."

Chandra's voice dissipated. Mom and Dad—talking to him either in the nightmare or in reality, he couldn't tell—looked at him with sullen, lost expressions. A vein appeared in his mother's head.

"You were a mistake," she said. "We should have never adopted you."

Mom, please don't say that! Stop!

"I'm sorry, kid." Dad shook his head. "You did kinda ruin our lives."

I'm sorry! I'll do whatever I can to fix things, I swear!

"You just ain't the son I wanted," Dad said. "I wanted a kid I could play baseball with, a real boy. Not some little nerd. Definitely not whatever brainless animal you are now."

"No kidding." Mom's teeth were gritted. "Why don't you just die already, Adam, so we can move on with our lives?"

Then the darkness cleared, though, and the nightmare lifted. He was awake again. Sweat soaked his armpits. *Oh my God, nightmares can happen to me at any time. I can't predict them. I'll just fall asleep randomly.* Everything was still blurry. His body was still heavy, but he was in a warm hospital bed in a white room. At that point, just having a nice bed was a relief—just knowing he didn't have to hold his head up any longer, that he could just sink into a mattress and do nothing else. A young woman wearing seafoam green threw back his blanket, and goosebumps popped up on his cold, naked flesh. She changed him into itchy pajamas that felt like sandpaper on his skin, rolling him back and forth to pull up his pants. He wriggled around, trying to show his discomfort, and she pushed him back down with a groan. His monumental effort of movement was nothing but a minor inconvenience for her.

"Relax, Adam, it's going to be okay." She shook her blurry, featureless head. "I wish I knew what was upsetting you today. If only you could talk."

I'm right here!

"They don't hear you." The Destroyer growled. "No one will ever hear you again. Just you and me. Together forever."

Adam used all his strength, every ounce of it, to fling his arm forward and catch the girl's hand. "Gllungh. Diss... oy... dss..."

Just kill me, if nothing else. Smother my face with a pillow. Don't let me live like this. Please! Anything but this.

The girl didn't kill him, though—didn't hear him, didn't know what to do. She pulled the blanket up to his neck, leaned down, and kissed his cheek. His rage simmered down into an annoyed appreciation. *At least she knows I'm a person.* A hard stone formed in his throat, and he swallowed it bitterly. *Things like kisses on the cheek are all I can hope for now.*

Then her blurry shape gestured toward a black blur in the window. "It was nice of your parents," she said, "to bring your old telescope here to your new home. We're going to take good care of you here."

New home, what? What about my old home? Where are Mom and Dad? Why did they bring me to—

"They set it up in the window here," the nice girl said, gesturing toward the black blur. "They said you've had it since you were a little kid. Is that true? That you used to spend all your nights just staring into it, looking up at the night sky? It's too bad you'll never be able to look out it again."

"Skkkllunn..." Adam peered into the black blur that was supposed to be his telescope. *Never again. I can't believe it. She's right. Never again.*

"Really sad," the nurse said. "It must be really painful looking at that telescope, knowing you can't ever use it again. Wow. I'm sorry, I... shouldn't have brought it up."

Above Adam, the Destroyer snickered. The invisible blades of the Nothing Spot serrated Adam's soul like a cheese grinder, slicing dozens of little pieces out at a time. *Never again. No more telescope. No more...*

He strained to look at the telescope. *I have to look through it again... even if I have to throw myself on the floor to do it.* The memories rushed back to him. *I was seven years old. Mom woke me up at the crack of dawn.* He remembered the excitement he'd felt and the way his parents had beamed at him as he looked into that telescope for the first time. *They loved me. They were proud of me, proud of who I was. No, not quite.*

Not just who I was. Who I am.

I do matter.

Six little lights appeared up in the Nothing Spot, six little glow-worms.

Adam gasped. *Did I do that? Just with a thought?* Adam ignored what the nice young woman was saying to him, and he instead focused on the memory of himself as a little boy, staring up into space, looking into that telescope for the first time with a beaming smile. *That's the real me.* When he looked at the Nothing Spot again, the six lights were drawing closer.

I do matter.

The blurry room was darkening, becoming even cloudier, but Adam felt the six lights touch down on him, swimming around his face. He repeated the thought. *I do matter.* The lights jumped down his open mouth, and oxygen flooded his lungs.

He inhaled deeply then erupted. "I matter! My imagination matters!"

Adam squeezed his fists, feeling blood coursing through them again. His head was too heavy to lift from the pillow, but he kept trying. He gritted his teeth. "I am the Courage!" he shouted.

And with that declaration, he lifted himself from the hospital bed, screaming through closed teeth as pain coursed through his legs. He stood up, shaky on his feet but resolute in his will. The not-so-nice nurse towered over Adam. The skin of her face pulled apart into thick scales, and her blushing cheeks darkened from red to violet.

"You're nothing," she said. Her lips pulled back, gums splitting open, pierced by jagged, sharp teeth.

Adam wavered. *She's not a nurse anymore. Never was. All of this is the Destroyer.* The nurse's jaw fell from her chin as a crocodilian snout pushed from the torn remains of the fake human face. Tendrils sprouted from the creature's midsection. Spines puffed out from its back. Adam faced the Destroyer, legs wobbling beneath him but fists balled up.

"I'm the Courage," he repeated in a whisper.

"You're just a paralyzed animal." The Destroyer's violet tendrils twisted toward him.

Adam stepped forward, every movement tearing the atrophied muscles in his legs. *Keep going. Fear can become strength.* He smiled, stubbornly marching toward the tentacled alien. "I am who I choose to be," he said, "and I know my own... my own Face."

Adam's skin hardened. His sweat formed a cementlike armor around his skin, from head to toe. He stepped forward, pushing through the extra weight, fighting the pain.

The Destroyer whipped Adam's legs with a tendril, knocking him to the floor. He crashed down, heavy as a rock, and the floor cracked beneath his weight. Tears formed in his eyes. *I have to keep going!* The Destroyer pounced on top of him, pinning him down to the linoleum. Its eyeless head moved inches away from his face, its drool trickling down his ear.

"You're *mine*," the Destroyer whispered. "I'm the only thing in the universe that understands how pitiful you really are."

"No." Adam's teeth were still clenched. "No... you..."

"I'm the only one that truly *knows* you." The Destroyer's hot exhalations smelled of vomit. "Your best friend in the universe."

The floor beneath Adam's body cracked so loudly that he winced. He felt heavier. His limbs hardened as if the blood was compressing, getting tighter, denser. His skin and muscles became solid, rocklike. Heat wafted out of him, a gentle blue mist rising from the shimmering obsidian that his body was hardening into. He smiled. *Okay, I get it now. I can't be just one at a time. I have to be... to be...*

"I know myself," Adam said, "and I know"—he squeezed his fists until they were rocks—"that I am an Optimist!"

Adam swung an obsidian fist into the Destroyer's jaw, shattering its teeth like a glass window. The Destroyer recoiled, throwing its head back and shrieking. As Adam's heart pounded like a jackhammer, he slammed the Destroyer with the other fist, breaking the creature's jawbone with a loud crack. The Destroyer leapt back, yellow blood pouring from its lips. It looked different. *It's smaller now. Smaller than me, even.* The pathetic, shrunken creature scurried away from him.

"You don't know anything!" it sputtered.

Adam stood up, strong enough to support the weight of his entire obsidian body. As he stepped toward the Destroyer, it scuttled beneath the hospital bed. It had shrunk to the size of a dog. *It's afraid of me.*

"You're wrong, Destroyer." Adam reached under the bed. "Because I know that with these sparks inside me, I'm also the Motherboard." Adam's voice shook with renewed energy, excitement, and terror at the power flowing within him. He grabbed the Destroyer by its long neck and dragged it into the open. "And I'm even the Mad Glee too!"

Adam kicked the Destroyer in the ribs, and the creature shrieked in pain. Blue flames erupted from inside Adam's obsidian shape, spiraling across his back, flowing through his veins like blood. He seized the Destroyer's shoulders and lifted the creature to eye level.

"But when it comes to monsters like you"—Adam squeezed—"monsters that want to hurt innocent aliens and pretend to be my parents..." Adam growled, glaring into the scarred, eyeless sockets of the cringing creature before him. "I am the Rage!" Adam tore off the Destroyer's tentacles as though plucking the legs off a spider.

The Destroyer screamed in anger, spittle flying from its bleeding, toothless lips. "You're nothing but a miserable little Earth Boy. You don't matter!"

The room's overhead lights flickered. Adam winced, feeling the Destroyer's words pierce him. The stars outside the window pulsed in and out with Adam's heartbeat. *Don't lose focus. I'm inside my mind. My imagination.* Adam seized the Destroyer's serpentine throat.

"You're wrong, Destroyer," he said. "I am the Galaxy Seeker. *You're* the one who doesn't matter."

Adam twisted the Destroyer's head until it tore free from the creature's shoulders, splattering yellow bile onto his feet. Its body slumped down onto the linoleum floor. The lights went dark, and Adam stood there in the shadows, panting for air. His heart was pounding so loudly that he could barely hear.

"It's done," he whispered.

Chapter 35: The Consciousness

A dam shivered on the edge of the hospital bed, his legs pulled up to his chest. Hours had passed as he waited there in the darkness, staring at the night sky outside the window and hoping something would change.

The Destroyer's broken corpse lay in the pile where he had left it, but Adam hadn't looked at it since it had fallen. He didn't want to see any more bloodshed, not even when it was the dead body of such a despicable creature. Behind him was a closed door, which presumably would bring him to other rooms in the nursing home, hospital, or wherever he was, but Adam wasn't interested in any more adventures. He didn't want to risk his life again. He longed for home, the *old* home that he remembered from before the broken brain, the broken car, the broken family.

That place is gone now. All that's left is the new home that the Destroyer showed me in the Nothing Spot.

"Can anyone hear me?" Adam asked the shadows. "Please, someone answer."

Nothing replied—not a whisper, not a light, nothing. He no longer felt the six aliens inside his chest. *I killed the Destroyer, and now they've left me behind. Moved on to the next world or something. No thank you or anything.* He didn't know what was supposed to happen next. A terrible loneliness darkened his heart. Outside the window, the stars rolled out before him but offered no answers. He looked at his hands—imaginary hands—and wondered if he was perhaps trapped on the vessel now, no longer connected to the aliens but too far away from his old mind to ever go back to Earth. *Do I have to spend the rest of my life in space?*

Adam stared outward for a long time. He rubbed his eyes, struggling not to cry.

He stood up, tiptoeing around the Destroyer's corpse. *Okay, it's time to stop moping around. I can't let myself just give up.* If the Consciousness had taught him one lesson, in all of its six forms, it was that he had a stronger will than he'd ever thought possible. He faced the exit door and took a deep breath. *It might be scary. It might be bad. But I can't hide behind doors any longer. The shy little boy is gone. A car crash killed him, and the Destroyer buried him. I'm something new now. Something better, maybe.*

I'm a new Adam.

Adam opened the door, and the light behind it was so bright that he shielded his eyes. The corridor stretching before him was filled with blue flames. At the end was another open door leading to an even brighter light. Inside the blue flames were voices, laughter, and music.

Then the voice of the Consciousness spoke up above all the others, bringing a smile to Adam's face. *"Come to me, Galaxy Seeker."*

Adam walked down the hallway, and his footsteps echoed. The flames circled around his legs like playful dogs. *I swear, it sounds like they're even giggling.* With every step, he felt the weights the Destroyer had tied to his soul being unbound, loosened until he moved into the light at the other side of the corridor.

He stepped out onto the surface of an enormous brain floating in the sky like a cloud. A dark hole was carved into the broken section of the brain, right in the place of his TBI. The healthier gray matter squished beneath his feet. He turned around, but the glowing hallway had disappeared.

"Oh man," he said. "I'm standing on my brain again? Great. That was so much fun the last time."

The floating brain-cloud hovered miles above a craggy black mountain range, right in the center of an enormous valley. The mountains stretched on for miles, some of them jutting out of the earth in sharp spirals while others sloped into downward-plunging curlicues that could've come from a Dr. Seuss book. Above him, the sky was so bright that he could barely look at it, and it was streaked in colors that the human race had never invented words for. *Ultraviolet ones, maybe? That's kinda cool.*

Adam bent down. He was so high up that his legs twitched. For support, he patted his brain like a favorite pet. "Well, hi, Mr. Brain." He smiled. "You gonna talk to me too?"

He perched on the edge of the brain-cloud to get a better view of the valley, and when he saw flashing images of himself staring up from below, he jumped back in shock. "Whoa," he whispered.

He looked again. In the valley between the mountains, Adam's entire life played out beneath him, every single moment occurring simultaneously like a comic book compilation of his story. He closed his eyes, overwhelmed and mystified. *I can't even take this in.*

He looked again. *Crap, there goes my sanity.* Deep within the center of the enormous valley, an American couple adopted a little boy from India. At seven years old, the same little boy was receiving the gift of a telescope from his mother and, a few days later, jumping around in a Jupiter Man costume. Playing games on the computer. Sneaking up to the roof of his house. Staring at the sky through his telescope night after night. At the same time all that was happening, though, other events were taking place in higher stretches of the valley: the car crash, the current operation, the Adam of a few weeks ago building his bicycle while Chandra Goswami kissed another Adam, and another one defending her from Joe Sanderson. The cardboard boundaries that time created were being broken down and shown for the arbitrary structure that they were.

"This is *nuts.*" Adam shook his head.

The colors of the sky glowed and darkened, displaying weather patterns Adam could neither describe nor understand. Drops of water flowed upward instead of downward. Fractals blinked and danced around each other. Adam gasped and turned away from the landscape beneath him, overwhelmed beyond belief. *I can't deal with this. It's too much. Too fast.*

The brain-cloud was descending toward the valley. Adam walked from one side to another, his feet squelching against brain matter, trying to figure out if he needed to jump off. The black mountains were towering above him, but the valley was still many miles below. If he jumped, he'd die from the impact. *Or maybe it'd teleport me back into the past or something bizarre like that. Seems too risky, either way.*

However, something about the dark mountains beckoned to him. *That's the path ahead. Darkness. They're going to send me back to my brain-damaged body, and I'll never have a clear thought again.* As Adam stepped toward the edge of the brain-cloud, a light appeared within the mountains and floated toward him. As it came closer, it revealed itself as a blurry humanoid figure walking through the sky in his direction.

The sky-walker descended to the brain-cloud and stood across from Adam with its hands on its hips and a smile on its face. As the figure approached, as the light within it dimmed and revealed its features, Adam saw that, despite its phosphorescence, it *was* a human being—a young man wearing a T-shirt and jeans that were too baggy for his slender frame.

"Hello there," the man said.

The sky-walker was probably no more than twenty years old. He had dark skin, straight black hair, and dark eyes. His cheekbones and fingers were long, and though he was tall, he walked with both a self-conscious slouch and a noticeable limp.

"Oh my... my God," Adam stammered.

"Hey, Adam." The young man flashed him a warm smile, as if he were the older brother that Adam had never had.

Adam swallowed. "You're... ah..."

The man stepped closer. The glowing fractals illuminated deep surgical scars running along the young man's arms, neck, and forehead, with one especially deep scar that started at his temple and disappeared behind his hairline. Adam stared down at the brain beneath him, then examined the man's grinning face. "You're...you're..."

"I'm the Consciousness." The man looked down shyly then laughed. "Or the Star Voice, if you prefer."

"Actually, I was gonna say that you're *me*." Adam's voice was small and frail. "But yeah, the Consciousness. Or both. Or... ah..."

The older Adam grinned at that, and the man's good-humored nature calmed Adam's speeding heart.

Adam stepped forward, moved to touch the Consciousness, then pulled back. "Can I...?"

"Of course."

Adam ran his fingertips along the older Adam's shoulder then moved his hand down his arm. He drew back at the prickly hair there then nervously touched the puffy surgical scars and drew back again. The man watched him with no judgement, no resistance. Taking a deep breath, Adam stood on his tiptoes, briefly touched the man's stubble... and finally ran his fingers along the puffy scar on his head. *He's walking. He's alive. Does that mean...?*

The Consciousness kept looking at Adam with that same understanding smile. "It's okay," he said. "I know this is a lot to take in."

"Are you real?" Adam stepped back, crossing his arms to hide how much he was shaking, to pretend he wasn't scared.

"All of this is real. It has been since the beginning," the Consciousness answered. "All of *us* are real too."

"I wanted to say goodbye to the other aliens. I never got to see them again."

"That's okay because I *am* all of the aliens. Just like you were, for a bit. But hey, I'm sorry that we all disappeared on you after you took care of our Destroyer problem. I guess we probably seemed rude." The Consciousness shook Adam's hand. "So let me speak for all of us when I say this: thank you saving our lives, Galaxy Seeker. Without you, our entire species would be dead. That Jupiter Man guy you love, the one from your comic books, would be really proud of you, I'll bet."

"Entire species?" Adam frowned. "But there were only six of you."

"Oh, that?" The Consciousness scratched his stubbly chin. "Well, hmm. I guess you could say that there were six specific shapes that could be imprinted onto your imagination, based on six specific shapes that already existed within your psyche. But the number of beings that existed *within* each shape, whether that shape was a Motherboard or a Mad Glee, varied tremendously. Some of the figures you met contained many thousands of unique entities merged into one overall shape. What you encountered was a version of our species that you could process because—"

"I know that part. The Face told me." Adam looked down. "I mean, uh... *you* told me, I guess? When you became the Face? Or when *some* of you became the Face, or a few of you, or... whatever." Adam threw up his hands. "Crap, I don't get this."

Adam turned away, fighting the tears that threatened to emerge from him. After the epic journey he had been on, his little human brain was craving resolution, enlightenment, answers. He wanted simple, concrete scientific explanations. He faced the valley, staring back on the total accumulation of moments from his life, seeing firsthand how circular it all was, how many times certain life lessons had been repeated and not learned. He stepped up to the ledge.

"I still don't know why you chose me," Adam said. "I know that I did beat the Destroyer and all, but I also created him, so whatever. I still think I'm a mess."

"Every conscious being in the universe is a mess. That's what's so beautiful about life. Clean things are boring things." The Consciousness stepped beside Adam and put an arm around his shoulders.

Weird, feels like I'm giving myself a hug. Adam moved closer to him.

"Listen," the Consciousness continued, "you just saved us, kid. And everyone has their own Destroyer, not just you. You can't beat yourself up over that. I think we did a pretty good job of picking you out to be our Galaxy Seeker, based on the evidence."

Adam looked up at the older version of himself and wiped the tears from his own eyes. "But I feel so lost. Nothing that I did makes any... I can't... I don't know. It's so hard not to just write everything off as a dream."

"You want to understand the whole thing better." The Consciousness nodded, letting go of him. "Well, look below."

"Which part?"

The Consciousness pointed down at the valley, his finger aiming at the replay of the first time Adam had peered through his telescope on the dawn of his seventh birthday. "We chose you," the Consciousness said, "because of your imagination, because you aren't afraid to dream, and because you have the rare stubbornness that makes dreams into realities."

The Consciousness pointed at another section of the valley, and Adam saw the time he fixed up that old bicycle that the guy on Craigslist wanted to get rid of, the bike that had meant so much to him. He watched himself running away after fixing it to make sure the owner wouldn't be able to pay him. Playing out beside that was Adam encountering each of the alien beings he had met on his quest, finding their sparks, collecting them, and saving them from the Destroyer.

The Consciousness smiled at Adam, his cheek dimpling in the same place Adam's always did. "You might not be innocent, kid, but you *are* noble. You are kind and giving but also humble and strong. You take care of others, and they love you for it. You won't take credit for it, but you sacrificed a lot to stay on our vessel, surrounded by beings you didn't know or understand, saving us from a terrible entity—all because you thought it was the right thing to do. That's pretty amazing, Adam. Pretty heroic. Take credit for it."

Adam stared up at his older mirror image. Then he looked down and saw the hospital waiting room, a small lobby filled with not just his parents, but most of his classmates and all his teachers.

He rubbed his eyes. "They're all there for *me?*"

The Consciousness smiled and nodded. He clapped Adam's shoulder. "You know why you became the Galaxy Seeker, Adam?"

"Because you picked me."

"No." The adult Adam's grin widened. "Because you *believed* you were the Galaxy Seeker."

The Consciousness turned Adam away from the past images of his life and forced him to face the dark mountain range looming above the brain-cloud. Flickering between the mountains, a fissure opened in the sky, a hole in the fabric of reality. *A portal.* Adam shadowed his eyes, but the fissure was impossible to focus on as it constantly changed shape, form, and color from one instant to the next.

"Adam Helios," the Consciousness said, "I thank you for saving us, from the bottom of our many hearts. But it's time for you to go home."

Adam cringed away from the massive black giants towering above him. "Consciousness, sir." His voice cracked. "I'm scared that I'll be trapped in a brain that isn't me anymore." He shook his head. "Can I stay with you a little bit longer, maybe? What if you bring me to see your home world?"

"Human beings are not meant for our world," the Consciousness said. "Your senses could not process our true physiology, not yet, not at this point in your evolution. Maybe a thousand years from now, but at the moment—"

"Please!" Adam seized his older self's shoulders and nearly crumpled to the brainy floor. "On Earth, back in those dark mountains... I know what's waiting for me. I'll be a vegetable on Earth. I love my family. I love Earth, but you guys... you guys have changed me. I don't know what I'll do without you."

The Consciousness smiled. "And that's why you won't be without us."

Adam blinked. "What?"

"We'll be with you, Adam. We'll give you a light to keep you going when the times are hard. We'll be the extra energy you need to get through every day with a smile—until the time comes when you're ready to do it on your own."

The Consciousness's skin hardened into rock. He grew taller, his facial features disappeared, and blue flames burned from the edges of his body. As the hulking figure of the Optimist stood before him again, Adam dove forward and hugged his obsidian companion.

"Optimist!" he cried. "I missed you!"

The Optimist enfolded him within his massive arms. The hole in the Optimist's chest was filled with a craggy chunk of black rock that emitted rainbow reflections whenever the light hit it just right.

"Galaxy Seeker, do not be afraid," the Optimist said, rubbing Adam's back. "We understand that you have a challenging road ahead, and in return for saving us, we shall leave you with a gift."

The Optimist reached to his chest and removed the chunk of rock that was his spark, with an audible click. He placed it into Adam's hand.

Adam pushed it away. "Oh, no. No, no, no. That's yours."

"Take it," the Optimist said. "Use my spark to guide you back to consciousness. If you believe that you are the Galaxy Seeker, you will be okay."

Adam stared out at the fissure flickering between the sharp black mountains, moving from crevice to crevice. He was beginning to understand. "But I can't—"

"You can." The Optimist placed the rock in Adam's hands again. "Take my spark with you, back to your world. Challenges await you. Use it to heal your wounds, to repair your mind, to shelter your soul. And then, someday, when you are ready to face the universe on your own, you may return it to us."

"But I just spent all this time wrestling this piece of rock away from the Destroyer so I could give it back to you!" Adam returned the rock.

"The spark is just a symbol of something far greater, a thing that resides within each one of us, including you. Take it, use it, turn your life around, and improve the quality of your world for everyone on it." The Optimist nudged Adam's chest, tapped it twice, and dropped the craggy obsidian rock back into his hands. "We will miss you, Adam."

Adam turned the rock over in his hands. "I'll miss you, too. You're probably the best friend I've ever had."

"And you are the best friend that we have ever had, as well. Take care, Galaxy Seeker. Your true journey shall now begin."

"But maybe I shouldn't—"

Before Adam could finish speaking, Optimist pushed him off the side of the brain-cloud. Adam toppled through the air, screaming at the top of his lungs, in shock that his friend could have betrayed him. He hurtled toward the sharp rocks below. The wind whistled through his ears as he flipped through the sky like a rag doll. Then Adam remembered what the Consciousness had said. *He didn't betray me, did he? He set me free.* He held the obsidian rock in both hands. Energy pulsed from it, spreading into Adam's heart then shooting down his legs—and burning into his soles. As Adam fell into the valley, radiant energy shimmered beneath his feet.

The lightboard burst into existence.

Adam shot into the sky like a jet, weaving through the clouds. His laughter flew with him as the lightboard zoomed back down, shooting past the floating brain-cloud and deep into the mountain range. *I'm free!* Adam waved at the distant figure of the Consciousness, who waved back.

"You are the Galaxy Seeker!" the Consciousness shouted.

"You bet I am!" Adam laughed as he swooped down over the valley replaying his past and zoomed up into the dark mountains of his future.

He gripped the black rock, pressed it to his chest, and smiled. *I am the Galaxy Seeker.*

A boulder toppled from the peak of a curlicue mountain, and the lightboard sailed past it. One of the mountains exploded, throwing more boulders in their direction, and Adam zigzagged between them.

"Let's do this, lightboard!" Adam cried. "One more time!"

The glowing fissure flickered in a narrow opening between two cliffs, teleported to the peak of another mountain then scuttled around the back of it. Adam curved between sharp cliff edges on his lightboard, following the fissure's tail, grinning with excitement.

"That way!" he called out to the lightboard, as if it too possessed a mind—and perhaps it did.

The lightboard swept downward, cutting closely under a rocky bridge. It dodged another falling boulder. They were closing the distance. The fissure would soon be in reach.

He could see inside it. Even though its shape and color changed with every moment, the inside of the fissure was a portal back to the world he knew, back to a room full of white coats and rubber gloves, a room where his brain was being operated on. Fear swept through Adam, and the lightboard started to fade—but instead of giving in, Adam squeezed the obsidian rock. *I am the Galaxy Seeker.*

The fissure dove deeper into the mountain range, trying to escape. *I am the Galaxy Seeker.* The lightboard followed, sweeping high into the sky then plummeting down, beating the fissure at its own game. As it hovered above the fissure, the lightboard came to a halt. Adam knew what he had to do.

"Thank you, my friend," Adam said, and he leapt off the lightboard.

He toppled down, free-falling between giant cliff drops, swooping right into the fissure's radiant center. The light swallowed him. As he disappeared within it, plunging into its depths as if he'd jumped into the deep end of a pool, his body felt heavier and heavier. His limbs became sore and tired. His bones became brittle. He smelled the stench of sweat, blood, and rubbing alcohol. The air became cold. *I am the Galaxy Seeker. I am.*

I am the Galaxy Seeker.

He squeezed the rock then closed his eyes.

Chapter 36: Earthly Happenings

The door to the waiting room opened, and all the murmuring among teachers, students, and parents went dead silent. Camille clenched her fists. Dr. Benjamin Blake stepped in, his head bowed, hands in his pockets. Camille gnawed on the inside of her cheek, thinking, *Oh God damn it, that's not the look of a good outcome.* The door clicked shut behind the doctor, and all eyes in the room followed him as he moved toward Camille and John.

"Camille? John?" Ben scanned the room. "Er... everyone?"

He's not smiling. Shit. She squeezed John's hand so tightly that veins bulged out. "Ben, is Adam... you know. Is he?" She bit her cheek, and it bled.

Ben blushed, looking at the crowd again. Principal Hamer stood up, gesturing for the doctor to take his seat, which he did.

Finally, Ben shook his head. "I don't know." He folded his face into his hands. "I have no idea what happened. The outcome, I mean to say. I don't get it."

"Ben," Camille said, "what happened?"

Please be alive, Adam. Please. Please. Camille was tempted to send out everyone in the waiting room, to ease Ben's tension, but that felt wrong. Most of them were just kids, and they'd waited there. They cared. They'd earned answers.

"Yeah." Ben cleared his throat. "Yeah, okay. He's alive. First person who has ever survived." Before Camille could even form a smile, Ben flashed his eyes at her. "But I don't know if the operation worked. His brain is sending mixed signals. It's in flux. Not doing what it's supposed to."

All across the room, heads dropped to the floor. Some children whispered to each other.

That Chandra girl started crying. "Is Adam going to come back?"

Ben faced the crowd, his face redder than a beet. "I'm sorry, everyone. I know you've all waited, and you deserve a better answer than the terrible one I've got, but I just don't know if the news is good or bad. X-rays show some regrowth, but it's unclear if any of it is going to stick. We had to revive him twice, which isn't a good sign. Adam himself is unresponsive. I'm sorry. I wish I could say something more conclusive, but this is uncharted territory."

A young boy inched forward. "What does that mean?"

"This is either going to be a groundbreaking moment in medical history, or it's going to be another failure. I have no idea what's going to happen or how long it's going to take. Could be days. I'm sorry, I just don't know."

Ben was shivering, a nervous man forced to stand onstage. His eyes zoomed around the room. *He's terrified.* Camille swallowed her fears, took a deep breath, and stood up. She took Ben's hand, pulled him up onto his feet, and then hugged him. He melted into her, and Camille rubbed his back. "Thank you, Doctor," she said.

"I don't know if I—"

"You gave it your best shot." Camille kissed his cheek and pulled away. "You're a fantastic human being. Thank you for taking care of my son."

Then, following her lead, John stood up and shook the doctor's hand. Principal Hamer followed, as did his wife. On the inside, Camille was shaking, terrified. The lack of answers was tearing her apart. She didn't, wouldn't, *couldn't* know if her son would be okay. *But other people matter too. All of them. Not just me.* Ben stood a little taller and less red-faced as all the children gathered around him and asked questions. Camille went up to the Keurig, made a coffee, and gave it to Ben. He thanked her.

"Go do whatever you need to do, Ben," Camille said. "We'll be waiting."

Chapter 37: Synapses

Every day felt like a year. By the time a couple weeks had passed, Camille was ready to start checking for gray hairs. Adam was never far from her thoughts. When she was near him, standing over his hospital bed, she watched for signs of recovery. When she *wasn't* near him, when she slept in her bed at night, she woke up every morning wondering if maybe she'd missed something, if maybe that day would be the one he came back.

Today. Tomorrow. The next day.

John had been discharged from the hospital shortly after Adam's operation, and he was spending most of his time relaxing in front of the TV at home. He visited Adam for a few hours every day and wanted to stay longer, but his pain medication made it hard for him to stay awake long enough.

Camille, on the other hand, spent almost every waking hour in that hospital room, right at Adam's side. After a few days, she brought her laptop in and telecommuted to work. Once her work was done, she spent every afternoon talking to Adam, updating him on current events and reading Isaac Asimov novels to him.

I know you're in there, Adam. I love you. I'll never give up on you.

Ben came in often, checking to see if Adam's status had changed. Adam's brain had yet to be responsive, but the rest of his body was recovering: every night, the nurses came in and peeled off another bandage. He looked good—skinnier than he should be, but good—handsome as ever. The most noticeable scars were on his chest, arms, and legs. The scars on his face were minimal, other than a puffy surgical scar that started at his temple and stretched back behind his ear.

By the end of the third week, Camille had read him the last lines of *Foundation and Empire*. Right as she finished, Adam started choking, as he often did when he had too much mucus in his throat. *Damn it, the nurse put his head too low again.* Camille bolted upright and pressed the button that raised the head of his bed. The choking immediately stopped, and he coughed out phlegm.

Camille wiped the drool from his lower lip. "Jeez, Adam, be careful," she said. "You gotta be careful with that, remember?"

His mouth moved a bit, but his eyes remained closed. Ever since the operation, they hadn't opened. Camille's stomach knotted at the realization that she'd just scolded him for something he couldn't control, even though she'd done it gently. *It's not his fault he choked.*

Camille kissed his forehead. "I'm sorry." She ran her finger along the scar on his head. "Not your fault. I should've noticed earlier. Cough anytime you need to. I'll be here. Every day. All day."

She heard nurses outside the room, hustling to the next room over. Adam's heart-rate monitor beeped softly, with that little flashing blue light. She sat down in the chair again, realized the Asimov book was underneath her, and pulled it out.

"Did you like the book?" She paused and looked down at the cover. "The Foundation Series is one of my favorites. I figured it'd be up your alley, what with all that sci-fi stuff you like. Hope you enjoyed it."

Adam coughed again. *Hell!* Camille shot upright, moving to raise his head even higher, and Adam's eyes flipped open.

He coughed again, but it was a gentle cough. His chapped lips puckered up, sucked in air, then fell loose again.

Camille leaned in close, staring into his dark pupils, looking for a spark. *Don't get your hopes up, you stupid woman. It might just be a reflex. But maybe...*

Adam closed his eyes, but before Camille could panic, he reopened them. He turned his head to face her, his eyes wide open and unblinking. *He's looking at me, I swear, he's looking at me!*

Adam swallowed, and from the depths of his dried-out throat, a barely audible rasp emerged. "Mom."

"Adam?" Her voice shook.

He smiled. "I'm back, Mom."

Camille shrieked in excitement, no longer able to restrain herself. She leapt forward and hugged Adam, squeezing him tight. "Adam! I love you, Adam. Oh my God, I love you!" She kissed the side of his face numerous times then pulled back to make sure she hadn't jarred him. "Are you okay?"

He said nothing, but she could see his smile—*oh yes, there it is*—Adam's beautiful old smile, with the dimple in his cheek, the glow in his eyes. She squeezed him as hard as she could, making sure he wouldn't go away again, making sure he was real. His arms shakily embraced her but then dropped.

"Can't... breathe..." he groaned.

Camille pulled back and let go. Her eyes widened. "Oh my God. Are you okay? Adam, please tell me that you're—"

"Oh yeah, I'm good." He laughed, which became a cough.

God, I missed the sound of that laugh.

She patted him on the back, and he smiled again. "Just... hard to move. Stiff. I'm good."

"You don't have to move if you don't want to." She nodded. "Holy shit, Adam. I love you so much. I've been so worried. You have no idea. I'm so sorry about what happened. I can't believe—"

"Mom... calm down." He reached out to her with his weak, shaky hand, and she took it. "Everything's okay now. It's all gonna be A-okay."

"Yeah." Camille grinned, and she realized with some astonishment that she'd been sobbing so hard that both her shirt and Adam's hospital gown were soaked with tears. Her excitement had been so intense that she hadn't even noticed the tears until then.

Adam laughed, and Camille laughed with him. "You're right, Adam. Everything's A-okay now."

Chapter 38: After the End

After months of recovery, physical therapy, and checkups, the hospital exit was finally almost within reach—just down the hall, just at the end of the lobby. The glass doors stood there, glaring at Adam, daring him to take them on. He looked at those doors, breathing heavily, in disbelief that the moment had come.

I know it's time to go home... but am I ready? His hands were so shaky that he almost dropped his crutches. Beads of sweat ran down the sides of his face. *I don't know.* Staring at those doors that he'd dreamed about walking out of for months, he felt that passing through them—into a future life so different from the past, but probably so similar—was every bit as intimidating as climbing up the Rage had been.

You can do this. Adam exhaled. He rubbed the tender skin of his armpits, which were constantly being worn down by the crutches. Physical therapy had been rough that day, and the therapist had suggested taking it easy that afternoon, but Adam was firmly against leaving the hospital in a wheelchair. *I came in on a stretcher. I've gotta leave on my feet.* He'd dreamed of walking out ever since the day he'd woken up from his coma. When he'd relearned how to walk, every successful step had felt like another move closer to this day.

Adam pushed ahead, crutches punched to the ground, each forward movement a mountain unto itself. *Keep going.* Every time he took a step, every time a crutch slid beneath him—threatening to send him crashing down—he focused on everything he had been through. *I survived. My brain survived—so can my body.*

His brain had made an almost full recovery, in fact. Language, reading, logic, social cues, all of it, though he sometimes had a weird difficulty remembering people's names. Regardless, his recovery not only astonished Dr. Benjamin Blake, but also got the attention of local news outlets, which blasted the story across the Internet and turned both him and Dr. Blake into social-media heroes for a few weeks.

He pushed forward on his crutches again, the exit just a little bit closer. *I survived.* Adam had enjoyed getting interviewed in his hospital room and praised Ben for saving him. Deep inside though, Adam wasn't entirely sure if it *had* been the medical procedure that saved his life. He alone knew what had really happened to him during his brain injury, though he also knew he could never expect anyone else in the world to believe some wacky true story about aliens. As time went on and the once-fiery memories of the Consciousness, the Optimist, and the others faded, believing some parts of it became harder and harder for even *him*.

He lifted his body and pushed forward. He did it again. Again. Every extra inch felt like another little victory. Outside the door, Mom's new car waited, and she watched him with a nervous expression.

"Let me help you—"

"No." He stopped, panting. "I have to do this myself."

Mom stared at him, her arms crossed and her mouth a thin line.

Adam smiled. "It's okay." He launched forward on his crutches again, sharp pains rippling down his back.

Keep moving. Move through the pain. Gotta get used to it anyway. His spine hadn't healed quite correctly, so a future career as an athlete was probably out of the question. He would probably have headaches for the rest of his life. The brain injury had given him epilepsy, so he would have to take AEDs.

None of that held him back, though. After his experience on the vessel, Adam swore to himself that he'd never be held back again.

Adam's armpits ached. His arms wobbled. The doors were no longer so far away, just a few more lunges. *Almost there.* Adam wavered a bit, catching a fearful glance from his mom, and as anxiety rose within him, he closed his eyes—just for a moment, a brief second. He focused on the spark that the Consciousness had given him, focused on the hope inside it, and he remembered that *nothing* was impossible.

Then he pushed himself through the hospital doors. He was outside, in the beaming sunlight, free from the place that, only a few months before, had been intent on imprisoning him forever. Mom hugged him, and he laughed.

"I made it," he said.

She opened the car door. "You sure did." She laughed with him. "Come on. Let's go home."

As he walked out to the hospital parking lot on his crutches, the sight of moving cars on the roads ahead sent his heart racing. *I don't know if I can get in a car. It might happen again.* However, he pushed that fear aside, focused on the spark, and climbed into his mom's new Subaru.

ADAM STARED OUT THE car window. The sensation of being in a moving vehicle still gave him pins and needles in his feet, but he tried to get past it. When Mom finally pulled into the old cul-de-sac where he had grown up, Adam barely recognized it. *It's been so long. I was a different person the last time I saw this.* After having been in the hospital for so many months, he saw his old surroundings as just as alien as anything he'd experienced in the Consciousness.

"This is so weird," he said when she parked in the driveway.

"You okay?"

"Yeah."

An even weirder revelation greeted Adam as he opened the door and climbed out, balancing on his crutches: sitting there in the driveway was his old bicycle, the same one Joe had torn apart, fully repaired and repainted. Adam hobbled forward to get a closer look. The gears looked brand new.

He laughed and turned to his mom. "How did you do this? Who...? Was it Dad?"

His mom pointed toward the front porch. Adam jumped back at the sight of Joe Sanderson sitting on the railing, dressed in a T-shirt and nylon shorts, swinging his feet back and forth. Adam stared at him. *What is he doing here? The bike, did he...?*

Adam walked up to Joe on his crutches as Mom stood back and watched with her arms crossed. All the bruises on Joe's face were healed, and his hair was longer than before.

Joe hung his head over his chest, just as Adam had used to do at school. "Hi, Adam." He pointed at the repaired bike. "I, ah... I kinda fixed it up for you."

Adam couldn't quite climb up on the railing beside him, but he leaned next to it. "Wow, dude. That's really cool."

Mom went to the back of the car and pretended to clean out the trunk, though Adam knew she was actually listening in. She didn't need to worry about him so much, but he understood, considering she'd been inches away from losing her son only a few months before. *Can't blame her for feeling overprotective at this point.* Adam looked into Joe's pleading eyes and couldn't help thinking how surreal the universe really was, how circular, and how somehow the two of them—mortal enemies, bully and outcast, fierce combatants—were now sitting together on the porch, *his* porch.

"It's all my fault, man." Joe swallowed back tears. "Everything that happened to you happened because of me. I'm real sorry, man. Real sorry. I don't blame you for hating me."

"I don't hate you," Adam said.

"But I teased you and crap." Joe breathed in. "I was an *asshole* to you, man. For no good reason."

"Whatever." Adam smiled. "Listen, dude, you fixed my bike. I can't believe you really fixed it. That's awesome."

Joe looked up hesitantly, made eye contact, then looked away. "Yeah. You got no idea how many online videos I had to watch to figure that crap out. You're really smart for putting it together the first time. I hope you can, um... *Can* you still ride a bike? When you heal up, I mean?"

Adam laughed and grabbed Joe's shoulder. "Joe, are you kidding me? Hell yeah, I'm gonna ride that bike again." Swaying a bit on the railing, he winced and readjusted the crutch under his arm. "Probably not today, though."

Joe laughed, his face bright red. "I'll help you get back on it when you're ready. If you want my help, I mean. If not, it's okay."

"Cool." Adam stood up on his crutches again. "Hey, you wanna come inside and play some video games or something? I haven't done *that* in months. I probably need to get my skills back up."

Joe smiled. "That'd be real cool, man."

"Let's do it."

Adam walked back inside, and Joe followed him.

Chapter 39: Graduation

The weather was so perfect that it seemed unreal: warm but with a breeze and just enough clouds in the sky to make a perfect landscape painting. The bird of summer was starting to spread its wings but hadn't laid its eggs yet.

Adam shivered and sweated, perched upright in the front row of a crowd of 215 students filling what was normally the football stadium. He sweated inside his heavy robe. The cap didn't fit right on his head. He didn't know how to deal with a tie, so he'd picked up a clip-on at a thrift store on the way. His mind was lost in a buzzing mixture of anxiety and exhilaration as the school's alma mater blasted through the speakers, then his social-studies teacher, Mr. Johnson, began reading the names.

"Adam Helios!" he announced.

Adam's heart went still. He looked to both sides. *That's my name. Me.* He stood up, breathing heavily, beaming with what felt like the goofiest smile he'd ever shown in public. *It's me. I did it!* He looked back toward the bleachers, trying to see his parents, as the crowd roared his name.

Adam limped toward the stage on his bad knee, his back slightly hunched. He normally never blushed about walking like an old man—he'd been doing that for years—but the heat of the crowd's eyes felt awkward, and he stumbled a bit more than usual. Then the crowd cheered louder, though, and as the pulsing repetition of his name blasted across the field, Adam's chest swelled with pride. *They know me. To them, they'll just always remember me as the boy who survived the car crash... and hey, if that gives them hope, then maybe that's a pretty cool thing.* His graduation cords dangled from his neck.

He strode onto the stage with a huge grin on his face, raised his fists in an expression of triumph, and the crowd screamed in excitement. Then Adam spotted his parents, standing tall on the highest bleacher, both of them cheering at the top of their lungs. Dad's camera was snapping hundreds of photos. Mom's red hair was sprinkled with so much white that it glowed in the sunlight. Both of them were wearing T-shirts with his face screen-printed on them and the slogan *Team Adam* under the collar—the same gaudy shirts they'd been threatening to wear all week. That was their idea of a practical joke, and although it should've been embarrassing, it made him laugh.

"I made it!" Adam cried, and the stadium applauded.

He shook Mr. Johnson's hand, and the teacher spoke into the microphone, "Adam is graduating with a 4.0 GPA, and he'll be chasing his dreams when he heads off to MIT this fall!"

The cheers became so loud that Adam could barely think. *Wow, are they seriously cheering for me? There's no way. That's nuts.* He kept his head down, but he was smiling so hard that his cheeks hurt. He seized his high school diploma, held it over his head, and heard his dad whistle with excitement.

"You did good, Adam," Mr. Johnson whispered in his ear.

"Congratulations," said Principal Kelly, shaking his hand.

Adam strode across the stage, went down the other side, and returned to his seat with a slight stagger. He tried to stop smiling, his cheeks so hot he felt as if he was melting. *So many people looking at me.* He was just too happy, though, and the smile only grew wider. *I'm really here.* He couldn't believe he'd done it. Back in the early days after the accident—*have five years really gone by that fast?*—back when the physical therapy had been so painful, when the toll of the accident had been so high, he'd always feared he might never make it here.

But I made it. Wow, man. I really did.

As the next graduate was called, Adam stole one more glance back at his parents, snuggling together on the bleachers, both of them laughing as they went through the photos on Dad's camera. Catching his glance, Dad closed his glass eye in a wink, and Adam winked back at him. Mom dabbed at her eyes with her sleeves. She pointed down at his camera screen, seeming to be especially impressed by one photo.

Adam loved seeing them together, side by side. He found it funny that the older they got, as their hair had gone white, the more they resembled twins. He loved listening to them sneak out together at night, as if they were the teenagers and he was the parent, until they'd come home from the bars at midnight, laughing at the tops of their lungs.

I love them. I'll tell them that, after this whole silly ceremony is done, when the three of us grab lunch together. He was going to miss them when he moved to Boston, but he thought that having so much more time together would be good for the two of them, especially as they headed toward retirement. They were so happy together that he found it hard to believe they'd ever argued so much. Adam wasn't sure if the car accident was responsible for their happiness, but if it was—if his permanent limp, bent spine, and scarred forehead was the price to pay for their renewed joy in one another—then he was *glad* it had happened to him.

When the ceremony ended, Adam said goodbye to some of his classmates. A hand clapped his shoulder from behind, and Adam turned around to see the smile of his best friend, Joe Sanderson. Joe had that mischievous look in his eyes, the look that usually meant he was scheming something.

"Hey, big shot." Joe shook Adam's hand. "You coming to the party tonight?"

Adam chuckled. "No, thanks. I'll be busy tonight."

"Ah, man, why not?" Joe sipped from a coffee thermos filled with some combination of tequila and ginger ale. He offered it to Adam, who waved it away. "Aren't you flying to India, like, two days from now?"

"Yeah." Adam smiled. *I can't wait.* "But I'll only be gone for a few weeks."

"Ah, *man.*" Joe laughed. "That's really cool. Don't get me wrong. I'm glad you're doing that. But then it's only a month until we both move to Boston—"

"Where we'll be roommates." Adam wrapped his arm around Joe's shoulders, and they walked side by side. "Don't worry, dude, you'll be seeing me all the time. Too much, probably. We'll get sick of each other. We're going to be sharing a bathroom soon. Hopefully not a toothbrush, though."

"Great. Then people will probably think that we're a couple."

"They already make jokes about that." Adam laughed.

"True, that. None of which has helped my efforts to get Rachel Mathis to go out with me." Joe sipped his secret tequila again, eyeing Rachel across the field. "So what are you so busy with tonight, then? What's so important you need to blow off your poor, poor old best friend, who is always so loyal to you?"

Adam smiled and punched Joe in the shoulder. "I have an appointment with some old friends from a long time ago."

"Who?"

"Uh, well..." Adam shrugged. "You don't know them. I'll tell you about it later."

Chapter 40: One More Time Again

Later that night, Adam took off his robe, stepped out into the night, hopped into his beat-up old coupe—with its 210,000 miles, oil leak, and balding tires—and took a drive through town. He passed by his old middle school, took a turn by the high school, and parked for a bit in front of the hospital. He stared at the lit-up window where Dr. Blake's office was, wondering if the doctor was still at work. *Hey there, Ben. Hope you're doing good, dude.* Then he lowered his gaze to the grassy hill, which was covered in dewdrops... just as it had been on that fateful night when some astral version of him had stood there.

Five years. The entirety of high school had passed by in a heartbeat. It all seemed so long ago.

He started the car again and drove off, his mind torn between nostalgia for the hometown he hadn't quite left, excitement for MIT, and wonderment at the thought that, in a few days, he would be in India. He didn't remember anything about his birthplace. He didn't know anyone there, but ever since he'd bought tickets, he browsed pictures of all the places he was going to go: Kolkata, Mumbai, and yes, the Dharavi slum, the place where his story had begun.

As he drove past the outskirts of town, everything around him seemed as though it belonged to his past instead of his present. *I guess it kinda does, now that I've graduated.* Finally, he stopped in a dirt parking lot and got out of the car. He'd reached his destination. The junkyard spread out before him, hundreds of busted cars dotting the landscape, their shiny surfaces reflecting silver moonlight.

Before he did anything else, Adam searched his pocket for his cheesy old-school MP3 player, the same one he'd had back in middle school. *I haven't used this thing in years. I'm surprised it still turns on.* He plugged in the earbuds, earnestly proud of how nerdy he probably looked. After searching through the old playlists that his thirteen-year-old self had loved, scrolling through one song at a time, he stopped at Soundgarden's "The Day I Tried to Live."

He'd always liked that song. For a few years after the accident, Adam had found it difficult to listen to. Five years later, though, he rediscovered it. He liked that it brought him back, that it made him remember.

As the chorus blasted in, he shivered with recognition. *One more time again.* That was his favorite song, yes.

He walked through the junkyard, touching the rusty leftovers of automobiles, the dirty tires, the cracked windshields, the scenery lit only by the full moon in the sky. He reminisced on the time he'd walked down that same path with Chandra Goswami, back when they were still shy and little. He'd ended up dating her for six months back in his freshman year of high school, back before she moved to Connecticut. They still kept in touch via e-mail, and though Adam had dated other girls since, something about her stuck with him, and he wondered, not for the first time, if they should reconnect when he got to Boston, which was only an hour or so from her new town. *We'll see. I'll e-mail her when I move up there.*

He walked up the hill and then stopped. The treacherous slope pained his sciatic nerve, sending a lightning bolt down his legs. The hill had never been that difficult when he'd been a kid. Back then, he used to climb it almost every day on his regular hunt for bicycle parts. He paused to catch his breath.

He panted for a few minutes then kept going. *Don't give up.* Using the shattered remnants of cars for balance, he limped all the way to the top, where Mom's old SUV lay crumpled beside a similarly battered old school bus. Adam ran his fingers along the length of the old SUV, a shudder passing through him when he reached where the back door had buckled inward in the spot he'd been sitting. Through the broken window, he peered in with his cell-phone light and saw the seat belt he'd never buckled.

Adam climbed onto the SUV's hood. He lay back on his arms, legs crossed, and stared down at the landscape of cars spreading out before him like a valley of memories. Above him, above everything he considered home, was the universe, darkness covered with stars. The flashing red lights of a satellite blinked in the sky. A full moon, its craters gloriously revealed, shone down on Earth like a spotlight.

Adam stared at the sky for half an hour. Finally, the first shooting star painted a long white streak across the cosmos. *It's time.*

When he'd first read about the meteor shower predicted for that night, he knew the time had finally come. He'd been waiting for that night for a long time, waiting for the moment it felt right. *Tonight.* He thought it just too perfect that his graduation night coincided with a night when stars fell from the sky. *No way that's a coincidence.* He'd felt it in his gut, so he came back to the place where it had all begun, back to the same automobile that had sacrificed itself so that the real Adam could come to life.

"I made it," he whispered.

Adam reached into his pocket and took out the spark. The jagged obsidian rock glimmered in the moonlight. He smiled at it, bouncing the weight up and down in his palm, feeling its warmth course through his bloodstream. Through all his darkest days in recovery, the spark had always been right in his pocket, guiding him back to the light. Whenever he'd needed help, he gave it a squeeze, and hope refilled his heart. The Consciousness's promise had been true.

He'd never told anyone about it. No one would ever believe it was anything more than a black rock. That was okay because *he* knew.

Adam looked up at the night sky as a racetrack of comets streaked through the darkness and found their way to Earth. "Hey, guys." He smiled up at outer space. *Sometimes, I still feel it. Space. Coursing through my fingers. Like I'm still out there.*

"I just want to let you guys know... I made it." He squeezed the rock. "Made it here. To this day. Because of you." He inhaled deeply as the stars twinkled down at him. *So hard to believe I was out there.* "Just like I saved your lives," Adam continued, "all of you saved mine. Because of your help, I was able to get out of my shell, to become who I am today, and now I'm the person I dreamed I could be. You taught me that I'm not a creation of external events but of my own perception, and because I control my own perception, I control my universe. Yeah, you know, it's like... you taught me that if I choose to be strong, I *am* strong. If I *want* to matter, then I do matter."

Adam turned the spark around in his hands. "Guys, I don't want to let go of it." Tears tugged at the corners of his eyes. "I miss you, all of you, every day, and this weird space rock has always reminded me that it *did* happen, that I did make it back to Earth... that I didn't imagine it. But I know you guys said a long time ago that someday, when I was ready, it'd be time to give it back."

He wiped his eyes. "I'm now doing what I always wanted to do in life. I've made my own way. I have my own spark now."

Another meteor sailed down from space. Adam imagined how, out there in the distance, so many others were witnessing the same phenomenon, how somewhere out there, maybe in the same town or maybe somewhere else, another little kid—just like he had once been—was sitting in his bedroom window, staring out a telescope for the first time.

"I'm ready," he said. "I'm not sure how all of this alien business works, so all I've got is my intuition. But my intuition tells me that it's time for this spark to help someone else, maybe here or maybe on some other planet, someone in the same lonely place that I was when all of you first contacted me."

A dazzling array of shooting stars were dropping from the sky, lighting up the darkness like fireworks. Adam smiled. *This feels right.* Warmth pulsed from the obsidian rock, and it began to emit enormous rainbow reflections across the cars, trees, and hillside.

Adam laughed. "Thanks for helping me."

Adam tossed the glowing spark into the sky. Instead of dropping, it hovered over Adam's palm. It hesitated for a second, as if either gravity or indecision weighed it down, then floated upward. Luminescent signals flashed all over the entirety of the junkyard as the spark slowly propelled itself through the atmosphere.

A powerful radiance appeared in the night, more beautiful than any of the meteors and brighter than the sun itself. Adam shielded his eyes, and after a moment, he saw the radiance was emitting from a triangle of six individual lights, working together to achieve a common goal. The spark floated up into the sky and returned to the triangle that had created it.

Adam waved at it. "Later, guys."

The triangle of lights blasted off across the sky and disappeared into the farthest reaches of space. Somewhere else in the universe, the aliens were out there, finding new worlds, meeting other beings.

Stars came down to earth, and rocks went up to the sky. Adam Helios, a native of the dirt, had touched the heavens in a way no man in history ever had before, as far as he knew. However, sitting on the hood of a single automobile perched on Earth's crust, Adam felt like an ant that wanted to be an elephant. He smiled, proud that out of everyone on Earth, he was the one whom the sky had touched. Out of all the human beings in the world, they had chosen *him*, a fact that would never become any less overwhelming.

In his heart, he would always be the Galaxy Seeker.

About the Author

Originally from California, Nicholas Conley has currently made his home in the colder temperatures of New Hampshire. He considers himself to be a uniquely alien creature with mysterious literary ambitions, a passion for fiction, and a whole slew of terrific stories he'd like to share with others.

When not busy writing, Nicholas is an obsessive reader, a truth seeker, a sarcastic idealist, a traveler, and—like many writers—a coffee addict.

Also by Nicholas Conley

Pale Highway
Intraterrestrial